I0817788

We Come as Girls, We Leave as Women

We Come as Girls, We Leave as Women

a novel

Chrishaunda Lee Perez

Alpharetta, GA

This is a work of fiction. Names, characters, businesses, places, and events are either the products of the author's imagination or are used in a fictitious manner. Any resemblance to actual persons, living or dead, or actual events is purely coincidental.

ISBN: 978-1-63183-365-6 – Paperback
ISBN: 978-1-63183-366-3 – Hardcover
eISBN: 978-1-63183-367-0 – ePub
eISBN: 978-1-63183-368-7 – mobi

Library of Congress Control Number: 2018957424

♾This paper meets the requirements of ANSI/NISO Z39.48-1992 (Permanence of Paper)

Book cover concept by Chrishaunda Lee Perez and design by Taylor Brown
Photo credit: Tina Rowden

0 5 3 1 2 4

Dear gracious reader,

It is because of you and people like you who chose to consider this story, "We Come as Girls, We Leave as Women", that this book continues to be shared far and wide for so long. I spent 7 remarkable years writing this novel, pouring into the girls, and even growing with them, too. Throughout the time of crafting the individual personalities and lives, relatability and authenticity served as my north stars. It was paramount for me that readers could see themselves or someone they knew in a character, which makes the read that much more endearing. You will learn that each girl is unique, and each girl is perfect as she is, simply because she IS. As are we all. The cultures in this story are distinctive, yet the themes of each journey and each girl's feelings about them are what keep us all connected. For me, this experience was indeed a proud one.

After you read about the lives of these worthy girls, hold them up, champion their evolutions, and pass on their triumphant energy to others. Each of us can be resilient. It is also true that together, we are mighty.

You honor me by reading, I honor you with gratitude.

For my "two number ones," who will in time be women. Your roads will not always be fun or fair, but by believing in yourselves and in each other, you will rise. You will.

I am there with you every step of the way.

To the two left-handed heroines who
raised me from girl to woman:
I salute you for giving me the kind of love and
growing-up tools that were clearly right for me.

Keep watch over us, dear Obidimma.

Sisterhood is a funny thing. It's easy to recognize, but hard to define.

—Pearl Cleage

Contents

Preface

I remember waking up that magical morning feeling particularly strong. I think it was a combination of me finally being over the nausea meant to fortify the second stage of flourishing for the second brilliant female being to grow in my belly, and my eagerness to elevate to a new level of authorship. "I'm ready," I proclaimed aloud before I approached my husband, confiding that I was prepared to write a long story. By then, I'd written enough pages to perhaps amount to three books or more, but I'd written nothing good enough to call them such a thing. At the time I'd been penning copious essays, three-to-five-thousand-word topic-driven observations and opinions that I cut and pasted onto a web blog in which I took great pleasure. My column was called "Yes, i Brought It Up," writings meant to ignite conversations about certain funny and/or taboo topics involving women, like "What Do You Do When Your Child Publicly Acknowledges That Your Breasts Are Long?" or simply finding everyday extraordinary women to celebrate. I was having a ball writing these ideas and points of view that each soon came to an end after a few pages, and had "laugh-out-loud" moments with the comments section. I felt proud to be helping to strengthen our community through open and honest words that were not about "redeeming" who we are as women. We have nothing for which to apologize or compensate. Enough of that. We are incredible just as we all are.

Still, I was eager for something altogether different. I felt inclined and passionate, after years of scrawling on paper and tapping on my keyboard, to approach a writing that would not be "soon to end." I felt ready to grow with a work not only for days and weeks, but for months, even years.

Then came the Girls.

They appeared in my mind and heart at the stoplight, in car pool, on the phone with a friend; they even interrupted essays where they did not necessarily fit. They were coming alive, each one, from places all over the world. Each whispered of a different story filled with trials and feats and challenges, and gains, and loss. Each girl developed through her own journey, and I was in awe to realize that over the course of taking notes about their, at times, parallel lives, the subconscious goal in unison was the same: how to get to the place where I sit today—womanhood.

I reached back to my own challenges as an upper teenager and also related those that I know happen, and those that have happened to many of us women, the kinds of hurdles that when we were teenagers we felt that we could not succeed without compromising ourselves. I created a world where winning was possible by being one's self as they knew it, and to celebrate only that, much like the world I experienced at the remarkable boarding school I attended called Miss Porter's School. Boarding school is where I made my transition into womanhood along with my friends, and it is an ideal environment to house a variety of cultures and perspectives, but I believe that maturing girls can bond anyplace where they are free to dialogue. Sharing stories amongst one another is how parallel experiences can converge in a most beautiful way. The more varied the outlook shared, the stronger our sense of empathy can become. And I created a world where despite the extremely diverse population of girls, the idea of living like one is an island is the only foreign thing. No matter from where a girl derives, we all come from the same root, like the oldest and strongest baobab tree. I wanted to reaffirm that like the baobab tree's sprouting, a girl's bloom into womanhood is not to be taken for granted, for it is plentiful and essential.

I know that when I read about the development of girls today in highly publicized text, often the focus is about a girl's physical advancements, not spending enough time on what is going on with them inside. I wanted to use this book to inspire a broader conversation about their various milestones, concerns that might not receive as much attention by the adults around them. What goes on in the mind of a girl in transition to womanhood? How are they affected when they feel overlooked? How much does a need to please impact their choices in life? Why don't they feel comfortable sharing their feelings with people whom they have known all of their life? Is there one thing that can bring fundamental fulfillment to any and all of them, regardless of any racial, ethnic, or economical difference? How do they feel at their core? I was once an upper teen girl, and I envisioned a story that would have made me think about the possibilities of my own life in a different way, and one that would truly encourage me to consider "all of me" while progressing into adulthood.

After several years evolving with this one story, We Come as Girls, We Leave as Women was the gratifying outcome. Though the story had to eventually come to an end, in my mind and heart, it is still ongoing.

Introduction: All Can Be Favored

Contrary to popular belief, a teenaged girl's development into a proper woman has little to do with her looks.

There, I said it.

A smart teenaged girl might grow to be an intellectual woman, but her God-given instinct and gut will always serve her more in her life. To gain intellect, you must learn how to read. To gain instinct and an ability to trust your gut, you must learn how to LIVE.

To be a woman, you have to be able to get through, move past, and forgive with your anger being shown the door through the tears that fall from your eyes. After this, you have to be humbled enough to REBUILD. You must know how to inhale with gumption vigorous enough to move sedimentary rock, and exhale with your arms open wide and tender enough to comfort a naked baby skin to skin.

To be a real woman is to be a complex and powerful creature so full of herself on the inside that her considered "womanness" on the outside is without question divine, sensual, and RIGHT.

Big booty, flat booty. A cup, D cup, no cup.

You can be fat, thin, short, tall, long hair, no hair, kinky hair, straight hair, brown eyed, freckled faced, round faced, blue eyed, green eyed, four eyed, cross eyed, thin lipped, big lipped, straight hips, wide hips, long torso, long legged, long arms, long nails, bitten-off nails, short legs, short torso, short legged, big teeth, gapped teeth, no teeth, too many teeth, not enough teeth, brown skin, pale skin, olive skin, yellow skin, dark skin . . .

You can live with courage, loving yourself just the way you are, and be a fierce woman.

Girls Are the Filaments of Our World.
When We Help Them Connect to Their True Sense of Womanhood, We Have Light.

Legend

Though the weather was inching its way into the fall season, trees were still proudly green, and the summer's flowers continued to thrive in full bloom. No petal had yet to drop from the rows of daisies that lined the front of the Main Building at the Madame Ellington School for Girls. In fact, to Ingrid Knoll, headmistress of MES, it seemed as though the eye of each daisy shone wide with anticipation of the arrival of the student body for the new school year.

It was early, just after sunrise, the last Saturday of summer. The girls would begin arriving in a matter of hours. Ingrid had awakened excited for her annual tradition—to walk the entire campus in the last moments before the students came and brought the campus back to life after a sleepy three-month break. She thought of it as "inspecting the grounds," though of course this was not part of her job description. The grounds were, as always, perfection—all the landscaping expertly tended by the local company that had been working with the school for years, since before Ingrid's arrival.

Ingrid mused, as she did every year on this morning, about the people—the young women—who had walked these paths in the school's near one-hundred-thirty-year history. The year the school was founded, 1875, Alexander Graham Bell transmitted sound through a wire using his "acoustic telegraph," the famed opera *Carmen* premiered in Paris, and five years after the first anti-slavery society was dissolved. In spite of the advancements in the world, when Margaret Ellington opened the doors of her small schoolhouse that year, she had plenty of doubters. She was often warned that her "women's education" movement would fade as fast as the twenty-cent coin (which was also authorized that year), but Margaret held strong for her students—her "girls." Ingrid idolized Margaret, and when faced with a difficult situation as headmistress, she tried to imagine what Margaret Ellington would want her to do.

As a young girl, Ingrid had discovered a biography of Margaret Ellington, and she had become fascinated by Margaret's daring story. When Ingrid was appointed headmistress, one of the first things she did was go to the archives and read Margaret's journals and letters, which had been donated by her estate after her death. It was amazing to touch the paper, to see the handwriting, and to read the words of this forward-thinking woman. Though Margaret had doubts about her vision in those first years, before long, the twenty-cent coin would, in fact, be recalled, and Margaret Ellington would present her first graduating class.

Margaret was the youngest child and only daughter of Charles Stafford Ellington. Her father was the town's pastor and rarely separated Margaret from her two older brothers, perhaps because Charles was overwhelmed with his own teachings at the church, and the loss of his wife shortly after Margaret's fourth birthday rendered him more protective over her. Charles did not know that by keeping Margaret so close to her brothers, Margaret was exposed to parts of herself that would have been kept dormant had she spent more time with the other girls. Whatever her brothers read, she read. Whatever games or sports they took part in, Margaret tried her best to keep up, often returning home scratched and bruised, but never crying, and her father did not deter her spirit. Some people in their town criticized Charles for allowing his daughter to behave so wildly with her brothers, commenting that Margaret would never grow to be a suitable wife to anyone. A few old friends of her mother took pity on the busy and precocious girl and tried to take Margaret under their wings. "A primary concern for a girl is to handle well a domesticated life," she was told by her mother's dear friend Susan Locke, but Margaret resisted and her father Charles did not forbid her to do so.

Margaret watched her brothers grow up and become outspoken, educated men who commanded the attention of groups through their chosen professions of medicine and law. While Margaret never wished to follow in her brothers' footsteps in those ways, she did have an inclination to lead. After joining her brothers at Yale and completing its fine arts program for women in 1873, Margaret returned home and began offering tutoring courses for reading to young girls who lived nearby. She would have the girls take turns reading aloud, and even these simple interactions touched both students and teacher, many expressing that the first time they felt truly heard was in her class. Girls spread the word amongst their friends and families, and Margaret's tutoring class for reading eventually evolved into a full-day school located in a small house on Main Street in the neighboring town of Ruralton. The wealthy families, even her own, referred to Margaret and her "eccentric, yet tasteful manner of education," and through that very exclusive word of mouth, Margaret Ellington became a household name in her corner of the world. Year after year parents could not believe how much their daughters were blossoming, especially the shy ones. What they did not see was how Margaret simply mirrored the teachings of her father: she gave the girls an open window to explore. With this freedom, they grew more confident. They were energetic, and inquisitive, and bold. Margaret, like her father before her, welcomed it all. Some called it magic. Many wanted their daughters to benefit from that magic.

Letters began arriving from various European countries to request her "training" for daughters of affluent and influential families alike. Margaret did not know what the future had in store for young women, but she wanted to prepare her students for what she believed could be a fuller life. She infused in her faculty her belief that what they did each year was more than teach academics—it was their jobs to ensure that each girl graduated "on the right path to her own journey into a successful womanhood." And so, that is what her teachers did then and every year since.

Ingrid was proud that the school was now comprised of girls from all over the globe, reaching from California to Australia, Russia, and Argentina. By the 1960s the school had a surge of applicants, and though the school became highly competitive, the maximum student body had never surpassed two hundred-eighty students, taking heed from Madame Ellington's creed of individualized education. To reflect its founder's spirit of inclusivity, recruitment had long welcomed and even sought out students of color, which inspired the administration to widen its financial aid and scholarship opportunities. Now, girls from every walk of life graduated arm in arm, conjoined by a calla-lily chain that symbolized their oneness.

Ingrid was approaching the Main Building, which was the center of the Madame Ellington campus today, but had once served as the lone schoolhouse in 1875. It had since been rebuilt and pushed slightly closer to the road, renovated and expanded and redefined with a vast surrounding campus and a wealth of added buildings and dorm houses. Ingrid liked to begin and finish her journey at this iconic spot. Her connection to Margaret Ellington filled her with pride, and never more than in this spot, where thus far, nearly seven thousand girls had embarked on a momentous journey that culminated with them being forever changed and on the right path to their own journeys into womanhood.

1

Meet the Girls Prepping for Arrival

11:00 a.m., Connecticut: Stephanie

After spending nearly forty minutes in her own shower, Stephanie could not resist the urge to have a look at herself for the fourteenth time in two weeks in the best mirror of the house: Her parent's full-length bathroom mirror. She was rarely disturbed, except the time when her mother had stepped in one day during her third self-evaluation, startling both of them. Stephanie's parents were keen on Stephanie having private grown-up girl time.

Acutely studying her sturdy, statuesque, and voluptuous naked body, Stephanie approached her left breast with her hand, gently squeezing it as if it were not her own. Throughout these newfound self-examinations, she remained in awe of how her body had transformed so suddenly. How did her breasts get so FULL? She tilted her head while squeezing both breasts together, then returned her head center and squinted her eyes and puckered her lips at her reflection. Giving her best beauty-queen/pinup-girl pose, complete with her right foot in front of the left, she stood there, robust with all the roots of a flower soon to be in luxurious bloom.

Her legs had lengthened, more powerful and lean. This Stephanie could attribute to years of squash, which her father happily introduced to her when she was five because, as he told his wife, "Squash is an excellent bonding tool for a father with a son or a daughter." Stephanie's seventeen-year-old arms could give Serena Williams a run for her money from serving as a star varsity volleyball player for two years. Her juvenile acne was practically gone, and her greenish-gold eyes gave her face a unique look that her father said came from his side—the Irish side—of the family. Stephanie's cherubic cheeks let on that she was still rather young, however, and her waistline had yet to completely be chiseled. Otherwise, the overall shape of herself had evolved. She had recently bid adieu to her orthodontist along with her braces and headgear, and the consequence of that farewell was a smile free of lifeless metal, and one full of a natural, vibrant glow. After a few up-and-downs on her tippy toes, she reached to the floor to pick up her cucumber bath sheet to rewrap herself, also enveloping her wet, cape-like brunette tresses. Standing there, Stephanie could not believe that after all of this time, she was actually HERE.

4:00 p.m., London: Brooklyn

While Stephanie stood in front of her mirror admiring her exposed beauty and reflecting on how her new finds were going to relate to her senior year experience, Brooklyn tucked her own anxiety about the new year into a swimming cap and commenced to perform a double front flip off the diving board into the indoor pool at her family's home. Her twin sister, Manhattan, yelled, "Bloody showoff!" as she walked past, sporting a pair of huge headphones blasting rap music. When Manhattan realized that their longtime nanny, Maude, was within earshot of her comment, her face immediately simmered red, but she did not apologize.

Brooklyn later joined her sister at the kitchen counter to receive her usual and final late-afternoon snack for that summer prepared by Maude, delivered less than a minute after she sat down. As pool water dripped from both her hair and body onto their kitchen floor, Maude reminded Brooklyn to cover up better, "So I won't have a load of wiping up after you both leave the kitchen." Brooklyn acknowledged her with a nod that she had heard this request, took a huge bite of her sandwich, and smiled back at her nanny.

The house phone rang loud enough to alert even a headphoned Manhattan, who, while rapping along to OutKast's "So Fresh, So Clean," swung around on the stool to retrieve the telephone from the wall without missing a beat. She pushed up one headphone from her ear and replaced it with the receiver. "Hello-o-oooo?" Manhattan sang.

Winsome, Brooklyn's best friend and only roommate since freshman year, was on the other end. Since she'd spent such concentrated time with Brooklyn, Winsome had yet to confuse one sister for the other, though the girls' own parents often confused their voices.

"Mate, where's your brizilliant sister?"

"Showing off in the bloody pool, of course, now smashing a sandwich down her bloody throat . . . *mate*."

Maude looked up from the corner of her eye while standing at the kitchen sink. Manhattan sensed Maude's disapproving glare and lowered the mouthpiece. "Sorry, Maudey. Shall I pass the phone, Winnie?"

"Not unless you want to continue the muffled OutKast concert in my ear!"

"Well, in case you didn't know, they kick ass!" Manhattan quickly readjusted her tone. "Okay, you all be safe in the wild and crazy Ameeerica!"

Holding half of her sandwich, Brooklyn eased up to her sister and grabbed the phone, consciously dripping water onto Manhattan's sneakers. Manhattan flipped her the bird with a grin, readjusted her headphones, and swung back around. Brooklyn, slightly stretching the phone cord, turned the corner to the sitting room to achieve more privacy.

"Winnie! Are you there? What's our room look like? You are still giving me the wall this year, right?"

Winsome was sitting at the dorm payphone, which had a clear view of their shared bedroom. She stared at the only uncovered bed pushed against the wall, wishing Brooklyn was there with her, outfitting her mattress with linen from her chosen shade of red for the year.

"Yeah, Brookie. All set."

"Dude, what's irkin' you? You seem low."

"Yeah, my dad has been on me since the morning all the

way to school about theater. I think he wishes I were more like Claire. He told me that it is a waste of time to put so much energy into something that will only result in me becoming a career waitress, or worse, a waitress at our restaurant . . . Not all actresses end up waiting tables."

Brooklyn laughed. "Not forever, anyway! Look, Winnie, you are so bloody brilliant. And your dad knows. He just wants you to put your brilliance in a place he understands more. What does your mom have to say?" Brooklyn took a bite of her sandwich, feeling good that she might have calmed Winsome's anxiety problem.

"You know my mom. She tries to make the both of us happy. She helps to cool my dad's head all the while reminding me that I'm 'his child' to convince me that we are so alike, and that he sees so much of himself in me. Honestly, save for this cleft in my chin, I don't see it. I have never wanted to follow his way for me."

Brooklyn put down her mostly eaten sandwich and grabbed a towel to wrap it around her still-dripping suit. She wished she could somehow appear in front of Winsome in this moment, to give her best friend a hug and distract her from her father's disapproving eye. "My dad says the same thing. I'm my *mother's* child. What. Ever. Winnie, we are our own people, you and me. And we are gonna show the world what we are made of. Your dad loves you, he just has to *see.* And he will. And by this time tomorrow, I will be there to see YOU!" She picked up the last bite of her sandwich and stuffed it in her mouth.

"Why are you the best?" Winsome asked.

"Because you are!" Even over the phone, Brooklyn could hear the squeals of glee in the dorm—girls were arriving, re-uniting after a long summer apart. She missed Winsome, like a part of herself. But when she was at school, she missed Manhattan—her true other half.

"Look, you've got to get on over here before I explode from not having anyone to crack jokes with. Plus, I would really like to get a head start on our project."

"Already? You're not wasting any time!"

"Yeah, with my dad on my heels, just like you said, he needs to SEE!"

Back in the kitchen, Maude was wiping up the countertop, and Manhattan was skimming through the latest issue of *Rolling Stone*.

"What kind of room did you get this year? Hopefully not that sloped-wall monstrosity you all were forced to sleep in as juniors!"

"Give it a rest, Manhattan! Anyway, Winsome said the room is lovely, we got the one we wanted. And they even took down the wallpaper."

"Don't you think it's odd that you haven't given anybody else a shot? I mean, you've roomed with Winsome for three years already."

"Don't you think it's odd that you rarely want to leave Europe? Only if it's demanded of you by Mummy and Daddy." Brooklyn reached into the fridge for a bottle of water.

"Why do I care about going somewhere where every time I go I feel like I'm in some sort of televised bubble. I don't get the Americans, so dim—their preoccupation with fame and celebrity."

"England is not far off from them. Our paparazzi end up getting people killed, lest we forget. And being educated there is quite different."

"Speculation! And yeah, the education is different. It's all the more BORING."

"Is not!"

"Is so!"

Maude interrupted the two by reminding them that Brooklyn had a flight to catch the next morning and therefore they should spend their last day together acting civil toward one another. They agreed.

Brooklyn and Manhattan shared a studio apartment–sized bedroom together with their line of division being their color choice for each identical twin's half of the room. Manhattan favored multilayered hues of blue over Brooklyn's choice of crimson and gray. Her room at school also reflected a love for the deep reddish color, primarily because she thought being surrounded by that which resembled the "drapes of the stage" would bring her closer to success as an actress. Brooklyn naturally inherited her mother's love of acting, having been cast as a last-minute choice for a bit part while visiting her mother on set when she was seven. Manhattan preferred existing in a world where she didn't have to be poked and prodded at, which she considered the life of both their famous parents.

Manhattan didn't like performing like her mother, or competing in sports like her father. Her natural gifts derived from her late maternal grandmother, Grande Dame, in her day, having served as one of England's most prominent photographers. Manhattan would rather shoot stills of her pet fish than have a moving camera record her every motivation.

Brooklyn's wall was an ode to theater. She had fashioned a collage of many of the world's greatest stage icons, from Julie Andrews to Elaine Stritch. Her vanity table showcased a vintage hat designed by Edith Head given to her by her father on her sixteenth birthday, and replica gloves worn by Judy Garland in *A Star Is Born*, given to her by her mother when she turned twelve. The wall of Manhattan, the minimalist, was much less decorated, showcasing only a single, mural-sized photograph taken by her late grandmother of a mostly hidden snail under a leaf on a forest bed. That single photograph of the snail reflected much about Manhattan: deliberate, precise, and private.

Brooklyn was feverishly enthralled in repacking the right clothes for the school year, often taking things out of her monogrammed suitcase and placing them back again into her drawer due to a sudden change of heart. But something else preoccupied her, and not even that detailed task could prevent anxiety from finding its way to her heartbeat. To calm herself down, she thought about her boyfriend, Chris, how inseparable they were every day, and about the two nights in a row she shared with him during the summer. They originally only planned for one, but the previous evening had been so passionate, they had to find a way to rendezvous again. Manhattan covered for Brooklyn the first night, and she was prepared to keep Maude out of their room after Brooklyn snuck out and until she snuck back in. The second night, however, Brooklyn told Maude she was spending the night with a friend. Chris's bedroom was located on the first floor of his family's townhome, with an entire floor separating him from the others, so it was not difficult to sneak Brooklyn in and out. Brooklyn knew she would see Chris in Connecticut because he attended the neighboring boys school, but that time shared stealing moments on either campus would be nothing like what they had for nearly three months straight in their hometown.

Brooklyn and Chris loved each other, and they both believed that the other was their "forever." Thinking of Chris removed some of Brooklyn's nervousness, yet a bit of anxiety lingered on. She took a deep breath, turned around, and stared at her twin, who was lying on her own bed analyzing film slides entranced in music. Brooklyn crossed the imaginary boundary line to get to Manhattan's bed and stood there directly in front of her sister. Feeling her presence, Manhattan's blue eyes met with Brooklyn's, and just like the older sibling that she was (by a full minute and a half), Manhattan made room for her younger twin to cuddle up beside her.

11:00 a.m., Massachusetts: Elaine

"Elaine!" her mother yelled as loudly as she could to prevent being drowned out by the vast waves gathering every second on the beach. "Your father has packed the car and is ready to head out! I've had Rinalda prepare a snack for you to eat on the way to the city!"

Elaine, busy writing in her journal, turned around and returned a smile with a hand wave to her mother.

"Okay! I'm coming in!"

Elaine was not exactly looking forward to the hour or so drive home listening to what had become of her parents' conversation since the dismal ride out. For that matter, she was not optimistic about the overall state of her parents' current relationship. There was a time when friends of her parents would comment about their connection, calling them Romeo and Juliet, because they were deeply passionate lovers who came from opposite worlds. Today there was something forcing them to be distant and argumentative with each other. Sure, her parents were going through all of the "right" motions of playing their respective dual roles of a married couple, but it no longer appeared as if they cared about being in love. Their car rides used to be filled with the sound of her mother ripping past pages of a smart publication, then sharing with Elaine's father the latest on everything in the world, and her father adding his perspective. At times their chats would develop into serious yet endearing banter that culminated with one of them asking for Elaine's opinion to break their debate. In the end, they would pull up to their house with Elaine's mother exiting the car, exclaiming something like "*Zut alors!*" still clutching the publication and holding strong to her position. Her father was sweetly amused about how riled up she always got.

But lately, her father's usual enthusiasm had turned into what Elaine had labeled in her journal as "excruciating silence." On the way home, Elaine attempted to break that silence, bringing up a subject she was sure would interest both of her parents. Sadly, her mother, in a mixture of French and English, swiftly disapproved the first comment her father offered, as if her mother had been simmering, waiting for a trigger to pull. That disapproval then opened a can of worms that would not close all the way up the stairs to the back entrance of their home in Cambridge, and re-erupted about a half hour away from dropping off Elaine to school in Connecticut the next day. The enormous "Welcome Back" sign that hung on the traffic lights in front of the Main Building saved them all from the climax of that argument, and Elaine had no clue if her parents had continued their argument after they unpacked her things in her room and returned to Cambridge. Yet if she had to put money on it, she would bet her easily earned A in French that they had.

11:00 a.m., New York City: Sagrario

This was a tough time of day to take the Peter Pan bus to Connecticut, and Sagrario knew it. She had intended to catch the 8:00 or 9:00 a.m. bus at the latest, just because there would be fewer people, and she knew that those who traveled earlier in the morning, like her, "would be more calm." She prayed that the college kids on their way to UCONN would be tired out and would not ruin her two hours of tranquility. She really needed this space in between her arrival to campus to rejuvenate, having just left home practically depleted from one set of ill-given responsibilities to take on the ones she chose to handle at school.

Luckily, Sagrario was the first and only one in line because she had managed to arrive early. After loading her luggage at the bottom of the bus, she ventured up the stairs, anticipating heading straight for her lucky row and sitting on the inside seat. Even if someone had to share the seat with her, leaning on that window just above the bus's engine put her to sleep almost immediately, and the engine's hum could drown out just about anything. She hoped that regardless of what other kind of energy entered the bus, a little music and the engine's hum would overpower that, too.

When she reached the top of the stairs, she smiled at the bus driver, who seemed to recognize her from the year before.

"Headed back to school, eh?"

"Yeah, my final year."

"What are you going to do afterward? What kind of job will you get?"

"Oh, I'm sorry, sir, I'm only in high school. Next year I head to college."

"You go to one of those fancy high schools, right? You look so grown up to be only in high school, though."

Embarrassed, Sagrario looked to the floor. "Yeah . . . Well, thank you." She sped up her walk toward her seat because a line was beginning to form at the bottom of the stairs of people waiting to load.

When Sagrario sat down, she commenced her routine checklist: Homemade bag lunch? Check. Music fully charged? Check. Datebook? Check. Fully charged mobile phone? On vibrate? Check. She reached down to feel for her belted wallet, folded her carry-on sweater to use as a pillow, placed her book and brown-bagged meal on her lap, and leaned her head on the window.

She caught eyes with a blue-eyed, blond girl who reminded her of a fellow senior at Madame Ellington, Caitlyn Lovette, though Sagrario believed that Caitlyn Lovette wouldn't be caught dead using public transportation. Sagrario was sure, as she adjusted her body into the best position on the soon-to-be cramped bus, that Caitlyn was right now having her monogrammed sheets placed in her suitcase by her black nanny, whom Caitlyn always referred to as "Our sweet Annabelle." At school, Caitlyn often spoke of Annabelle like she was some sort of adorable, reliable house pet. "Annabelle always does this and that . . . Annabelle never leaves crust on any of my sandwiches, and she wouldn't dare put a slice of pizza with crust in front of my brother, Carl. He'd freak out!" Sagrario would not be surprised if one day Caitlyn declared to her friends that *Annabelle can even sit when told to AND roll over! She's just like part of the family!* Caitlyn did not need a bag lunch because she would likely be fed a classy, hot meal on her first-class flight from Houston to Connecticut, and she did not need a belted wallet because she would never be in a place where someone might pick her pockets, which were no doubt filled not with cash, but with high-limit credit cards.

Imagining Caitlyn's presumed routines made Sagrario annoyed, but then she chuckled to herself at the thought of having such a life. "I'm doing all right all on my own," she almost affirmed aloud.

Not long after the bus was half filled, to Sagrario's surprise, NOT with a bunch of loud co-eds, but with students like her—reserved and prepared—her phone began to buzz. She saw the word "Ma" appear on her phone screen and she smiled to herself. The bus was calm, and Sagrario believed she was receiving a call of appreciation and well-wishes from her mother. The ride was turning out not to be so bad after all.

She answered the phone in a quiet, cheerful voice. "Hey, Ma!"

"Sagrario. *Yo no sé porque* you didn't give me *dinero para pagar el bill de teléfono*!"

Sagrario was stunned. She thought her mother would be grateful because Sagrario had somehow, between tuition and all of her supplies, paid both the electric and telephone bills two months in advance IN ADDITION to giving her mother two hundred fifty dollars—fifty dollars more than she did before she started school last year. She hadn't asked her mother for one dollar all summer, and had done more than her share of providing for the family all while saving up for school. Paying those two extra bills in advance coupled with the extra money Sagrario thought would have helped out tremendously, especially since her younger sister had recently become pregnant. Yet because of Isabella's pregnancy, Sagrario's mother had grown more and more frustrated and took out her anger and disappointments on Sagrario, as if all of their family's troubles were her fault.

Sagrario tried to speak in as low a tone as she could. Now it was she who felt like the loud one who might ruin the chance of a quiet bus ride.

"Ma, that is all I could do. I had to pay my school bill or else I would not be able to attend this year. *Es mi año final.*"

"And this school *mierda* is getting on my last nerves. You should be here, right now, taking care of your brother and sister so I don't have to pay all of this extra money! Who will be responsible for your *hermana* and her new baby that will be coming *PRONTO*? Not you! *Dime*, are you too *importante para tu familia*?!"

It was as if spending the entire summer (every summer since she was fourteen) without a life of her own meant nothing to anyone in her family, especially her mother. From the moment Sagrario returned home for the summer each spring, there were no welcoming arms, only passing of babies for her to babysit for slightly older relatives who had recently delivered and could not afford childcare. After sophomore year, she began an annual summer-job program at a law firm offered through a connection at "A Better Chance" that provided some relief. Securing that summer job only gave her family two weeks to use her before Sagrario was required to head downtown five days a week to work in an air-conditioned building with people who complimented her work and spoke to her like she mattered, just like at school. It was a double-edged sword for her family, who half wanted her near home to tend to all of the children being born, and half loved that Sagrario was making more money than many of her adult relatives. Both school and work were very, very demanding for Sagrario, but they were also rewarding in some way. Home life was thankless.

Sagrario's father could not take the pressure of having to feed a family that included three children in a small two-bedroom apartment. He was often arrested, usually after getting drunk at a bar to avoid his crowded house, which ended with him starting a fight with someone on the crowded streets. The most recent time, he had broken a bottle over someone's head while he was still on probation. And for that offense he was sentenced to serve eight months in jail. Sagrario had decided a long time ago that her father was jailed on purpose, just so he could be given some time away from his responsibilities at home. She thought he looked at what she was doing as almost a vacation, and soon after Sagrario began boarding school, he found a place to escape to as well.

Now, with her father gone, Sagrario's mother had no one to whom she could direct her anger, except Sagrario. "Ma, I am sorry that you feel that this is not enough to last you, but I don't have any more money. I gave you all I had. I have only thirty dollars to deposit into my bank account at school, and I will have to begin working at school right away to pay for books. I still owe from last year."

"Well no *es mi problema.* If you stayed home and went to *escuela pública*, you wouldn't have to pay for books."

Sagrario had heard this all before. She sighed. "Ma, the best I can do is see what is left over after I pay for books and send something to you then. This year is going to be tough because I have to also pay for a graduation dress, and a few other extra things. But I will figure it out."

"*Bueno*, Sagrario. *Así espero.*" She hung up.

Sagrario opened her datebook, and beginning with an asterisk, she wrote, "Family needs more money" under the day's date. She closed her book, put on her headphones, and began to think good thoughts about the school year to come, and how exciting it was going to be to serve as Student First Head of School. Despite the interruption from her mother, Sagrario was able to let go of the stressful reality she was leaving and focus on the great possibilities of what could be. By now the bus had become completely filled with the exception of a few seats, including the one next to her. A teenaged Hispanic girl was making her way up the stairs carrying a bassinet and a diaper bag. The girl seemed fatigued and appeared way too young to have a baby, like Sagrario's fifteen-year-old sister, Isabella. The thought of Isabella having to travel from state to state alone on a crowded bus with an infant in tow brought on thoughts of sadness for Sagrario. As far as she was concerned, that would never be Isabella's fate because Sagrario would ensure that her sister and baby would be taken care of, even if it that meant she had to take on Isabella fully when she graduated from Madame Ellington. Despite being away the past few years, Sagrario practically raised her younger sister, and so she felt that Isabella, more than anyone, was her responsibility.

Searching around for a seat, the young mother blew her bangs up from her forehead to cool her face, and Sagrario gestured for the girl to sit next to her. When the girl sat down, Sagrario smiled warmly at her, then again leaned her head on the bus window. It had to be a sign. Though the girl initially brought Sagrario's sister to mind, Sagrario also knew that had she remained at home, that young girl could easily have been herself carrying the bassinet and exhaustingly blowing her bangs up off of her face. Sagrario felt reassured that she was doing the right thing.

2

Back on Campus

4:00 p.m. the following day, Connecticut, Madame Ellington School Chapel

Stephanie felt extremely self-conscious as she gathered with the group of seniors, many accompanied by their New Girls, to a predetermined section of the chapel, where they would listen to speeches from those who presided over the Madame Ellington School. She chose to wear a button-down shirt, leaving open only one button to hide her newfound cleavage, but the blue Lacoste oxford shirt still accentuated her upper body curves. None of her peers had yet commented, but Stephanie took detailed stock of everyone else. She noticed who let their hair grow out a little over the summer and who arrived with a fresh chop. She even noticed a girl who for three years presented herself as an introverted bookworm appear without braces and reveal her legs for what seemed like the first time. Stephanie wondered why she all of a sudden emerged so liberated. Had she lost her virginity over the summer? Stephanie had never considered the girl to be pretty, but now, after these changes, she could see how a guy might. Stephanie followed the new and improved scholar with her eyes all the way to her seat, until Ingrid Knoll, the school's headmistress, instantly stole away everyone's attention when she stepped up to the podium.

Stephanie switched her focus to see if, as with some of her peers, there were any changes with Dr. Knoll. *Not one*, she thought. Dr. Ingrid Knoll could not have made a more perfect bow of the school's signature silk handkerchief, which she wore around the flipped-up collar of her short-sleeved white blouse, complete with the school's gold pendant pinned on the knot. Her Princess Diana haircut, which looked fresh from a recent appointment, framed her gleaming brown eyes. Dr. Knoll's hair was flawless, as were her white-toothed smile and beautifully curved nails, which were always shined with a clear nail polish.

"Good afternoon and welcome back sophomores, juniors, NEW GIRLS, AND SENIORS!"

The part of the audience comprised of the nearly two hundred Old Girls knew the tradition—keep the cheers low for sophomores and juniors, a healthy uproar for New Girls, and leave the loudest cheers for the seniors.

"Hello, ladies. As most or hopefully all of you know by now, my name is Ingrid Knoll, headmistress of this esteemed Madame Ellington School for Girls. I am very proud to serve what will be my tenth year here, and my door is always open for each and every one of you."

The audience clapped.

"I expect our sophomores and juniors to have a delightful year as you press on to become the women this school can help you grow to be. New Girls, whether you are a freshman, sophomore, junior, or senior, I expect you, with the help of your senior Old Girl, to navigate our wondrous world here at the Madame Ellington School. Your Old Girl will assure you are on your way to understanding our traditions, our stellar curriculum, and that you have the confidence to truly fulfill your potential! MES student body, welcome to a new school year!"

The crowd roared with enthusiasm. Stephanie sat in the middle of the crowd of seniors gathered in the back. She looked to her New Girl, Hedda, from Berlin, who also happened to be a senior. Stephanie had been anticipating meeting Hedda since she received her information and photo by mail late that summer. Being a day student kept Stephanie a bit disconnected from the boarders, and she rarely slept overnight at school unless there was an early game on a Saturday and the weather was bad. Stephanie imagined that she would show Hedda the lay of the land at school, and that they would become inseparable because Hedda would depend on Stephanie as her closest ally. Their actual meeting was mild, but Stephanie chalked it up to Hedda's foreignness. In a short time, Hedda would warm up to her, Stephanie was certain. She energetically nudged Hedda when Ingrid referenced the "senior New Girl" as if she was talking specifically about Hedda. To count, there were actually two New Girls in the eldest class. The other was a day student who lived in town. When Hedda was nudged, she offered Stephanie a weak smile.

"Returning seniors, you've done the work, and this is your year!" The crowd cheered even louder, this time with special hoots and hollers from many of the seniors.

Dr. Knoll, with her uniform and delicate stature, looked nothing like Stephanie, but Stephanie admired her for her open heart and willingness to embrace everyone. When Stephanie attended a summer program at Madame Ellington the year before she officially became a student, it was Dr. Knoll who helped Stephanie through early feelings of awkwardness. Dr. Knoll encouraged Stephanie and other volleyball hopefuls to play soccer with her rising sophomore twin sons who were on summer break from Arthur Newgate, the neighboring boys school. Stephanie was a scrappy rising freshman and enjoyed competing with the boys. This calmed her a lot. Then, at the start of freshman year, Stephanie began experiencing different feelings of awkwardness, and though she did not pry, Stephanie felt Dr. Knoll understood. That unspoken understanding between the two, and reassuring smiles from Dr. Knoll, gave Stephanie added confidence that whatever she was feeling, she was okay. It was Ingrid Knoll's gentle way of letting a girl know that they had her support without making a big deal about it. Stephanie greatly appreciated that. This nuance did not feel like it was coming from an Oxford- and Princeton-educated headmistress of school. It felt like it was coming from a mom.

Since she had become an official student of the Madame Ellington School, Stephanie no longer needed hand-holding from Dr. Knoll, but it felt good to know she would be there if ever Stephanie needed her.

Ingrid Knoll was glowing. "Some of you New Girls might be feeling jitters because your parents have now left you here alone. Some of your parents are still camping out at the Old Inn for as long as they can to be near you . . ."

The crowd snickered on cue.

"But know that whether they are here or not, their confidence in you will always be in your heart, helping to guide you. They are only a phone call away, and you will soon learn that with all that happens on campus, school holidays seem to come up one right after the other. Many of you will find yourselves so wrapped up in your lives here that your newfound independence will inspire you to spend the shorter vacations with fellow students and their families, or take advantage of some of our programs abroad during the lengthier holidays when you become a junior or senior.

"We have paired each of you New Girls with a senior Old Girl whom we believed would best relate to you based on the information you sent to us about yourselves. Even if your chosen Old Girl is not from where you are, don't be alarmed. Give it time. There are other reasons why we thought the two of you would connect in a very real way."

Stephanie glanced at Hedda, who seemed to be trying to focus on understanding fully what her new headmistress was saying.

"I am sure you have all met your teachers with your parents earlier today and are becoming acclimated to your rooms and meeting your new roommates. I trust that everyone will be respectful of one another's things, and though there might be rough patches here and there, you will all do your best to get along. And I feel that all of you, returning darling sophomores, returning courageous juniors, and our triumphant seniors, will always do what you can to make every blossoming New Girl's experience a welcomed one. Every single student in this room is an Ellington girl now, and that fact means something very profound. You have all earned your way here, and thus you are starting an exciting journey. I know I speak for our entire faculty when I say we are already beaming with pride for you.

"Now without further ado, I am very pleased to introduce to you your new First and Second Student Heads of School. Ms. Sagrario Nuñez and Ms. Abigail Turner!" Ingrid stood aside while clapping along with the audience and then took her seat behind the podium.

Sagrario approached the stage poised, professional, and confident. She'd adjusted into her school self the moment she reached campus the day before. She was able to stay sane at school by somehow convincing her family that the students could not take calls on their mobile phones during the week (only half true), and she did not give her family her dorm phone number. She faithfully called home every weekend at the same time, when her mother would give her a laundry list of problems she knew Sagrario could not solve from afar, and problems that Sagrario should not have been made privy to in the first place. But Sagrario always took it in, sifted through the muck, and honestly tried to help as best as she could, even if it was only to give her mother an opportunity to vent. The once-per-week call setup made it possible for Sagrario to keep her family at bay so that she could fulfill all of the things Headmistress Knoll always talked about. Followed by her fellow Second Student Head of School, who smiled and offered her best pageantry wave, Sagrario stood behind the podium and adjusted the microphone upward.

"Good afternoon, everyone. My name is Sagrario Nuñez, and I am this year's First Student Head of School. My excellent co-head, Abigail, and I would like to thank all of you who voted for us to be in this position. We will not take it lightly."

Abigail smiled in agreement.

"We have a very exciting year ahead, filled with traditions, excursions, and opportunities to further our growth into intelligent, responsible young women. I remember like it was yesterday the first day I sat where you are sitting, New Girls, anxious and anticipating what life would be like for me here at the Madame Ellington School. I entered this school a very shy girl from the Bronx, and in one semester, I matured out of my shell and two years later built the courage to campaign for myself to serve all of you in this way. This is more than a dream come true, and all of you will experience your own dreams come true in the days, weeks, and months to come."

Winsome and Brooklyn were seated in the balcony with their New Girls, who both were like little versions of the pair—only reversed races. Like Winsome and Brooklyn had three years prior, their New Girls bonded the moment they met, and when one whispered into the other's ear after Sagrario mentioned "dreams coming true," they slapped fives quietly. Winsome and Brooklyn smiled to each other over their heads, but then Brooklyn shifted her attention and whispered in Winsome's ear while gesturing toward Sagrario, "She is such a pet for Dr. Knoll!" Winsome nodded in agreement.

"I cannot tell you all of what you can expect, because all of your experiences will only belong to you, and you will never forget them. Many of the friendships you make here will last a lifetime. And many of the things that made you nervous will evolve and become your strong suits. I know that some or all of your friends at home attend school with boys, and some of you might find it challenging to adjust to single-sex education at first. Accept it as a gift. And don't worry, we do not shun boys in every way. There will be plenty of opportunities to spend time in recreation with them."

Winsome began to drift while listening to Sagrario. Both she and Brooklyn took issue with Sagrario's angelic image and believed her rise to popularity at the school was contrived. Winsome's boredom led her eyes to continue to wander, and finally her eyes landed on Victoria Lee, a Korean senior who was San Francisco and Busan based. For all of the qualities Winsome's and Brooklyn's New Girls shared with them, Winsome wondered why the androgynous Victoria, who instantly seemed embarrassed after Sagrario mentioned boys, as if she had something to hide, would be paired with an Asian beauty queen. Even Caitlyn Lovette's New Girl, sitting with Caitlyn's crew of Southern belles and their New Girls, was practically color-coordinated with Caitlyn. Perched with their shoulders so upright that their spines wouldn't touch the sloped backs of the chapel pews, they looked like a welcoming committee for a country club in springtime. Victoria, who dressed in nondescript, plain, masculine clothes all of the time, paired with her glamorous New Girl, exemplified more one of those drastic "before-and-after" pictures from a talk-show makeover.

Winsome again took inventory of Caitlyn's group, then looked back to Sagrario, hoping her speech would soon come to a close.

Sagrario continued.

"What I would like to impart upon you on your official first day here, and it is something that I will reiterate to you all throughout the year, is above all things, try to be yourself. If you do not know exactly who that self is within you yet, make it a priority to find out. Knowing that will make all of the rest fall into place. You might come as a girl, but you will leave as a woman. Thank you."

Brooklyn breathed a sigh of relief—she was *this* close to discreetly plugging her ears. Of the two best friends, Brooklyn was always most irritated by Sagrario. Yet she realized that the remainder of her peers did not feel the same when she watched them all stand up and cheer on Sagrario, including the faculty and Headmistress Ingrid Knoll, who gave Sagrario an approving wink. Brooklyn rolled her eyes, but she and Winsome stood with the crowd anyway, so as not to appear mean-spirited. Brooklyn always wanted to be a well-known face on the Broadway circuit, but they all knew that at Madame Ellington, Sagrario was the only breakout star. Brooklyn had heard through the campus grapevine that, for various financial and family reasons, Sagrario almost didn't make it back to campus after every long holiday during her first year, and that she legally emancipated herself from her parents the year after that. Though she still chose to live with them, the move catapulted Sagrario into a new realm of independence. Her place at the Madame Ellington School was no longer in jeopardy, and the young, exceptionally intelligent girl from the South Bronx could finally shine. Most of the students and seemingly all faculty genuinely liked Sagrario, for she acted as a mentor and role model for a number of the younger girls there. Brooklyn knew all of this, but it was hard for her to believe that Sagrario was in truth so well put together. Brooklyn had never witnessed firsthand, nor understood, how anyone who'd been through so much could stand so strong and tall.

Dr. Knoll returned to the podium after Sagrario and Abigail stepped down, introduced the school song for all to sing together, and then dismissed the school for free time until all of the students were expected to reconvene at the Main Building for dinner at 6:00 p.m.

Walking back from the chapel to the senior dorms, Stephanie remained silent until, surprisingly, Hedda broke the ice.

"I don't understand. Everyone acts like this school is the best thing in the world."

Stephanie tried to shed some light. "Well, many people say that it is. I just know that it's an amazing school. Did you like the school you attended in Germany?"

"Not really."

"Is that why you came here?"

"No."

"All righty . . . Well, just like Sagrario said, this is an awesome place to help you figure out what you do like, and that helps you know who you are better. When I first came here, I was so nervous. I didn't think I would make any friends. I was short, tubby, and I wore headgear, sometimes even during the day. Do you know how long it took for boys to stop making fun of me at the other schools? I, for one, was so happy that at least I didn't have to add boys to my problems! Unless it's competing in sports, I don't get them and they don't get me."

Hedda didn't laugh.

They had almost arrived at the senior dorms, and Stephanie wanted to spend more time with Hedda. She didn't want Hedda to retreat to her dorm room without inviting her in. When Stephanie realized that Hedda was not interested in hearing more about her boy complex and that the conversation was rapidly heading south, she quickly changed the subject.

"Um, what classes are you taking again?"

Hedda, who by now had become almost completely withdrawn from Stephanie, and was actually walking slightly ahead of her, reached the threshold of the senior dorms. She said without turning around, "Honestly, I cannot quite remember. An English class to help me communicate better . . ."

Stephanie chimed in. "Yes, that's an ESL class! English as a second language . . ." Stephanie was losing confidence.

They ascended the stairs of the dorm. Once on the second

floor, Hedda stopped in front of her dorm room, which was located right off of the staircase. Stephanie continued.

"Well, that's good. If you ever need any help, I am here for you."

Hedda stared at Stephanie for a moment, then turned to open her door. She stood in the doorway, gave a small wave goodbye to Stephanie, and gently closed the door. Stephanie stood there, feeling bewildered and embarrassed in front of Hedda's closed door. As she heard other seniors begin to arrive into the building, she placed herself back into the bustling pedestrian traffic of the second-floor Senior Building Two hallway until she arrived at the huge and already populated common room reserved for senior day students. There she could, as usual, attempt to relate in some way to those other nonboarders as they gabbed about going to see their boyfriends after school.

"Being a boarder really blows," declared one.

"I know, I could not imagine having to get 'permission' from my parents just to hang out at a guy's house. My mom doesn't know where I'm going half the time. I just get the keys," confided another.

"Since I got my car, I drove to New York practically every weekend last month."

"No way!" declared one.

"To see that artist who lives in the East Village?" asked another.

"Stop bragging, loser!" cried a third.

Stephanie pretended to be searching for something in her

book bag while her peers gossiped. She had received her license and driving privileges of the family car when she was sixteen and could drive alone if she wanted to. But she never tried to sneak out to see a boy, or steal away to New York City. The most she'd done since being given driving liberty was take a handful of boarders to the mall to scout for boys. Even then she could barely connect with the surges of emotions each time a student would see one to which they were attracted. She instead would excuse herself to look for something sports related.

One of the gabbers reached to include Stephanie in the gossip session. "Stephanie, I'll bet that you'll get hit on a lot this year. Just look at your boobs!"

Stephanie wanted to button the top button on her oxford shirt and would have appreciated if there were more to button up past her head, too. Stephanie wished that she, like Hedda, had a private door to quietly enter and close herself off from everyone else.

Just two doors down from the senior-day-student common room resided Brooklyn and Winsome, who had brought their freshmen New Girls with them to show all that would be theirs in just three short years.

Because Winsome arrived a day earlier than Brooklyn, her mom had already put away most of her clothes, and Winsome's bed was made. Nothing was placed on the walls because she and Brooklyn liked to decorate their walls together. From the day they were paired as roommates they decorated their room in sync as if they were old friends. Brooklyn's signature crimson colors always complemented what Winsome brought to the new space, as she slightly changed her style each fall.

The New Girls oohed and aahed their way into their Old Girls' rooms, which to them was more like a fortress compared to the quaint room they shared with one other freshman that made their room a "triple." Winsome and Brooklyn had desk nooks carved in two separate corners of their room, walk-in closets, and the center of their room was spacious enough to do a cartwheel.

"So, how'd you guys do with the Name-Writing Tradition?" inquired Brooklyn as she plopped down onto her bare bed.

Winsome's New Girl was bold. "I hated it. I mean, it's bad enough that we have to lug all of our things in and unpack, but then we get interrupted for some friggin' exercise to see how well we can spell our dorm mate's names?"

"Whoa, girl, you are talking to two seniors." Winsome warned her New Girl.

"Well, she's not all wrong," chimed in Brooklyn's New Girl. "I believe I am an excellent speller, but some of these names, you've gotta give us a moment to at least pronounce them well first. We've got TWO Indians and one Taiwanese girl in our dorm! Their names are more complicated than my cousins in Lagos!"

"Calm down, little ladies, don't get your knickers in a bunch. If you missed some, you aren't going to get expelled!" offered Brooklyn with a grin.

"At least not right away!" teased Winsome.

The blood in Winsome's New Girl's face rushed to her cheeks.

"She's kidding!" added Brooklyn, beginning to laugh.

"All right, all right, I think we're pushing a little too hard. It's cool, girls. You'll be fine. Let's change the subject," continued Brooklyn. "What really brought you guys to MES?"

Brooklyn's New Girl was the first to answer. "My mother and father travel a lot, especially my mom because she helped to fund a school in our family's native country of Nigeria, and my older brother is about to graduate from college in two years, so I spent a lot of time alone. My mom said I would make plenty of new friends here, and because the school is close to where my brother attends school, we can all spend more time together as a family when my parents come to visit."

"Fair enough," Brooklyn responded. "And what do you think you want to become?"

"Well, my mom thinks I'm going to be an attorney like she is, but she's got it wrong. I'm gonna sing at Carnegie Hall someday."

Winsome's eyes widened.

"And as for you, leggy beauty, what do you want to be? Some kind of equestrian cover girl?" Brooklyn asked sarcastically.

"No. I'd like to become a chef," Winsome's tall, fresh-faced and freckled, ginger-headed New Girl answered matter-of-factly.

"Oh?" Winsome questioned.

"Yes, my inspirations are Julia Child and Alice Waters."

"Yes, and her company will cater all of my grand singing engagements," chimed in Brooklyn's New Girl.

"Sounds like us, Winnie," laughed Brooklyn. "Except, I never knew that your new version would be quite so . . . tall!"

"And a new version of you . . . with so much hair!"

Brooklyn's New Girl had lush, black, thick curls that trailed down her back, like a wavy lion's mane. Winsome and Brooklyn laughed.

Brooklyn recalled, "Remember when we both decided we would become actresses, and that we'd finish Madame Ellington, then head to London for the British Acting Academy?"

"And you were going to design many of our costumes if we made it to Broadway," added Winsome.

"Yes, I will, *when* we get to Broadway," assured Brooklyn to Winsome.

"It will happen," responded Winsome, with a bit of apprehension, then she quickly focused her attention to the floor.

Entering MES as a sophomore, Elaine would not share the full four-year experience with best friends Brooklyn and Winsome, or Sagrario and Stephanie. She stayed largely to herself and blended in with the crowd most of the time just so she could people-watch. It seemed to Elaine that the girls who had freshman year in common shared a bond to which she could not relate. There were only two other girls who entered as sophomores the same year as Elaine, but they were Panamanian fraternal twins, Ursula and Andrea, and they had each other. Elaine decided that she would remain on the margins and be happy with that. Today, alone in her dorm room looking out her window, Elaine watched Victoria Lee as she walked carefully from the senior dorms to the Main Building across the street. She noticed how safe Victoria played it while waiting for the light to change, how she did not project her foot out into the street until the light literally turned green, although vehicular traffic was practically dry. This observation was not particularly interesting to Elaine, but she would rather have searched for Victoria's *raison d'être* than consider what she'd just escaped the day before at home. Staring through people was Elaine's way of exploring her own life. When she felt down, she was attracted to those who looked equally as melancholy, and she imagined what they might be going through as a way to soothe her pain. In the same way, when she was happy, she often celebrated by bearing witness to the joyfulness in others. She'd spent a good part of her childhood in France, her mother's native country, and feeling so in-between made it challenging to relate to her American peers much of the time, or others, though Madame Ellington also had a healthy international student population. Elaine had the privilege of choosing either side when she wanted. Rather, she mostly chose to be kept at a safe distance, which allowed her to exist at Madame Ellington on her own terms.

Elaine nearly became lost in her thoughts about Victoria but was jolted back to the present by two students laughing loudly in the hallway as they passed by her bedroom door. As Elaine turned to close her door, she caught a glimpse of a framed photo of her parents she'd just placed that morning on her bookshelf. It was a candid shot that she had taken of them sitting on teak beach chairs at their second home on Nantucket the summer before. Elaine remembered when her father had coated the brand-new chairs with a protective sealant when she was twelve years old, which made them glisten in the sunlight. At the time that photo was taken by Elaine, years had passed, and the chairs had now faded to a grayish color. The wind was almost visible, with clouds hovering nearby. Looking closer at the photograph, Elaine recognized that her mother's usual "feel-good" smile appeared forced. Her parents looked dated like those teak chairs.

While lingering in the old corridors of the Main Building waiting to attend the first Student Heads meeting of the year, Sagrario caught herself fixated on a Latina New Girl having a talk with the head chef in the dining hall. When the chef spotted Sagrario, she paused her conversation with the student and whisked the smiling girl over to Sagrario.

"It is you, my dear Sagrario!"

"Chef Jackson!"

Sagrario initiated the embrace with the tiny, short-haired brunette. The younger student looked on.

"Have you personally met your Student Head of School, Sagrario Nuñez?"

The student humbly shook her head no.

"Well, this is your lucky day! Sagrario has been one of my worker bees since she was a freshman, like you are now! She will tell you about all of the fun we have in here, won't you, Sagrario?!"

"Oh yes, what is your name again?"

"Sara."

"Well, Sara, yes, working with Chef Jackson is *work*, but she makes it fun." Sagrario smiled.

"You bet I do. No sense of trudging through the day. Routine or not, you've gotta enjoy what you do. It's gotta have purpose."

"Yes, it was Chef Jackson who made me more than conscious of why it is so important to wash my hands before handling food. If you saw what we transport from our hands to our mouths throughout the day . . . That video still gives me chills."

"Keeps you washing your hands, doesn't it?"

"Um, yes."

"Mission accomplished!" Chef Jackson laughed. "Well, anyway, I wanted to make you both acquainted, as I suppose you won't be with me much this year with all that you have on your senior year plate, Sagrario."

"True. I will be taking advantage of library work study."

"That's fine. Everything has its place."

"Something else valuable I learned from you, Chef Jackson."

"See, Sara, Sagrario was just like you, and now she's Student Head of School. You could be that one day."

Sagrario nodded and smiled at Sara again. "This is true."

Sagrario wished Sara well for her first year, and Chef Jackson ushered her back into the dining hall. Watching Chef Jackson walk the New Girl back into the dining hall, hand placed on Sara's shoulder, made Sagrario think about how far she'd come.

Sagrario, running late to be early for a Student Heads meeting, hurried to the second floor of the Main Building. Victoria, appearing almost out of nowhere, tripped and fell onto Sagrario as she touched the first stair to head to the second floor.

"Whoa, looks like somebody is more than ready to get the meeting started, huh, Victoria *L'Artista*?"

Victoria smiled at Sagrario. "Sorry, Sagrario. I think I have my head in the sand."

"It's cool. I am excited, too. I really like the 'Welcome New Girls' poster you put up in front of Main. For someone as quiet as you are, you have a very big voice when it comes to art. I am so happy that you were chosen for head of the Arts Program."

Victoria smiled again and allowed Sagrario to lead the way to the Student Heads meeting.

3

School Is in Session

Stephanie's grand plan was not coming together at all. Feeling rebuffed by her New Girl, Hedda, compelled Stephanie to try harder to win her camaraderie. After all, Stephanie was a star athlete who thrived from competition. In order to win Hedda's approval, Stephanie thought she had to create an environment where the language barrier would not prohibit Hedda from fully participating. Because Hedda was tall like Stephanie, she decided she would convince Hedda to try out for the varsity volleyball team where Stephanie reigned as captain. It worked.

During tryouts, all of the hopefuls watched in irritation as Stephanie practically performed Hedda's drills for her. Hedda was horrible. She had no real coordination and her muscle endurance was remedial. The students expected Stephanie to give some sort of preference to Hedda because she was Stephanie's New Girl, but this was ridiculous. One of the hopefuls whispered to another if Stephanie could be less obvious.

At the end of the tryouts, it was clear that Hedda was not equipped to play varsity volleyball. She was so clumsy that she probably couldn't play dodgeball if she tried.

Stephanie hinted to Hedda about becoming the team's water girl, but Hedda, from what she could understand, was not impressed.

The next day, stumbling into American Classics two minutes late due to traffic and her little sister's breakdown about her new braces, Stephanie was relieved to see Hedda, but disappointed that she'd already found someone she felt comfortable sitting next to. It was the Ukrainian girl who entered Madame Ellington the year before. The two girls were engaged in quiet chatter in German because the Ukrainian girl spoke five languages. The teacher, a jovial, wiry, bearded man with no mustache named Gary Milikin, cheerfully called the class of ten to attention.

Stephanie tried to focus on this first-day teacher monologue, but her mind was all a blur. The students were supposed to be taking notes and paying attention to what was explained would be the scope of their first semester as they were gearing up for standardized tests and beginning the college-application process. Stephanie could only focus on Hedda's fingers as she swirled wisps of her ringlets around them while smiling back and forth with the Ukrainian girl. Hedda had barely acknowledged Stephanie's arrival—less like she did not like Stephanie, more like she just did not consider her.

While writing down what she did hear, Stephanie became off and on fixated with Hedda's sea-blue eyes that seemed to open and shut underneath an umbrella of blond eyelashes. Stephanie stole several glances at Hedda's smile, though not made up of pearly white, impeccably straight, newly-freed-from-braces teeth like her own, and sighed. To Stephanie, Hedda's smile had character. She imagined the two of them playing volleyball together, laughing together about Hedda's missteps. Laughing together when Hedda would try to hit a ball over the net and trip. Stephanie, the agile one, would catch her fall. Hedda's full crown of highlighted waves and ringlets would cascade over Stephanie's face.

Stephanie's mind was nowhere near the time and place required of her and the class, and when Mr. Milikin grinned his way through inquiring about Stephanie's summer vacation, Stephanie replied, "Golden."

"That's quite poetic of you, Stephanie. Anyone else here have a golden summer?"

Brooklyn and Winsome were relieved that they were closing out their final year in the same theater class, though they had been known in the past to whisper during a presentation or while the teacher was talking. They'd already decided that they would complete a joint project for their senior thesis, a two-woman show they began writing after Winsome hitched a ride to London with Brooklyn's mom on a rented private jet from New York earlier that summer.

The girls performed the third draft of the first scene in front of Brooklyn's mother and paternal grandmother. Before they finished, Brooklyn's grandmother was in tears.

BJ Fortunato, their theater teacher, was one of the most difficult teachers at the Madame Ellington School overall. Her intimidating personality did not derive from being dramatic; it was her constant matter-of-factness that imbalanced the nerves of even a few colleagues. BJ Fortunato hailed from England and had received a master's degree from the prestigious Royal Academy of Dramatic Art. She made no apology for her grand declarations, many times ending sentences in an aloof monotone that threatened to be challenged. Unlike her teacher's assistant, who flailed her arms to express any given emotion, BJ Fortunato communicated through her words alone. She folded her hands over her knees and sat atop a high stool placed center stage while the students occupied the center front row of the audience.

"All right, girls. This year is your last hoorah, and this semester will be your chance to get it right during this stage of your lives before you have to really prove yourselves next semester. I urge you to approach your chosen projects vehemently, with the dedication of a hawk to a mouse. Seek, target, attack. I want you to peel away every layer of emotion, break down the dialogues and monologues as if they are buildings made of sand, and then rebuild them with stone bricks. Through this practice, you will not only fully learn the characters you create or choose to portray, but you will also come closer to uncovering who you really are."

Winsome felt a lump in her throat. She turned to Brooklyn with a frightened look in her eyes, and Brooklyn nudged her. Without her saying a word, Brooklyn understood. She grabbed Winsome's hand.

"He just has to *see*. And he will," Brooklyn whispered.

"I know," Winsome whispered back, mustering her most confident tone.

BJ Fortunato continued on with her speech.

"This is why many great actors attest that the art of acting is one of the most cathartic experiences a human being can have. This is why a few of the students who said prior to university that they wanted to attend RADA, but when they received the chance to prove it, they failed. But even if you are allowed to enter the halls and study at the Royal Academy of Dramatic Art, and I do hope some of you dare, this still does not mean you will get it right. Those who are said to have gotten it right can be acknowledged through various citations and awards, but 'getting it right' is not ultimately determined by a panel of judges. It is by the aliveness of the piece itself. If you, as a chosen player of any piece, are dedicated enough and honest enough with yourselves, you will know if you've gotten it right, and no statuette will be able to make you believe it more or less. Because you have to give way to your own insecurities, fears, and strengths to create an undeniably authentic experience for the ones watching, you become the art, and this, my dear students, is what is considered 'getting it right.'"

The group of girls was mesmerized by BJ Fortunato's words.

Winsome and Brooklyn looked at each other. They felt inspired, yes, but were also withholding relative panic. They knew they were gifted, and they knew they made Brooklyn's grandmother cry. But BJ Fortunato was not talking about making your loved ones shed tears of support. She was talking about an ability to connect with a complete stranger. And unless the proper layers were pulled back, unless the real work of uncovering intention and meaning were accomplished, an authentic performance would not be achieved.

Not long after their feelings of fear settled in, it occurred to Brooklyn that there was no coincidence that they were paired one last time in theater class: BJ Fortunato wanted them to help each other find their own depths through concentrated practice. If they took their time to get it right, they just might find themselves on Broadway someday. BJ Fortunato believed in them.

❧

Believing in herself was why Sagrario was elevated to AP Calculus, where she sat next to her polar opposite, Caitlyn Lovette, who sat next to Victoria Lee. While Sagrario looked over her notes, Caitlyn pulled out her notebook. Taped to the cover's inside page was a photo of her boyfriend. Sagrario, looking up and over from her notes, noticed Caitlyn's portable shrine dedicated to him and shot her a semi-sincere smile. Sagrario believed that for all of the non-work Caitlyn had to do to get through the world, the fact that she had time to decorate her folder with photos of her boyfriend was not fair. While Sagrario had to work a student job to stay in school, Caitlyn's tuition was probably paid for with the interest from one of her trust fund accounts.

Both girls were gifted brainwise, though one's smarts were cultivated with privilege, and the other's were cultivated by beating the odds. And though Sagrario did believe that Caitlyn's math intelligence was God-given, she could not help but feel sensitivity about some people being more favored in the world than others. It pained Sagrario that she had to labor hard to understand things that girls like Caitlyn were exposed to in their everyday lives, yet Sagrario's common smarts were not equally valued. She felt ashamed that she was not innocent and naïve about certain things like Caitlyn. When a teacher suggested aloud that Sagrario and a couple other girls who were wealthy, and also from New York, had natural street smarts because they were from a big city, she felt that putting her name and the word "street" in the same sentence was demeaning. She did not believe that the teacher thought the other two wealthy girls from New York really had street smarts, that he was only referring to her, the "Bronx street girl." Part of Sagrario wondered why her life had to be so tough even though she spent so much time persevering, and why girls like Caitlyn Lovette, who could dillydally about a boy before a pop quiz, confident that she would most likely receive an A, and slide through life like it was covered with expensive, imported olive oil. People like Caitlyn didn't give people like Sagrario eye contact because they didn't have to. Sagrario remembered the handful of times she spoke directly to Caitlyn in four years, and in return, all Caitlyn ever showed Sagrario was a skittish smile. A smile filled with no substance, one that might not have even been sincerely directed at

Sagrario. An obligated, meaningless smile, like the ones you give to a stranger as the two of you enter and exit the same door. In Sagrario's mind, her kind of people were not really regarded or considered by Caitlyn's kind of people.

Sagrario lingered on about what she thought about Caitlyn's "kind of people" until their AP Calculus teacher caught her attention.

"So again, this quiz will not mean anything at all as it pertains to your grade. I simply want to know what you've retained from last year so I can determine how we should proceed," Mr. Mansher declared as he passed copies of the one-sheeted AP Calculus quiz.

An audible sigh of relief was heard throughout the small classroom.

"But that does not mean I want you to take it too lightly. You should still do your best to show me what you've got," he said after dropping a copy on Sagrario's desktop.

By this time, Caitlyn was flying through the pop quiz and twirling her hair. Sagrario glanced at Caitlyn and thought about the fact that Caitlyn did not really have to give her best, because her life would go well no matter how hard she did or did not try. She was probably even secretly engaged to that perfect boyfriend of hers whose face was taped to the inside of her notebook, and her parents probably already prebuilt a starter mini-mansion that was waiting for her and her new husband to move into after they graduated from college and became married. When Caitlyn did decide to have children, a proper nanny, not relatives who needed to earn money, would fill in her parenting gaps. Sagrario had the major details of Caitlyn's life all figured out before she could figure out the answer to the first quiz question.

Sagrario looked at the quiz and then at Mr. Mansher and smiled. He knew he could count on her to give her best at all times. Though on some level Sagrario thought she had nothing really to lose, yet everything to gain, her life heavily depended upon her giving one hundred percent.

In AP French class, reporting on her summer in her mother's native tongue, Elaine relished how effortlessly the language came to her. "And as usual, the last two weeks of my summer were spent with my parents at our Nantucket beach house. The only difference is, my father was in the middle of a deal that kept him on the phone a lot and he burned the pancakes three times."

Elaine gave a wry laugh, to which her classroom peers laughed back.

"*Bien, bien,* Elaine. It seems that you have been conversing with your mother more this summer. Your verb tenses were perfect."

"*Merci beaucoup.*" Elaine took one last look at her small audience of AP French peers and eagerly sat back down in her seat.

Elaine was the only other student to have an advantage in

AP French besides a French Canadian sophomore. Still, her way of communication was not as perfect as Elaine's, whose mother was born in a small village in Nice and had become one of the America's foremost educators in the language.

Because of this advantage, times like now when Elaine wanted to daydream did not affect her comprehension of what was being discussed. She could, just as easily as in English, catch the context of what was being said at the tail end and not skip a beat.

And because her teacher required all seven of the girls to take turns giving a full summary of their summer vacations, this made Elaine think deeply again about what she thought she overheard her mother asking her father the night before they were set to leave their beach house for the summer:

"And what do you suppose I should do with *that information*, Tom?"

Elaine repeated that question over and over again in her head but could not make out the full context. Why would such a random question linger in her mind? There were three specific details that aided Elaine's final assumption:

One: The timing of the question could not have been more suspicious. Elaine heard her mother ask her father this question shortly after she abruptly left the dinner table minutes after her father had to step away to tend to a call.

Two: The *way* her mother asked her father made it clear that whatever the *that information* was, it was a Very Important *that information.*

Three: Once her father responded (Elaine could not hear

his response), her mother retreated to their bathroom and did not come out for over an hour.

Elaine played over the scenario again and again in her head. All she could come up with was that her father must be very ill and her mother was worried sick over it. Their arguments exemplified how commonplace it was for her mother to manifest fear into anger. This assumption rendered Elaine anxious. Her parents were all she really had in the world. Her father's family's money tore his family apart, and her mother's family, namely her grandmother, resented Elaine's father, Tom, for convincing Elaine's mother, Madeleine, to forgo her dreams in France to be his wife and move to America. Though Elaine's mother had become successful as the chair of Harvard's French program, it took Elaine's grandmother nearly twelve years since Elaine was born for her to visit them in Cambridge. With deceased and estranged extended family, Elaine valued her parents unlike anyone she knew.

Just as Elaine was beginning to feel bad for her father, her teacher interrupted:

"*Votre famille maternelle est française, Elaine, pouvez-vous donner un peu de conseil à Jessica pour où elle peut chercher les boutiques de hanche à Paris?*"

Startled, Elaine winged it.

"*Bien sûr.* We can talk about it whenever you would like. Madame Howard, Jessica and I live down the hall from each other. Anytime." She smiled at the girl.

Elaine's French teacher complimented the gesture. "*Vous êtes très gentil d'offrir votre temps, Elaine.* You were raised well."

4

What Other People Think

Sagrario was happy that she did not have to preside over this evening's sit-down dinner. The first two months of school had already flown by in a blur, and she really wanted to take part in a social situation where she could blend in rather than stand out. Her co-head, Abigail, seated across the room, stood up to perform an appropriate, all-inclusive well-wishing over the meal. Sagrario watched as the students assigned to wait the tables all did their best to work in sync to serve their prospective tables. This was a new cycle of seating, as every month the table attendees shifted to encourage student engagement. There was also a faculty member assigned to sit at each table, and Sagrario had hoped that faculty member (in this case, the lead soccer coach, Jen Mathers) would find the new students interesting and lead a discussion about them and how their year had gone athletically. But as it always had been, superstar Sagrario was the topic of conversation.

"Wow, Sagrario, tell us about how this year is going for you? I mean, I remember when you were only fourteen years old with so many choices, and now you are a senior who has narrowed down to quite an impressive set of priorities, although I do wish there were an extra three hours in each day so you could have continued on with soccer." Coach Jen laughed, but only a little.

The well-wishing of the meal had just ended with everyone sitting down. Sagrario did not want to be rude, but she immediately reached to butter her roll, hoping no one would require her to talk with food in her mouth. She had planned on doing this with her food until the whole dinner itself was done. Simple nods and smiles between sips of water were all she was aiming to have to add to the conversation. Coach Jen did not catch Sagrario's hint, though. So Sagrario swallowed down hard a not-fully-chewed piece of bread.

"Oh, it's been really good. Actually, I have been getting more sleep than I thought I would . . . but that is because a few other things cannot be done. The days of late-night pranks on my friends are over!"

"That is called growing up, Sagrario. It's just like committing to a sport. You've got to get your rest. Even on Friday nights. The game depends on it. All the greats can speak to social sacrifice. It pays off."

The students at the table, mixed with all four grades, had faces of jade, aloofness, and sheer horror as Coach Jen declared this. She noticed.

"What's with the long faces? We're Ellington women! We aren't afraid of traveling the less traveled roads!"

Sagrario thought she was then off the hook. She cut a piece of her steak and shoved it in her mouth as fast as she could, wishing the other students would begin to challenge Coach

Jen in true Madame Ellington fashion. Instead, Coach Jen again turned to Sagrario for backup. Sagrario, having not savored the steak at all, chewed fast and swallowed.

"Well, I agree with Coach Jen, but I want you to know that that level of extreme social sacrifice did not happen for me until I entered junior year. Also, everyone has different lives, really, and so not everyone feels the need to make the kinds of priorities I did. You will all know what is right for you. Be cool."

Sagrario felt annoyed that Coach Jen would create the kind of platform of discussion where Sagrario would have to do what she does every day, all day on campus: peptalk younger students. Sagrario simply wanted to eat her steak and potatoes and salad, nod and smile a few times, and retreat to her room. She thought she had the evening off.

The stars must have heard Sagrario's inner cry, because just like that, Coach Jen seemed satisfied with Sagrario's answer, then added a couple more lines about how if students fit in a sport of choice early in their high school careers they would find it easier to excel academically and athletically. She offered the three freshmen at the table soccer support whenever they had questions. Then she changed the subject and asked one of the juniors about her upcoming squash tournaments.

Sagrario was grateful that she was able to spend the remainder of dinner eating in peace. She looked around the room at her fellow senior peers while they laughed and joked, and wondered if anyone else had as much on their mind as she did. Scanning the tables she saw Winsome and Brooklyn, who, although not sitting at the same table, sat at adjacent ones and still managed to find a way to talk to each other as if they were sitting side by side. *Those two,* she thought. What if she had found a best friend at Madame Ellington? Would she be as far along as she was in her journey? Would she have been able to be First Student Head of School? Would she have had the time? What if she had found someone just like her, the way Brooklyn and Winsome had found each other? Perhaps she and her like-minded, overachieving best friend could have ended up serving as Co-Student Heads of School, and because they would have been best friends, whoever won First or Second Head would not have mattered. She smiled at this idea, then shot to Abigail Turner, who actually was her Student Co-Head, but although she was very nice ALL of the time, she and Sagrario had very little in common.

Turning her head from Abigail, Sagrario caught eyes with Elaine. Elaine smiled, and Sagrario smiled back. Sagrario had never considered befriending Elaine when she entered Madame Ellington as a sophomore, but if Sagrario had to think about it, she did find Elaine interesting. Elaine wasn't a sports girl, she wasn't a theater girl, and she wasn't deep into visual arts. She was simply this undeniably intelligent girl who lived in the world on her terms. Elaine was able to move in and out of things without issue. Her comments were valued during class discussions, but she was also respected and given peace if she chose not to engage. *For a girl who moved through life like that, what kind of woman would she become?* wondered Sagrario. *With such a wide array of options, most likely anything she wanted.* Sagrario could value a friend like that because someone like Elaine would remind her not to sweat the small stuff, but still keep her eye on excellence. "That would be cool," Sagrario heard herself muttering aloud. This was not the first time Elaine and Sagrario had caught eyes, but Sagrario was always so busy moving along that a quick "hi" was all she could ever muster. And in these moments, though busy with her own agenda, Sagrario recognized that Elaine had always given her eye contact. Sagrario's what-ifs lingered on until a student grabbed everyone's attention by standing up and clinking her spoon on her glass to salute someone's birthday.

As that singled-out birthday girl performed the Madame Ellington birthday tradition of hopping around the room while being serenaded a special birthday song by students, Sagrario continued to muse about her life in the present, and areas that could evolve for the better.

Brooklyn and Winsome rushed back to their dorm together to continue their conversation from dinner, and Brooklyn was set to have a chat with her boyfriend, Chris. When they arrived at their dorm room, Brooklyn checked her phone and realized that Chris had already called. "Bollocks," she fumed. "Why doesn't he ever listen to me when I tell him the days that I cannot talk during supper?"

"Because he's a boy, that's why," Winsome joked.

"I'm gonna ring him back . . . Winnie, can I have a moment?"

"Oh, sure. I need to do some laundry anyway."

When Winsome dragged her oversized bag full of clothes across their dorm room floor, Brooklyn had to comment.

"How is it that you have any clean underwear at all?"

"Trust me, I might have one pair left. Why do you think I had to get back here so fast?"

Winsome closed their door behind her.

Brooklyn dialed Chris.

"Love . . . Yes, I told you I had sit-down tonight! One day you will listen to me."

"Right, I thought you said that was optional. Sorry," Chris apologized.

There was a brief silence and then Brooklyn spoke up. "I miss you."

"I miss you, too. And the fact that you are not going to be with me during Long Fall Break makes me feel awful. Can you change your plans?"

"Chris, I wish I could. I have not been to Winnie's in ages, and her mom is looking forward to seeing me. If by some reason we decide to return early, I'll let you know. Or meet with you in the city. Are you still going to your friend's place?"

"Yeah, he wants to take me to some clubs, some early Halloween parties, or something. I don't really care for raves, but what the hell."

"I will talk to Winsome and see if she wants to do our last day in the city. About your friend . . . where does he live?"

"Central Park West. Ginormous flat with his own wing. You guys can even spend the night."

"Wouldn't I love that. Along with a couple other things!" Brooklyn flirted.

"See if Winsome is in. Hey, my friend just broke with his girlfriend. Winsome's pretty. My friend's into exotic."

"Exotic? How ignorant, Chris! Winsome's not exotic. She's Winsome. Gorgeous just because."

"No harm, love. You know I mean it as only a compliment. See if she'd be into it."

"I'll ask, but I doubt if Winnie'd be into that."

Just then, Winsome walked in carrying her now deflated oversized laundry bag. "Into what?"

"Oh, Chris is staying with a friend who just broke up with his girlfriend and would be open to hanging out with an 'exotic' beauty like yourself."

Winsome laughed. "Meeeeee? *Exotic?* To what do I owe? You know, Brooklyn, you should start telling all of Chris's friends who are interested in 'exotic' girls after they break up with their girlfriends that I'm totally open!"

Winsome grabbed the phone from Brooklyn. "Fuck off, Chris." She handed Brooklyn back the phone, laughing hysterically.

Chris was not amused. "Brookie! Why did you paint me like that?! You know what I meant!"

"Take a chill pill. Winsome is fine about it. But that was a silly statement, love. And you know every silly statement is just begging to be attacked!"

"Yeah, yeah. Just apologize for me, all right?"

Brooklyn yelled to Winsome, "Chris says he's sorry, love. Like really sorry."

"Like, sorry like, face-red sorry?" Winsome rubbed it in.

"Like red-face-never-gonna-say-or-think-something-like-that-again sorry. Right, Chris?" Brooklyn demanded. Chris humbly agreed.

Brooklyn still tried to close the deal. "But still, Winnie, let's see if we can hang out in the city the last day of Long Fall Break. You might not want to meet his friend, but I do want to see 'Sorry Chris.'"

"That should be cool, especially if Chris begins every greeting to me with 'I'm sorry, Winsome.'"

"That can be arranged." Brooklyn brought the conversation with Chris to a close.

"Winnie?"

"Yeah?"

"How does it make you feel to be called exotic, really? You always handle these kinds of terms so well, but does it hurt, or make you mad?"

"I guess it feels the same as it would feel if you were being objectified as a woman, with another layer of shitty crap talk added on top. Like you, as a woman I have had to develop a thick skin and build a sort of immunity to the inevitable objectification. Being black, though, having to deal with shitty crap talk piled on top, that same thick skin has to also become scratch proof."

Stephanie tore open a bag of potato chips and slouched on the family room sofa. She was happy she'd completed her homework for the day before eleven o'clock. Dinner was good, but often after dinner she'd help put away dishes, finish her homework, and be hungry again. When she was younger, eating late-night snacks added pudge to her short frame. Now that she had grown almost four and a half inches between sophomore and senior year, and she trained athletically twice as hard, everything she ate she burned off as quickly as she consumed it. Stephanie turned on the television, looking for nothing in particular, and settled on an old *Seinfeld* rerun. In it, *Seinfeld* and a friend looked on as two women stood in a video store holding hands in front of an *A Few Good Men* DVD. Stephanie's father, unbeknownst to Stephanie, walked into the room and offered a comment to what he saw on screen.

"Get a load of that!"

Stephanie, startled, turned around when he said this.

Stephanie's father gave no more commentary, rubbed Stephanie's head, and left the room. She quickly turned the channel. She stopped on a show that highlighted a flashback interview of Jay Leno with Britney Spears when she was first introduced to the public. She wore a yellow pantsuit, and Stephanie was surprised to note that Britney was shy in person. Her manner of speaking was contrary to the big persona she presented on stage. When performing, Britney belted out songs that moved the crowd. Sitting with only one other person, though, compelled Britney to retreat into a bubble, answering questions with enough protective and distant language that would keep her safe. On stage, the crowd before her consisted of thousands, sometimes tens of thousands, of people. But there were security guards lined in front of the stage, and actual barricades lined in front of those guards. With Leno, there was no safe partition, and no bodyguards. And with the fact that he sat less than a foot away, Stephanie understood how Britney could have felt pressured. Stephanie empathized with the idea of feeling the need to protect one's true self. *Sometimes,* she thought, *not everyone is entitled to experience what is real. Maybe they wouldn't understand it. What it takes to perform on a superior level, whatever that is, does not have to be shared with all.*

Stephanie understood Britney's dilemma. From the moment Stephanie served a ball, everything around her—the screams, even the grunts from opposing team players—acted as fuel. Stephanie came alive in a way that she could never accomplish when merely spending intimate time with a peer. She was not exactly shy, but something special happened to her when a game commenced. Like Britney, there were two sides to Stephanie, and in Britney's world, everyone was obviously okay with that. Stephanie realized then that being made up of more than one side did not have to be a bad thing. She celebrated this "Aha!" moment by stuffing a handful of chips in her mouth.

Before long, Stephanie grew tired and headed upstairs to go to bed. She overheard her parents talking in their bedroom.

"The big dance is in the spring. I think I'm going to fish for one of my old dresses and see if Stephanie wants to wear it," Stephanie's mother gushed.

"That is a great idea. She is really blossoming, dear. It will be no time before they'll come knocking down the door!" added her father.

"But you aren't going to be one of those fathers with the shotgun at the front steps, are you?"

"Of course not. I'm smarter than that. Shotguns are too loud!" laughed Stephanie's father.

"You crazy nut! You will do no such thing. Can you imagine? Our firstborn, how she has developed. She is practically out of our house." Stephanie's mother sounded like she was tearing up.

"She is going to live the dream. And as her father, I could not be more proud."

Stephanie retreated back to her room.

When she lay down to sleep, Stephanie thought about the two women on the *Seinfeld* episode who were brave enough to hold hands in public, leaving themselves wide open for silly comments like "Get a load of that!" by onlookers, or worse, mean-spirited ones and sometimes even physical harm, just for living their lives the way they felt they saw fit. The two women on the television show chose not to protect themselves as Britney Spears had done. Rather, they challenged the world around them. Stephanie knew that the women were actors, but that scene could easily have been real life. Could be her life. She was inspired. She immediately had second thoughts about her plan to protect herself as a knee-jerk reaction when she overhead her parents talking about the spring dance they were excited she would attend. Stephanie was a Madame Ellington girl, after all, and in every way she and her peers were being taught to stand up for what they believed in. Stephanie knew that her parents, especially her father, were a particular case. But it was only a matter of time. Protect herself she would, but she also knew the day would come when she would have to push aside the partition, stand face to face with the life she truly wanted to live, and live it.

5

Layers

Brooklyn slapped fives with Winsome as they sat down in the back seat of the taxi that was going to transport them to the bus that would drop them off in New York City, where they would catch the LIRR to Long Island and Winsome's family's home for the first school break: Long Fall Weekend. Though Brooklyn's family was loaded with "new money" wealth, her father, Robert, a street-seasoned, Brixton-born pro soccer player, instilled in his girls that they were never to become too good to ride the Tube in London, or any public transportation for that matter. He told them that everyone in the world was just one reality away from public transportation being their only travel option, and so no one should be unfamiliar with it. Brooklyn's mother, Melanie, an upper class–raised international stage and film actress, on the other hand, was opposed to this idea because she didn't want her family's image to be tarnished. Riding public transportation was something that she did not enjoy, and she thought it simply looked bad. Regardless of these differences, Brooklyn and her twin sister Manhattan could appreciate both perspectives about public transportation, and they chose to use it at times because bodyguards and tinted windows could prove to be a drag for the teenaged girls.

Once Winsome and Brooklyn arrived at the Peter Pan Bus station in Hartford, Brooklyn pulled out a pack of cigarettes and her lighter. Winsome urged her to wait.

"Why are you in such a rush? You know we have to make sure the coast is clear! We have all weekend, Brookie."

"Yeah, I know," stuttered Brooklyn, "but I am entirely stressed, mate."

"About what? I told you you've been weirded out lately, but you kept shutting down that idea."

"Let's just find a place to light up."

Upon gazing at the crowd to see any familiar stool pigeon–like faces, Winsome spotted Sagrario seated in a waiting area.

"See, look over there. I didn't know Santa Maria was going to be on the same bus ride. I forgot my rosary beads."

They both laughed. "Well, that means no striptease on the bus, eh, Winnie? We wouldn't want to offend the nun!"

"I told you to be careful. You know she would send in an anonymous letter to Dr. Knoll . . ."

"How long before the bus takes off?"

Brooklyn checked her watch. "We've got nearly forty minutes."

"Cool. Let's head for the coffee shop across the street, shall we?"

"We shall."

Brooklyn and Winsome breezed past Sagrario. Brooklyn rolled her eyes, and Winsome barely acknowledged her.

Sagrario couldn't be bothered. She thought the two of them were a waste of a boarding school education. She thought all they did was spend time going on about their "acting" careers. Who had time to bank their dreams on something as lofty as wanting to be a famous actress? Not her. Who could afford it? Certainly not her. Brooklyn came from lots of money, but Winsome? Her dad owned a restaurant, sure, and her mom was a nurse, but Sagrario knew that money was not enough to place Winsome in the ultra-privileged world that Brooklyn lived in. Like Caitlyn, Brooklyn could grow up and not be a success and still lead a perfectly good life. If Winsome did not make it in the world, Sagrario thought, she'd have to make the best of waiting tables or whatever it was that aspiring actresses did to get by.

For a moment, Sagrario wondered what their upcoming weekend would entail, because it was clear that they were going to spend it with Winsome's family. If they were spending it with Brooklyn's, she figured, they'd have been chauffeured in a town car.

Aside from that minor distraction, all Sagrario could really focus on was her own impending trip home. Part of her wanted to lie to her mother and say that she could not go home that weekend so as not to be bothered with her entire family, but the rest of her wanted to go home to provide a sense of protection and relief for her younger and pregnant sister, Isabella, even if for just four days. Sagrario's mother's voice still rang in her ears from the day she had to break the news to her.

"Are you kidding me? At fifteen years? Where the hell were you?"

"Mommy . . ."

"No, I know where you were, *studying*, like you always do when you come home. But who is providing the food to put on the table when you come home, huh? The least you could do was keep after your little sister so she wouldn't get pregnant, but now she is. So what you gotta tell me? Huh?"

Sagrario's mother rendered her speechless then, but she felt in some way she was right. When Isabella found out she was pregnant, the first person she told was her big sister, who promised not to tell their mother until the time was right. At the time that Isabella conceived her child, Sagrario's eyes were not on her younger sister, but were fixated on the prize of earning perfect test scores to make her a worthy candidate for an excellent high school student pre-law program. While Sagrario was busy studying to earn the sort of career that could really help support her family in the future, her younger sister was turning into an immediate liability. This new reality Sagrario neither resented nor rejected, though. It was simply added to the pile of other family responsibilities on her shoulders. Sagrario vacillated between a belief that she was doing the right thing by staying at the Madame Ellington School, and a belief that if she were attending a neighborhood high school like her mother desired, she could have prevented her little sister from facing such a life-altering situation. Besides Sagrario's mother, who worked all of the time, there were no other decent female role models in their family who could have steered Isabella in a direction away from boys. And because of her family's strong Catholic beliefs, if God deemed it so, that child would be born. This weekend also happened to be Isabella's baby shower/early sweet sixteen. Sagrario had to be there for her.

Chain-smoking three cigarettes brought on a perfect case of nausea in Brooklyn, and though she felt the sickness creeping in after crushing her first cigarette butt, the anxiety building up within her prompted her to prioritize satisfying one feeling over the other. Winsome announced that she was going to buy a couple of the "most likely dated" wrapped croissants from the aging storefront deli back at the bus station, and Brooklyn used the opportunity to take a dreaded walk to the bathroom and confirm what she believed was causing her anxiety. Three different brands and six pee-stick tests later, Brooklyn's wind was vacuumed clear out of her chest as each stick shouted at her, using plus signs and double stripes to give her the news. One was so bold that it practically stood on its own pedestal to proclaim the word: PREGNANT.

Meeting Winsome back at the waiting area of the bus station was harrowing. Brooklyn's frantic attempts to contradict what she'd read on each previous test were not successful. She even peed a second time on the last two, and those seemed to prove her condition the loudest. Taking a bite of her croissant back at the bus station, Winsome held out her hand to Brooklyn, offering one to her, yet the compounded anxiety mixed with severe nausea had Brooklyn way on edge, and she declined the pastry. She did not know whether she was going to throw up everywhere or have a nervous breakdown. Brooklyn, standing in the middle of a dizzying tornado of emotions, desperately searched the waiting room for Sagrario, hoping she was not within earshot or could not see her clearly. Brooklyn let out a small sigh of relief that Sagrario was seated far from them, closest to the bus entrance, as Brooklyn assumed, to be first on the line. But that tiny exhale really did nothing for the sheath of despair that shrouded Brooklyn's whole being. Brooklyn could not remember taking in any air since leaving the bathroom and imagined herself deflating completely.

Winsome acknowledged that Brooklyn did not look well. Brooklyn could only manage a few words of "feeling tired" in her own defense, and did her best to shrug it off. Oddly, Winsome seemed to buy the excuse and stuffed Brooklyn's croissant back in the shopping bag, packaging still intact. She warned Brooklyn that if she opened the packaging to have a bite, she'd have to eat the whole croissant at once because the waxy excuse for French bread was already half stale to begin with.

The moment Winsome and Brooklyn arrived at Winsome's parents' home by taxi, her little brother, Colin, greeted them at the door. He didn't speak at first, so Winsome broke the ice.

"Hi, Colin, how was school?"

"It was good."

"Colin, do you remember my friend Brooklyn?"

Colin nodded his head.

Brooklyn extended herself fully, hoping to absorb some of Colin's innocent energy, as her own felt muddled and soiled. Still covered with a cloud of anguish, Brooklyn took in what little air she could manage and put on her best act. "Hi, Colin! So glad to see you! You've gotten to be quite the tall one, eh? What's the grade now?"

Colin stared at her for a beat, then turned around to head back into the kitchen without responding.

"Give him a minute," Winsome suggested protectively.

In the kitchen, Winsome's mother was rinsing off a bushel of grapes.

"Winnie! Brooklyn! Who let you in? Colin? I know Winnie didn't have her keys!"

"You're wrong, Mommy, I just didn't have time to take them out of my bag. Colin could sense me arriving before the doorbell rang. You know how in tune we are." Winsome leaned down to her mother to give her an embrace. Then she stood to the side so Brooklyn could do the same.

Odetta Sinclair stood back to take a good look at both girls. "How you gals farin' at school, eh? Well?"

"Yes, Mommy, BJ Fortunato is gonna allow Brooklyn and me to complete our senior project together."

"Yes, and we've the perfect collaboration, which we've already begun. We performed our first scene in front of my mum and grandmum, and they loved it!" chimed in Brooklyn with all her might.

"Yes, Mommy, and Mrs. Abbott even cried!" added Winsome.

"That's all well and good. All well and good. Just keep at it, girls. Winsome, your father said that you are both to go over to the restaurant after you settle in. He'll be needin' a little help since two of his servers took sick today."

Winsome huffed, her jovial spirits having been rained on with this indirect request from her father.

Odetta sensed Winsome's frustration. "Winnie, it's just for today. He has coverage for tomorrow."

Brooklyn also felt Winsome's irritated energy mixed with a little embarrassment. "Win, it'll be cool. Do you think he'll let me work for free food, Mrs. Sinclair?"

Odetta laughed. "I'm sure that can be arranged."

As the girls were exiting the kitchen for Winsome's bedroom, Odetta grabbed Winsome's arm before she hit the staircase. "Oh, and Winnie, be sure to take a mint before you approach your father, eh? We don't want to give him one more thing to talk about. And all jokes aside, darlin', you've gotta cut out that smoking."

Winsome leaned down and hugged her mother again.

"Take my car," Odetta finished the whispered message in her ear.

Upstairs in Winsome's bedroom, Brooklyn's jacket and bag were hastily thrown to the floor and she bolted for the bathroom.

Winsome walked to the bathroom door and tapped. "Brookie, everything all right in there?"

"Yes, I'm fine. I think it was that awful croissant. I'll be ready to go in a bit. Sure I'll be hungry again."

Sucking on a mint, Winsome tiptoed into her father's restaurant office with Brooklyn lethargically tiptoeing behind her. Her father was handling business over the phone, and by the tone of his voice, the conversation was not smooth. When he noticed Winsome and Brooklyn walking in, he first shooed them away with his hand, then quickly waved them back in. They both sat down on the old-fashioned leather sofa across from his desk, and Winsome looked at the ceiling while Brooklyn looked around. Brooklyn had been inside of this space twice before. Once was an in-and-out experience following Winsome to grab her keys. The other time was standing by Winsome's father's desk while Winsome made a phone call. This time, sitting down, Brooklyn was really able to take it all in: the signed and framed Bob Marley poster on the wall, the tower of Jamaican newspapers stacked against the wall nearly as tall as Winsome, the Jamaican flag posted in the corner, framed childhood photos of Winsome and her siblings that surrounded a ten-by-thirteen framed photo of Mr. and Mrs. Sinclair circa the eighties.

Mr. Sinclair's office enveloped a rich history. From his bookshelf to the papers that covered his desk, Brooklyn could tell that he was extremely smart. He had five separate daily newspapers on his desk that looked like they'd all been read already. His literary collection varied from philosophy to business, and Winsome once told her how he created a computer program specifically for his business to track sales, profit, loss, and inventory at the click of one button. If Brooklyn were Winsome, Brooklyn thought, she would just sit at the restaurant to observe her father sometimes.

Brooklyn knew that Mr. Sinclair was intellectually driven, and she knew that he knew that her own younger parents were not. She knew that Mr. Sinclair was not like everyone else who was attracted to and impressed by her family's wealth. He was a bootstrap man: someone who brought up himself through a steady climb, armed with determination, wit, and instinct against adversity. His talents did not have to be a part of "pop culture" in order to be considered successful. Brooklyn overheard him telling Mrs. Sinclair on the way to dinner with her parents during parents' weekend last year, "I just don't know what I would talk about with them. I mean, does he even read?"

After cleaning off the counters and tabletops with Winsome, and heavily snacking in between, Brooklyn slid their to-go bags across the counter so they would not forget to bring them home. Winsome's father left earlier that day, and so it was her job to lock up for the evening. Just as Winsome turned off the kitchen light and lowered Bunny Wailer to a faint cry on the radio, the front door's bell jingled. Winsome yelled from the back, "Sorry, we're closed!" Brooklyn was in front with the man and smiled at him, naïvely assuming he was a customer. Yet the man ordered nothing and just stood there.

Winsome made her way to the front, thinking that

Brooklyn saw whomever it was out. She was surprised to see a man standing in front of the counter with an angered look on his face.

Brooklyn did not know what to do or say.

"Can I help you, sir?" Winsome asked politely.

Sarcastically, the man responded, "Yes, you can help me, MA'AM."

Winsome was nervous. This man did not look like anyone she'd ever met or remembered being a customer at her family's restaurant. And it was clear that his disposition wasn't a result of his displeasure with the curried goat. She tried to keep calm and handle the situation like an adult.

"I'm sorry sir, I've already shut off the oven. We've some beef patties I can quickly heat up for you."

"Mi nuh waan nuh damn beef patty, woman. Mi waan mi money!"

Brooklyn shuddered at his sudden uproar. She did not understand in full what the man was saying, so she stepped behind the counter. Winsome, who did understand all that the man was saying, trembled as she realized that he might be someone dangerous who had come straight from Jamaica. Her voice began to stammer.

"I'm sorry, sir. I don't have a key to the regis—"

"Get di fuckin' money or yuh restaurant ago bun dung!"

Brooklyn was stunned. She had never experienced anything like this before. She wasn't sure if Winsome had or not, because she seemed like she was handling it just fine.

Inside, though, Winsome was terrified, too. It did not seem

like the restaurant was being robbed randomly; it was clear that someone had a bone to pick with her father. Scared or not, Winsome's instincts told her not to let on that her father was the owner.

"Sir, we are the only ones here and we are just fill-ins. I can call my boss and let him know you are here."

The man edged into a booth while responding to Winsome's suggestion. "Sure, weh yuh nuh gwaan an do dat. Mi av time." He sat down at a nearby booth.

Winsome turned to head into her father's office to call the police, but the man abruptly stood up to stop her.

"Woman, mi tink yuh fi mek di fone call rite yah soh. Mi nuh waan nuh funny biz niz."

Winsome slowly returned to her previous position next to Brooklyn. She motioned to Brooklyn that she did not have her cell phone, so Brooklyn reached for hers in her back pocket and slid it to Winsome. Winsome's quivering fingers dialed her father.

Winsome spoke to her father as if she did not know him well, telling him that there was someone waiting for him at his restaurant, and her father quickly caught on. Within minutes, George Sinclair was charging through the front door.

Not intimidated by the man's lingering aggression, Mr. Sinclair yelled at him while walking straight toward him. "Weh dis fah?"

Mr. Sinclair's usual proper English instantly code-switched to Jamaican Patois, a common dialect that the angered man spoke to Winsome. Mr. Sinclair only reverted to this manner of speaking when his emotions were vital, which was not often. In a swift motion, he turned to Winsome, shooting her a look she had never seen before. His eyes were ferocious.

"Gwaan inna di office."

Winsome grabbed Brooklyn's arm and rushed her to her father's office. Once inside, she motioned for Brooklyn to sit on the sofa. Winsome walked to the door and cracked it while keeping an eye and ear on her father's confrontation.

Winsome watched her father stand face to face with the man, with a glare that Winsome was surprised did not make the man instantly disintegrate. Because of how he frightened her, Winsome knew that if he could have, her father would have sliced the man's throat with his eyes.

Mr. Sinclair whispered with brevity, something complex and threatening. Winsome was sure of this based upon how the man physically responded to her father. She watched the man unzip his jacket, revealing a gun tucked in his pants. This movement startled Mr. Sinclair, and he jumped back. Winsome, seeing all of this through the slit in the door, was jolted at the exact same time her father jumped back.

Winsome nearly fainted, anticipating what would come next. She watched her father hold up his hands to the man, and because she was so frantic, she could not hear all that was being said. Before she knew it, the man left their restaurant and her father summoned her to the front. Winsome obeyed, completely closing her father's office door with Brooklyn still inside.

Mr. Sinclair did not explain exactly what happened. He merely tried to assure Winsome that he had everything under control, and that she need not worry. Based upon what she witnessed, Winsome knew not to prod her father with questions, and as he did his best to balance convincing her and remaining calm, she noticed his hand tremble a bit. Winsome's natural inclination at this moment was to forego any unspoken protocol and plead with her father to tell her what was going on. And though it appeared that Winsome had a cool head, the truth was, her nerves were not only unstable like her father's hand, her heart was making its way to burst from her chest. Still, Winsome hesitated. As she observed her father's hand shaking, she felt his sense of embarrassment and guilt, and she did not want to force him to say something that would break him down any more than he already had been. Winsome nodded in agreement to everything her father instructed her to do, and he tapped her on her back a few times as the single act of physical comfort before hastily locking up the restaurant and driving home while the girls followed in Odetta's car.

"What was that?" Brooklyn questioned with a sincere concern, strangely grateful that she could focus on someone else's drama. She'd always looked up to Mr. Sinclair, and she was hoping that Winsome would tell her what they'd just experienced was all a dream.

"I don't know, Brookie. You saw as much as I did." Winsome knew that Brooklyn would begin asking questions the moment they were alone in her mom's car.

"No, that's not true, Winnie, you closed the door so tightly that only one pair of eyes could peer in. What did your father say that made the man leave?"

Winsome was becoming frustrated. "Look, I saw them, but could not hear them well. If you really want to know, why don't you ask my dad yourself?"

"Geez. Sorry I brought it up." Brooklyn could not remember when she and Winsome last had a serious spat, and she did not like the feeling of something brewing under the surface. She instantly regretted having mentioned anything.

The two girls took turns sighing in silence all the way back to Winsome's house. Winsome sighed because she was trying to keep from crying about her dad having possibly been killed. Brooklyn's sighs derived from her growing-by-the-second panic about having brought someone to life inside of her.

As the girls continued to follow Mr. Sinclair through the quiet residential traffic, he drove slowly and carefully so as to not be separated from them by drivers or traffic lights.

Elaine was so busy thinking about her parents that she missed the walk light entirely. She had hastily made the decision to remain on campus after becoming sandwiched between her mother and father during their latest argument when she called home a few nights before. She listened to her mother in tears as her father said damaging things to her in the background. Her mother threw down the phone and her father picked it up, not even acknowledging Elaine at the receiving end of the tumult, and hung up. Her mother called her later that night to apologize after her father fled to New York, but her father did not. Elaine, to her father, returned his favor and refused to call him also. Idle at the traffic light with nothing to do but stand, she was at once confronted with feelings of regret for not going home during Long Fall Weekend, at least to see about her mother. Elaine had watched fellow seniors prepare to hop in taxis and town cars and buses and, in some cases, fly across country to go home for the few days. There she stood, not even two full hours' driving distance from school to home, and Elaine chose to hide.

Hedda crept up behind Elaine with folded arms. When the two girls stood side by side, Elaine imagined that the slightest wave of wind could topple Hedda completely. Elaine had not ever focused on how thin Hedda was before. Back in France thin women were standard, but they were also petite from head to foot. Hedda's height magnified her frail frame.

Hedda turned around, looked Elaine in her eyes, and gave her a firm nod. Elaine whispered, "Hello."

The dining hall, at best, would be sparsely filled because most students were away for the weekend. Now it was practically empty since the doors had just been opened. Hedda and Elaine moved along the food stations, trays in hand, separated by a freshman dorm mother who attempted to manage holding a tray and keeping together two rambunctious toddlers. Elaine, who was first in line, ordered the chicken dish and made her way to a table to place her tray and choose something to drink from the beverage station. Hedda was already standing there filling her glass with water. Elaine glanced at Hedda's plate holding only one single small piece of chicken and sighed. Hedda shot back a look at Elaine, and Elaine's only defense was to invite her to sit at her table. Hedda agreed.

"Tell me." Elaine felt compelled to open the door for conversation after chewing her eighth bite of chicken, fork still in hand. "Why did you choose to attend Madame Ellington as a senior?"

"My parents wanted me to have an American school experience because all of my siblings did," Hedda responded dryly.

Elaine did not comment right away, for she could not relate to having siblings.

"Well, my mother and father feel the same about having a dual education, but I think my mother really would have preferred I did not begin my American process until much later. We moved back to the States when I was in the fourth grade, and although I went to a Lycée International in Boston, my mother says it still is not the same."

Hedda's eyes brightened. "You are European?"

"Yes, and no. I was born here in America, but I have dual citizenship because of my mother. She is from a small village near Nice."

"What village?" Hedda asked in French.

Elaine switched language, too. "It's called Cagnes-sur-Mer. Wait, you speak French? Aren't you from Hamburg?"

"No, I'm from Berlin, but I spent summers at a camp in Montreux."

Elaine was impressed. "Oh, I've been to the jazz festival there once when I was little. Michael Jackson's producer Quincy Jones brought a lot of American rappers with him. I did not understand what they were saying, but it was cool."

"I like Michael Jackson."

"Me, too."

Elaine was so shocked at the sudden connection between the two that she guffawed at her sudden, unknown connection to Hedda. To her surprise, Hedda did, too. They were both giddy for no reason at all.

This laughter prompted the toddlers who were finally sitting with their mother to jump from their seats and run around the room. The dorm parent gave the girls an accusatory look out of the corner of her eye as she leapt from her seat to capture her fleeing children. Her look made Elaine and Hedda laugh all the more.

Hedda, having let down her guard a little, returned her language of choice back to English, and lowered her volume. "Do you have a boyfriend?"

Startled, Elaine smiled. "No, haven't got one of those. What about you?"

"Yeah, I do, and he is an asshole," Hedda said, pushing her chicken, barely eaten, farther away from her on her plate.

"Well, my dad is an asshole, so we're even." Elaine was not about to explain how she put two and two together and that her earlier belief that father's supposed sickness was not what put her mother in a rut.

"Oh," Hedda said in a way that acknowledged Elaine's pain,

but also did not press for more. "You should be lucky not to have an asshole boyfriend. It seems the more you are in love with one, the harder it is to let them go, despite how they treat you."

By now Elaine had been moved into deep thought, and while semi-listening to Hedda, she replaced Hedda's head for her mother's and became angry inside. If Hedda felt that way about her asshole *boyfriend*, how must her mother feel about her longtime, asshole *husband*?

Later that night back at the senior dorms, Elaine walked into the bathroom and heard strong gagging sounds, and then a flush came from one of the stalls. Out walked Hedda, wiping her mouth, and she caught eyes with Elaine. Elaine stood still, unable to utter anything in English or in French to Hedda about what she'd just heard. Hedda made a sound, and whatever she was going to say was immediately interrupted by three Japanese girls laughing loudly about one thing or another as they set up their routine face cleansing. Elaine did not pursue what it was that Hedda was going to say.

Just as briskly as Elaine had made the decision to remain on campus during Long Fall Weekend, she made up her mind in that bathroom that she was going to catch the first train to New York City to prevent her father from possibly making her mother end up hurting herself, too.

As Elaine packed for her impromptu trip the next morning, back at Winsome's house, Winsome knew that she could not convince Brooklyn that what just happened was all a dream, so they both did the next best thing: pretended as though what they experienced earlier that day did not happen. It seemed like Winsome, who led the façade, shifted personalities as soon as she exited the front door of the restaurant. Brooklyn was feeling nauseous from eating nearly three full plates of rich Jamaican food, and from the stress of experiencing what they were pretending did not happen, but she went along with it as best as she could. When Winsome suggested they still head to a party in Brooklyn, the borough, despite it being so late, Brooklyn, the girl, agreed. During Winsome's search for the perfect outfit, Brooklyn knelt on Winsome's bathroom floor searching for the right octave in which to throw up and not disturb.

Somehow Brooklyn was able to pull herself together without suspicion from anyone and climbed into the passenger seat of Winsome's mother's car. When Winsome buckled herself in and searched her bag for cigarettes, she exclaimed that she'd run out. Brooklyn only nodded and leaned on the window. Winsome did not notice Brooklyn's sluggishness because she was wrapped into her own nicotine frenzy. Before heading to the highway, Winsome drove to the gas station to purchase a box of American Spirit Ultra Lights, and Brooklyn stumbled out of the car soon after to rush to the bathroom and relieve herself once again. When she returned, Winsome was leaning on her mother's car, inhaling from her cigarette that made Brooklyn yearn for her own long, deep drag, but she also wanted to gag at the very thought of doing so. Winsome smiled at her best friend and offered her the cigarette. Brooklyn began to tear up. Upon seeing this, Winsome joked, "Why the long face? I told you I was going to buy a new pack!"

Brooklyn did not respond, but her tears turned into cries, then long, desperate sobs. "Winnie! I don't know what to do!"

Seeing Brooklyn cry triggered Winsome's own tears. She flicked her cigarette, smashed it with her shoe, and rushed up to Brooklyn. "Brookie? What's wrong?"

By this time, Brooklyn was sobbing and stammering her words. None of what she was saying was intelligible, until she finally took in a real gust of air and came out with it. "Winnie, I think I'm pregnant!"

Winsome held Brooklyn tightly. This helped Brooklyn to take in more air and then breathe out without hyperventilating. Winsome drove them both back home, and during the drive, they cried uncontrollably, some for Brooklyn, some for what they saw at Winsome's family restaurant. They knew to settle down when they arrived and left Winsome to explain their change of plans to her parents while Brooklyn escaped to Winsome's room upstairs with her red eyes, flushed face, and smeared mascara.

Winsome and Brooklyn decided to talk very little about IT while in Winsome's parent's house. But Brooklyn cried quietly on and off all night long. She had a pillow shoved in her mouth, but Winsome could still hear her from the other side of the bed. Winsome turned around and cupped her best friend's body with her own, and Brooklyn let her. If Brooklyn could have, she would have balled up herself and disappeared.

Stephanie sat at dinner earlier that same evening trying not to cry about the fact that she was failing at winning over her New Girl. Stephanie wished that Hedda, who remained on campus during the break, would call her house and ask her to pick her up and show her around town. The only car Stephanie was allowed to drive was the family minivan, but she would totally clean it out and spray lots of Febreze inside so it wouldn't smell like musty cleats.

But Hedda never called. Stephanie thought Hedda was most likely spending her days being romanced over the phone by her German boyfriend, who looked like a younger Luke Perry. Stephanie stole a glance at a photo of him when she was helping Hedda bring some books into her room soon after school started. Stephanie was convinced that Hedda's displeasure about the Madame Ellington School was due to her missing the nonstop romance with the younger TV star lookalike.

Stephanie's heart ached thinking about how Hedda was slipping through her fingers each day. Following Stephanie's botched attempt to create a space for Hedda on the varsity volleyball team, their communication had been relegated to obligatory interactions: formal dinners, senior meetings, and school-tradition events. Being placed in the same American Classics class was of little help. Whenever she had a free moment to chat, Hedda used it to talk to the Ukrainian girl. For a minute, Stephanie was going to try to convince her parents to hire for her a German tutor after school. Stephanie was nearing a state of desperation.

All of these thoughts swam through her mind as she

swirled her spoon in the pumpkin soup her mother prepared for dinner in the spirit of fall.

Stephanie's father broke the silence at the dinner table.

"So, Eric, I hear that you made the Honor Roll all through junior year. Did you hear that, Stephanie?"

Stephanie looked up from her bowl. "Uh, yes, that's cool."

"I imagine you'll have your pick of schools, hey, Eric?"

Eric, a young man Stephanie had known since her family moved to their block nearly thirteen years ago, had always been extremely quiet around the neighborhood. He and Stephanie never crossed paths, except during universal holidays such as Halloween when all of the neighborhood children would be brought together. Stephanie remembered Eric always looked uncomfortable in his costume. Physically, he'd grown into an attractive young man. He had piercing blue eyes and curly jet-black hair, a perfect combination of his Syrian mother and Dutch father. Plus, Eric was tall, with broad shoulders to boot. Together, Stephanie and Eric looked like a Calvin Klein ad. Both were leggy and gorgeous. It was clear to Stephanie why her parents invited Eric over for dinner, but there was absolutely no way that she was going to date him. She didn't want to date anyone they wanted her to date for that matter. And even if she wanted to date someone, she couldn't be with the one she wanted to be with, even in secret.

Eric nervously made eye contact with Stephanie's father. "A—actually, I am applying early decision to Wesleyan University, sir."

"Staying in Connecticut! What a great idea! And Wesleyan

is a fine school. Lots of game-changers come out of there. Good for you! See, Stephanie, staying in Connecticut isn't so bad!"

Stephanie's father leaned across the table to give an impression of confiding in Eric something the family already knew.

"Stephanie wants to head west, Eric. The University of Connecticut is only a safety for her, but they've also got excellent sports!" he joked, half-whispering.

Stephanie's mother nudged her husband. Stephanie's younger sister snickered.

Stephanie and Eric remained silent.

At Stephanie's father's suggestion, "to better get to know each other without us folks in the room," Stephanie and Eric rinsed dishes and filled the dishwasher in the kitchen together. To her father's disappointed eavesdropping ears, Stephanie had few words for Eric while they were still physically in the house.

Stephanie needed some air and asked Eric if she could walk him home. When Stephanie told her father that she was going to do this, he smiled at her and clasped his hands like he'd just sealed a major deal. Stephanie loved her father very much, but she could not help rolling her eyes at him the minute she turned her head.

The autumn air proved to be just what Stephanie needed, and she expected to be left to her thoughts while walking down the block with Eric. They both knew there was zero chemistry between them, and Stephanie was not about to pretend like there was. To her surprise, it was quiet Eric who spoke up first.

"I hear UCLA has a huge LGBT community. Is that true?"

Stephanie's cheeks instantly lost all of the red the night air brought into them. "What? How would I know?"

Just like that, Eric turned into his most confident self. He walked slightly ahead of her, then turned to confront her head on. Stephanie paused, and Eric got close to her face, declaring in a calm, supportive tone.

"We all know you don't *do* boys! I can't believe your parents can't see! You are practically one yourself!"

Taken completely off guard, Stephanie steamed, "Fuck off, Eric!"

She sped up ahead of him, but Eric's longer legs soon caught up with her. "Look. Watching you in there with your parents made me sad. I saw myself in you. I was once where you are. I know how you feel."

Stephanie's eyes welled up with tears. "How would you know? What BIG secret do you have, huh?"

Eric put his hands on Stephanie's shoulders. "Darling, you are more boy than I could ever be."

The blood rushed back into Stephanie's face. "You? You?"

"Yes me, me. And until you are ready to say it out loud, your secret is safe with me, me!"

She did not know how to respond. Was this even happening to her? Was Stephanie just outed by a gay boy who was okay with being *out*?

All of a sudden Stephanie's lungs expanded wider than

they ever had. She took a serious deep breath, smiled, and embraced her new confidant.

On a crisp and sunny Saturday afternoon in the South Bronx, Sagrario had just finished taping the "Congratulations!" ribbons on the designated walls in her building's recreational center. She sat on one of the folding chairs and took stock of the decorations. She did her best to mix and match the colors from pastels for the baby to a little more sophisticated theme to also celebrate Isabella's sixteenth birthday. "Isa's gonna like this," she assured herself. "She'll feel good about this."

"Need help with anything?" Isabella wobbled into the room.

"Isa! *Muñeca!* What are you doing here? This was supposed to be *una sorpresa* for you!" Sagrario rushed to embrace her baby sister.

"It's okay. I knew all would be beautiful because you were doing everything, like you always do."

Sagrario looked to her younger sister.

"And you know, *hermana*, I appreciate everything you do for me."

"I know you do, *muñeca*."

"Mami does, too."

Sagrario bowed her head. "I know she does."

"I don't know about that. She prays for you. I hear her late at night sometimes when the baby wakes me up."

Sagrario lifted her head and looked her sister in the eyes. "I will never let anything bad happen to you. To any of you."

"I know you won't, *hermana*."

The sisters embraced. Sagrario gently pulled away, and she shed a few tears.

"So, you like what you see?"

"*Por supuesto* I do!"

"So many gifts coming for our baby."

"Where will we put everything?"

"We'll make do."

"Can you believe this is happening? *Mira* my belly! I have to pinch myself sometimes!

Sagrario leaned down to kiss Isabella's stomach. "It is a beautiful thing. You look beautiful."

"*Hermana*, do I really?"

"Like a *muñeca*."

Isabella laughed. "Well, this *muñeca* will need to find herself a place to sit down."

Sagrario rushed to unfold a folding chair and then placed it next to Isabella. Isabella slowly lowered herself onto the seat. Sagrario grabbed Isabella's hand, and both girls took stock of the room together. Isabella breathed deeply.

"Sagrario, you always make it happen."

The baby shower/sixteenth birthday was a success. With Sagrario's family combined, Isabella's little girl received all of her key essentials. If there was one thing Sagrario appreciated about her family, it was that they came together when it mattered most. But there were elements of her family's dysfunction that proved to threaten Sagrario's progression, which was why she sought legal emancipation from them. Sagrario's family drama showed early signs of destroying her chances at Madame Ellington during her freshman year. By the time she was to experience her very first Long Fall Weekend, her mother warned her father that she was going to take the children away and move to another state so he could not see them. Then her mother called the school and had words with Dr. Knoll about why was she taking Sagrario away. This behavior was so disturbing and embarrassing that Sagrario needed to find a sense of autonomy. Still, these acts never got in the way of the entire family banding together in support of one of their own when they needed help. So, though Sagrario was legally emancipated from her parents, she still stood by her family. Among the various cast of characters in Sagrario's family, Sagrario's father understood her better than anyone, and she missed him. He was not perfect, not even close, but he was all she had. She missed talking to him.

Sagrario did not talk much to her mother because her mother spoke to Sagrario as if she *were* her father, and that was not a good thing. And it did not help that Sagrario was her father's spitting image. Sagrario's mother's resentment toward her father stemmed from way back, before Sagrario was even a month old. When Sagrario was born, her father, nervous about how to fully support his new family, was arrested for stealing a car and trying to sell its parts with a friend. This unscrupulous move resulted in him having to serve three straight years in jail, and in the meantime, Sagrario's mother, who was only sixteen at the time, had to fend for herself and Sagrario. With all of her extended family around her, she still felt alone without Sagrario's father present. And she never forgave him for being gone during those tough times. Regardless, Sagrario's mother held out for him a solid year, and when he was denied early release, she fell into the arms of another neighborhood guy, who fathered Isabella and Louis, who was conceived the night after Sagrario's father was released from prison.

The father of Sagrario's two younger siblings was physically and mentally abusive to Sagrario's mother, and volatile in the streets. This behavior put him in an early grave. Sagrario's father, out of a mixture of guilt and sympathy, took on all three children as his own. But over time, the responsibility proved overwhelming for him, and so he continued a back-and-forth relationship with the Bronx Police Department. Sagrario's mother believed that if he had never landed himself in jail the first time, today they would be in a better place. Sagrario's face was a constant reminder of her father, and although her mother did love Sagrario, she could not help but misdirect her anger toward her oldest child.

And like her father, Sagrario did not verbally reject whatever her mother placed upon her shoulders. Also like her father, though, Sagrario was a dreamer and saw more for her life. From her mother she inherited a practical and stick-to-it attitude, which compelled her to take the proper steps to achieve her dreams. Sagrario watched her mother work at Albert Einstein Hospital for almost fifteen years, moving up to the head of housekeeping. Observing these consistent efforts influenced Sagrario's determined attitude. But Sagrario's *cojones* to reach for the sky came straight from her father. And when Sagrario was only thirteen, she reached up for the Madame Ellington School for Girls. By hook or by crook, Sagrario was going to finish well.

A day and a half later, the bus ride back to school was tranquil. Sagrario was able to read two chapters ahead in an assigned novel. Long Fall Weekend wasn't all that bad, she thought to herself, reminiscing. Sagrario accomplished what she wanted with Isabella, and was able to venture downtown to solidify a Christmas holiday job at the Gap in Rockefeller Center. It was always so pretty around there that time of year, and Sagrario, having worked two previous Christmas holidays there, would often leave work and walk around Midtown, dreaming of the day when she would call one of those doorman skyscrapers home.

6

The Dance

The next morning Sagrario entered the school chapel prepared to recite a schoolwide speech about the spirit of traditions that were soon to turn up a notch on campus. The "Name-Writing Tradition" was easy enough, but it served as a means to initiate bonding with the New Girls. Still, some of the New Girls thought they were being graded on how well they spelled the names of their fellow new dorm mates. The "Leafing Tradition" occurred on the Thursday before Long Fall Weekend. The entire group of New Girls had come together to rake and bag the mountain of leaves that had fallen in the square behind the Main Building. It brought on a few tears, only because the seniors allowed the rumor to float that no New Girl who was set to travel home could until all the leaves were bagged. Sagrario, considered the mother hen of all the students, could not help but giggle to herself at the sight of that frantic leaf-raking scene.

Sagrario and the rest of the Old Girls were the keepers of the traditions, and other than the generalized written description in the school handbook, the New Girls had only rumors to address suspicions or concerns. The concern was hardly ever about safety, yet there were Old Girls who could instill a certain level of fear in some of the New Girls as if they would suffer cruel acts like being trapped in a freezer for a full minute. One year, the rumors of traditions became so potent that the entire New Girl class protested against them before they even began, which meant, since the first official tradition occurred on the day the girls arrived to school in the fall, the protest was also held on that day. How a group of seventy-three New Girls were able to come together for one common cause within only a matter of hours of knowing each other remained a mystery. Some of the girls who had arrived late were literally yanked in the protest crowd without explanation to show solidarity. To this day, that class of 1994 prevailed as one of the most powerful. The bond held within that class served as a beacon for Sagrario, and she felt that the Madame Ellington school traditions were the catalyst for that powerful bond.

The best-kept tradition of all was that no student who'd experienced the year of traditions hardly ever spoiled it for the incoming girls the following year. They kept the magnificence of their first year a divine secret. Each year the New Girls waited nervously for each impending tradition and prank, and by the end of the year, they would have bonded so tightly with their peers that they finally, fully understood the purpose of the "rites of passage locked in secrecy." It was Sagrario's job, as it was those Student Heads of School before her, to calm everyone's anticipating, jittery nerves.

Sagrario remained in the chapel for a few moments after giving her speech to engage the small group of girls who had lingering questions for the Student Head of School, even after Sagrario had pretty much told them not to worry.

Sagrario noticed Brooklyn seated in the far back of the chapel, shuffling through her knapsack. Her trusted partner, Winsome, had already gone.

Brooklyn caught a glimpse of Sagrario as she chatted with a black New Girl from Wisconsin, and it was already widely known on campus that the girl's wealthy and famous aunt sent her to the Madame Ellington School to expose her young niece to its heightened educational experience. The girl had never spent any time in Connecticut, aside from visiting the school soon after she'd been accepted. She commented then that the environment felt like college.

"Um, Sagrario, what's going to happen if a student doesn't pass a tradition?"

"Don't worry about that, Chrisna, traditions aren't graded. It is all in good fun, and you will be fine."

"But what if I'm not?"

"You WILL be."

The girl smiled skittishly, understanding that although she was the last in line to speak to Sagrario, Sagrario might have her own school obligations she had to tend to.

"Well, thanks a lot . . . Just one more question, if I happen to not be okay, can I talk to you about it?"

Sagrario smiled at the New Girl. "Of course you can."

Sagrario watched the student walk away, understanding that it was not that long ago that she had the same fears. *How fast that fear passes*, she thought to herself.

The New Girl was in such a hurry to make it to class on time that she flung open the chapel door, almost making it swing in the face of Brooklyn, who was struggling to leave the chapel carrying loads of papers plus a messenger bag. Sagrario rushed to hold the door open for her. Brooklyn looked at Sagrario but did not say anything to her as she exited the building. After descending one of the three stairs of the chapel, Brooklyn staggered and collapsed. Sagrario broke her fall.

"Are you all right, Brooklyn?"

Brooklyn, on the brink of tears, held them back and said firmly to Sagrario, "Yes, yes, I am fine. I lost my footing, is all."

Brooklyn released herself from Sagrario's arms and repositioned herself to become upright. Walking away, she stopped, turned around, and uttered, "Thank you for helping me."

Sagrario did not know what to make of what had just happened. She responded, "Sure, anytime," and watched Brooklyn walk away.

Sagrario did not believe that Brooklyn all of a sudden became clumsy, for when she collapsed she seemed to faint, and her skin was as white as a sheet. Brooklyn did not appear to be starving herself, a common problem for some girls in classes past, but none in her class that she knew of. A little difficult to do at first, still, Sagrario decided to make it a passing thought.

Saturday could not have arrived any faster for Brooklyn.

She'd made it to Wednesday without a major issue since returning from Long Fall Weekend with Winsome, but the incident at the chapel with Sagrario was a close call. What if she had completely fallen? When Sagrario dashed to her rescue, it took everything for Brooklyn to not blurt out her problems to Sagrario in a barrage of tears. Despite what she'd always thought about Sagrario, in that moment, Sagrario's arms were entirely comforting, and her demeanor wasn't judgmental at all. In fact, Sagrario's energy was kind and embracing—just the kind of net into which Brooklyn would have liked to land and rest a while. Winsome was well aware of Brooklyn's pregnancy, but could not be available for every single ultra-vulnerable moment Brooklyn was sure to have each day.

Since that time of realization, the only feelings Brooklyn felt were nausea, irritation, uncertainty, and anxiety, all hovering under a giant awning of PANIC. Each day that she sat in secret unto herself proved to render her nerves more brittle. Her physical appearance had not changed much, but Brooklyn was definitely different. She knew it was her responsibility to remain as she always had been on the outside, regardless of how she felt.

Brooklyn also knew deep down that she desperately needed to see her boyfriend, Chris. After confiding in Winsome during Long Fall Weekend, Brooklyn decided not to join Chris and his friend in New York after all. Winsome offered to serve as the scapegoat. But Chris knew Brooklyn well, and did not accept the excuse. Every time he asked what was wrong, she declined to tell him over the phone. "Next Saturday'll be here, and I can hardly wait," Brooklyn would repeat. She barely wanted to talk to him on the phone, but she had to pass the time doing something. She'd spent nearly every day eating ridiculous amounts of food, soon after ejecting it all, only to have to soothe her stomach with crackers and ginger ale Winsome brought to her from the dining hall.

Brooklyn tried to remain upbeat, but hormones mixed with unsteadiness made her very testy. She did not notice how short she was being with fellow classmates, and when BJ Fortunato called her out during a run-through of the first scene of her and Winsome's senior project, the cat was almost let out of the bag.

"Brooklyn, are you all right? You seem ill."

"No, BJ. I'm fine."

"Let's have a look." BJ Fortunato stepped down from the high stool on which she usually sat perched during class and approached Brooklyn. She cupped Brooklyn's chin in her hand and angled her face so she could have a better look into Brooklyn's eyes.

"Are you sure?"

"Yes, I'm fine," Brooklyn responded nervously, looking away.

"Well, to me, you seem ill. You are entirely pale! I think you should head over to Nurse Foley at the infirm—"

Winsome used this moment as a cue to interrupt.

"I know what it is, BJ. I've had an awful cold all during holiday weekend and I must have passed it onto Brooklyn. We shared the same bed at my house."

Brooklyn caught eyes with Winsome while she was professing this quickly made-up lie to BJ Fortunato. Brooklyn's eyes expressed both gratitude and exhaustion.

Satisfied with Winsome's explanation, BJ Fortunato added, "Why didn't you say so? I'd heard there was something going around . . . Brooklyn, I know that you and Winsome have been working hard on your project, but I think you should go back to your room and rest for the remainder of the day. I will be sure to get word to the nurse so you can be cleared. You don't want to get worse, nor do you want to pass what you have on to anyone else."

Brooklyn nodded and complied with gratitude. Her only job was to make it to her dorm room without projectile vomiting along the way. BJ Fortunato did not know that what Brooklyn was carrying could not, in fact, be spread to anyone else by germ exchange, but she was right in stating that Brooklyn did not need to feel any worse than she already did.

The annual Fall Dance was always a hit, especially for the New Girls who'd barely interacted with the opposite sex as part of their experience at the Madame Ellington School, save for attending classes taught by the handful of male teachers, or greeting other school faculty who were men, or maybe if a school theater production required male students for the winter play, which it did not this term.

Yellow school buses lined up in a row along the back street

of the campus waiting to be refilled with the various ages of high school boys and young men. This was the time when many of the New Girl freshmen, having been just a few months released from the clutches of their parents, would poorly make up their faces, emulating their mothers or favorite film, pop, or TV stars. Some of them would dress too conservatively, wearing blazers with brooches and scarves, trying to appear mature. Others took a riskier approach, donning short spandex skirts. A couple of these girls would be asked by a school dorm parent or teacher to return to their room and change into something more appropriate. Then there were the girls who dressed like Stephanie, not looking to gain the attention of anyone in particular, at least not a boy.

Stephanie hung out on the outdoor stairs of the school theater, not far from where the dance was being held in the gymnasium. She wasn't going to go to the dance at first, but then she thought, *Who knows?* Maybe she would bump into Hedda and Hedda would choose to spend the rest of the evening hanging out with her. Just then, someone touched Stephanie's shoulder from behind.

"What a close call with your parents, hey?"

It was Eric. Now that he'd come out to her about being gay, Stephanie could no longer see the quote unquote attractive male peer about whom she could not have been more repulsed when her father tried to make them an item at dinner. Stephanie now embraced all of who Eric was. He already felt like a close friend.

"Hey . . . yeah. Who are you meeting here?"

"No one in particular. There is this boy who I think has the hots for me, but he won't show it. I'm hoping tonight he shows up and let's get it out in the air already." Eric confidently smoothed his tightish jeans.

"How do you know he has the hots for you?"

"Because I have caught eyes with him more than twice, and . . . a girl just knows these things."

"Then why do you think he won't show you his attraction?" Stephanie had yet to understand how the nuances of sexual attraction could work.

"Because it's not easy being the football team's biggest star!" Eric emphasized without heightening his volume.

"Whoa." Stephanie was in disbelief. To think, there was a football star hiding *his* sexuality. In the world of athletes, she wasn't alone. She wondered if the guy's parents made him eat soup with the neighborhood cheerleader in hopes of having a romantic union formed.

"Right. Who are you waiting for? A girl doesn't just WAIT outside for nothing. Looking to get noticed by someone?" Eric questioned with the tone of a gossip.

"Look. I haven't told this to anyone, but yes. But I don't think she is coming, and I don't think she has the 'hots' for me."

"That's a lot of negative talk, isn't it?"

"It's not negative, it's realistic. She has a boyfriend and she mostly keeps to herself about it, but I have heard her talking about him once or twice. When she says his name, *Raimund*, her entire face changes. There's this 'look' . . . I don't stand a chance." Just saying Hedda's boyfriend's name made Stephanie's shoulders slump.

"What I have learned in all of my years is one thing," Eric offered.

Stephanie laughed. "And what is that?"

"You can only be you."

Stephanie looked up at Eric and, again, allowed him to wrap an arm around her. This time, he kissed her on her forehead as she hugged his side.

Winsome had not dated anyone in nearly two semesters, after an emotional breakup with a boy who ended their relationship because he said they were becoming too close and his parents would not understand. She only understood that she loved him, and she had no doubt that he loved her. This is why up until now, neither of them could move on with anyone else. Winsome wanted to believe that one day he would grow some balls.

She instead searched around campus for another boyfriend, who was the love of her best friend. This was going to be the day when Brooklyn broke the news to Chris. Brooklyn declared this for three days straight, but in the end could not make her way out of bed to go to the dance. Winsome decided she would deliver Chris to Brooklyn instead. Chris had not exited any of the eight buses that arrived thus far, but Winsome saw the familiar sign of their neighboring brother school, Arthur Newgate, and stood near the pull-up station. Winsome noticed Caitlyn also standing at the station alone, and wondered why she wasn't inside the dance playing hookup queen for all of her friends. After a group of Euro seniors stepped off the bus, a handful of jocks did, too, and with them was Caitlyn's younger brother, Carl. At first he did not see Caitlyn, but she called out to him and he ran over to her. She said something like "I can't take it!" and fell onto him, sobbing. Carl walked Caitlyn back up the hill, and Winsome felt bad that she and EVERYONE knew that Caitlyn's longtime boyfriend had canceled their relationship, too. Winsome never spent any real time talking with Caitlyn, and they were not in any of the same classes that year, but she totally felt her pain. "What an asshole," she said to herself as she continued to wait for Chris.

After the final group of guys, a young class of Indian boys, stepped off the bus, Winsome learned from the driver that there was one more bus on the way.

~

Hedda had just gotten off her knees in a bathroom stall when she heard two girls elbow deep in campus gossip. She decided to sit cross-legged on a toilet seat and have a listen.

"Have you heard? Yeah, I think she's a dyke."

"How would you know? Have you ever seen her with a girl?"

"Have YOU ever seen her with a guy?"

"No, but she's a day student, she could have a boyfriend at home."

"Doubt it. She spends so much time in volleyball practice or just on campus in the day-student room."

"You sure know a lot about her . . ." One of them laughed. "Are you sure YOU'RE not the one who's gay?"

"Oh whatever! I'm just commenting, is all. I am the least gay person I know. I don't even like changing clothes in front of another girl!"

"YOU don't like changing your clothes in front of another girl not because you are so anti-gay, but because you're a weirdo!"

"Oh whatever! Anyway, who is weird is her New Girl, Hedda from Germany. She doesn't even talk to anyone."

"So true. I mean, why would anyone travel so far to go to a new school during their senior year when they don't care to make friends?"

"I hear that she doesn't talk, but she sure does pray a lot to the porcelain god!"

"You mean she's one of those?"

"One of what?" Elaine's voice startled Hedda. Who knew for how long she'd been listening?

"She's a total starve-girl! That's what she is! Her and her Old Girl over there are gettin' it on right before they throw up their lunch," declared the one who first initiated the gossip.

"What do you care?" Elaine asked, boldly. "Shouldn't the two of you be hidden someplace on campus taking turns giving blowjobs? I've heard about you, too!" The truth was, Elaine had not heard anything about them at all. She entered the bathroom right as they began slandering Hedda for no reason, and after the encounter she had with her father when she surprised him with a visit during Long Fall Weekend, Elaine was abundant with an avenging spirit.

The girls were so taken aback by Elaine, they could not even retort. Perhaps, Elaine thought, there was a bit of truth to the false rumor she'd conjured up.

As Elaine brushed past the girls on their way out, she headed into a stall, and soon realized that she was not alone. Hedda opened the neighboring stall and walked out with her head bowed.

"Hey," Elaine said to Hedda when they caught eyes.

"Thanks for that," responded Hedda with a weak smile and watering eyes.

"They were total losers. Don't sweat it."

"Don't sweat it?"

"Don't pay them any mind."

"Okay." Hedda began to walk away. Elaine called Hedda's name.

"Hedda . . ."

"Yes?"

"Take care of yourself."

Hedda did not respond, only mouthed the words "Thank you" once more as she walked away.

Winsome hummed to herself while waiting for the second

bus from the Arthur Newgate School, wondering how Chris would handle the news. If there was a guy who deserved an award for being wise beyond his years in his relationship, it was Chris. Winsome always felt that Brooklyn, like Brooklyn's mother, landed such a good guy. He was kind to her, did not try to stifle her, and was actually turned on by her independence. Most importantly, he was never afraid to show his affection for her, regardless of who was in the room. Winsome wished her ex-boyfriend was so confident about their union. He wasn't like Chris's friend who would have considered her "exotic." Winsome liked Chris, a lot, but her ex-boyfriend was not naïve like Chris was about race. He never made an insensitive comment unknowingly or otherwise, never stereotyped her. He was the only person she knew besides Brooklyn who was not her race who simply treated her as she wished to be treated. And like Brooklyn, if there was ever a question, he was never afraid to ask and educate himself. Winsome could not believe that someone raised by such linear-minded people could be so open and embracing. Yet for all of those attributes, he still caved when it came down to confronting his parents. "No-balls soft ass," Winsome muttered to herself. As she stared down the street, she saw a familiar face up ahead. It was Victoria, and she was with a boy. With all her androgynous behavior, Winsome could not believe that Victoria was interested in the opposite sex, or interested in anyone at all for that matter. From the looks of how they were carrying on behind the science building, it was clear that they believed they could not be seen.

Winsome's mouth was gaping open until she spotted the ultra-bright headlights from an oncoming school bus.

Elaine's boldness continued. This was the fifth swig of vodka and cranberry juice that Elaine had taken with a random male student from her brother school, whom she just encountered that evening. They met standing just outside of the gym, and he sparked up a conversation with her about his belief that the Madame Ellington School had the best campus of all the boarding-school campuses in the New England area. Elaine was impressed with the idea that he had seen that many other campuses to which he could compare hers, and she was also taken by his dark, wavy hair and single dimple in his left cheek. He looked French. He brought to mind her first instant crush on a boy named Victor, son of famed fashion photographer Patrick Demarchelier, to whom she was introduced by their parents at a gallery opening in New York the summer before. Alas, though, for Victor, there was no mutual instant anything. So, when this new boy asked her if there was somewhere farther away and private that they could talk, Elaine felt a delayed rebound and took him to just the place.

But by this time she couldn't remember his name. She kept thinking "Ian," but she wasn't sure. They were having such fun together she figured why create a ruffle by asking him his name again? Plus, this was the first time a boy paid her any serious attention since her sophomore summer on Nantucket. But that boy wasn't a regular on the island. "Ian" said she should drink more because he'd already consumed a lot on the school bus.

After she took another swig, she asked, "How are you able to disguise your breath? There's hardly any cranberry juice in this."

"It's easy. Just don't talk to anyone and speed past teachers. It's not the drinkers they catch. It's the sniffers. Want a cigarette?"

Elaine sobered up slightly. "We can't smoke here! This is a smoke-free campus!"

"Ian" shot back, "Do you think anybody cares tonight? I mean, who is gonna look for somebody smoking behind an old art shed on the night of a school dance? I think school dances give teachers a chance to check out, too."

"I suppose you're right. Just fan the smoke so it doesn't look like there's a fire brewing over here."

Elaine, hardly able to stand, leaned on the shed door, slid down, and sat on the ground. "Ian" followed. "Ian" took a few pulls of the cigarette and then passed it to Elaine. She took a pull and began to cough.

"You really are a prude, aren't you?"

Elaine became offended. "No! I just haven't smoked in a while!"

"Sure . . . So are your parents getting divorced over this 'mistress'?"

"What? Who knows."

Elaine had almost forgotten that less than fifteen minutes prior she'd told this stranger the grittiest details of discovering her father's mistress after she paid her father an unexpected visit over Long Fall Weekend. She said she realized that he wasn't physically sick, but sick in the head. Upon being reminded that she'd confided so much to "Ian," she felt regret, but just as quickly she forgave herself for having told him. Yet she wanted him to think she was cool, so she tried to sound dismissive and keep her emotions at bay.

"Maybe my parents already are divorced. I mean, my dad paraded the other woman around our apartment in New York like she lived there. She wasn't even nervous to meet me—she spoke to me as though we were friends! From the looks of her, she was not much older than I am. The nerve of him. I am only pissed off that I didn't say more to defend my mother, but I was so taken by surprise I could barely speak. I have been calling him an asshole for a few weeks, now I know exactly why. I don't know what's real anymore. Whatever."

"When my folks got divorced, we were all pretty happy. They argued all of the time when they were married. I actually don't have a good memory of them together except for when they entertained houseguests. The minute everyone left, slamming doors were my lullabies."

"That sucks. I actually do have really good memories of my parents together . . . I wonder what this is going to mean for Nantucket."

"Do you have a house there? Well, get ready. My parents couldn't agree on who should get what so they just liquidated everything. Including our summer home in the Hamptons."

"I can hardly think."

"Have another drink."

"Okay."

Elaine held the lit cigarette in one hand and the flask in the other like an amateur. Like a pro, "Ian" slid his hand up the back of Elaine's sweater and unhinged her brassiere, all while kissing her neck. The drunken Elaine liked it. The drunken Elaine took another pull of the cigarette and dropped it onto the concrete, which subsequently lost its heat from the wind. There was barely any light around the old shed, save for a streetlamp that shone almost a half block away. Before she knew it, "Ian" had pulled out a condom and was on top of her. The real Elaine knew better than to lose her virginity this way. The drunken Elaine engaged because she wanted to create something bigger for the real Elaine to think about than be preoccupied by her parents' possibility of divorce. So she gave herself, on the night of the Madame Ellington Fall Dance, to someone whom she believed was named "Ian."

Brooklyn was hysterical. Blowing her nose into a tissue, she tried to explain why she did not want to see Chris. She quickly covered her head with her duvet. Winsome, who'd returned from the dance as a last-ditch effort to get Brooklyn to leave their room, pleaded with her.

"Brookie, you've been wanting to see him all week. What's the deal?"

"Are you bloody serious? Look at me!"

"Brookie, you only look wrecked because you've been crying. Actually, you've lost weight. Who knows how you'll be feeling during the week to be able to see him then. I think you should tell him now while he's here on campus. He should know."

Brooklyn paused for a bit and thought about the fact that she was already nearly three months pregnant. She and Winsome read that you had to know what you wanted to do with the baby before three months, what is called a "first trimester."

Winsome edged closer to Brooklyn on her bed in order to ask her something she'd been wanting to ask her all along since she found out, something that she knew she had to approach delicately.

"Brooklyn, do you know what you want to do already?"

Brooklyn sat up and pulled the duvet down from her face. Her eyes welled up with tears again, and, lips trembling, she responded.

"As sick as I have been feeling . . . I can feel it inside of me. I can feel it Winnie . . . I'm so scared. I . . . I don't want to let go of my baby."

Winsome reached over to Brooklyn, and Brooklyn slowly fell into Winsome's arms. Brooklyn lay there and breathed hard. She couldn't cry anymore. But what she wanted most at that very moment was for another set of arms and hands to be wrapped around her: the arms and hands that looked exactly like her own.

Winsome walked Chris into the senior common room to a seated, track-suited Brooklyn. Chris, a tall, brown-eyed, Irish high school senior who attended Arthur Newgate, had no idea what was going on. He thought Brooklyn was just sick, so he stood with a distance between them. Although Winsome did her best to freshen up Brooklyn's face, her eyes were still red and puffy.

"Brookie, what's wrong?"

"Love, I'm not contagious. You can sit near me."

Chris looked to Winsome, who nodded her head in agreement, and so Chris nervously edged closer to Brooklyn, then sat down beside her. Winsome took that as her cue to exit the room.

"Brook, I'm going to hang around outside to keep everything cool, okay?"

Brooklyn nodded her head.

Chris reached over and put his hand atop Brooklyn's and took a deep breath. He looked to her with his downward-slanted eyes, mustered a sincere smile, and spoke again.

"Brookie, what's wrong?"

"I'm pregnant."

Chris's freckled face became instantly flushed, causing it to look blotchier than Brooklyn's.

He swallowed hard. "What? Preg—pregnant? H—how do you know?"

"Do you think I would look like this if I wasn't sure?"

Chris placed his head in his hands. "Oh my bloody God. What are we going to do?"

Chris lifted his head, looking at Brooklyn for an answer. She couldn't speak, but her face said it all.

Chris swallowed hard again. "Right."

Brooklyn added to what her facial expression introduced. "I'm due around graduation."

Chris stood up and began to pace the room. Brooklyn could see that he was scared, too. She knew he loved her, and believed that he had always been faithful to her. He was a decently sensible young man and always supported her. This news would scare off a lot of guys, but maybe not Chris, because his own mother was also very young when she gave birth to him. Chris had told Brooklyn about the hardships he endured with his young mother.

Brooklyn waited nervously. Would he offer her abortion money? Hastily propose? Brooklyn didn't know what she needed, but it wasn't either of those things. Instead, Chris wrapped his arms around Brooklyn and she felt something let loose in her chest. She put her head in his lap and cried, until she fell asleep. During that time, he stroked her hair in silence.

7

Bold

Elaine could not say if she was happy to have lost her virginity to the guy she believed was named Ian, but one thing was for sure: a strong dose of courage had cultivated inside of her as a result. After having sex for the first time with a complete stranger, Elaine was bereft of shame, anger, or fear. In fact, she felt oddly empowered. She had imagined *that day*, or the days leading up to *that day* (because of course in her previous mind, it would have all been planned), as an anxiety-filled occasion. Up until that night Elaine had never considered doing anything outside of the realms of her structured, governed life.

The sun had yet to truly rise when Elaine opened her eyes, and her dorm was like a ghost town. Dozens of seniors were still a few hours away from waking after the exciting event on campus the night before, and those who were awake were headed to mandatory sports activities and the like. After showering in the hollowed dorm bathroom, Elaine spoke a word aloud to hear if her voice would echo because the room was so empty. She took in her reflection while brushing her teeth. "I friggin' just lost my virginity," she whispered to herself as though she were confiding in a best friend.

Elaine walked quietly back to her bedroom and called her mother in Cambridge, who picked up on the second ring.

"*Bonjour*, Elaine, *n'est-ce pas comment?*"

"*Bien, bien, Maman, et vous?*"

Elaine's mother did not respond right away. After questioning her a second time, Elaine's mother finally responded in English.

"Fine . . . I'm fine."

Elaine felt bad about calling her mother with her newfound feelings of freedom, although she would not dare divulge the exactness of what brought on the giddy emotion. Elaine believed she should have been calling her mother with the sole intention of consoling her, because she could only imagine, though the two had yet to discuss, how her mother was feeling after finding out about her dad's affair.

It was clear that within her mother's withdrawn reply of being "fine," she was actually not fine, but was between-the-lines crying for help. Five days later, Elaine found herself riding first class on an Acela Express to Boston. When she arrived at her home from the train station via taxi, Elaine stopped short at who was sitting across from her mother at the kitchen nook: her maternal grandmother.

"Elaine!"

Madame Charton leapt to greet her granddaughter, Madame's aged, ultra-petite body still strong. Elaine dropped her weekend bag and they embraced with an unrelenting clutch, making up for lost time.

"*Bonne! Bonne!* We are all here! Come, sit down." Madame Charton began their conversation in French.

Before Elainc could sit down, though, she had to physically connect with her mother, who remained seated, diminutive, wearing a weak smile on her face like a mask. Elaine's mother desperately tried to keep a good head.

Elaine leaned down to kiss her mother, whose eyes closed when her daughter's lips touched her cheek. Elaine, almost upon instinct, then kissed her mother on her forehead.

"*Maman*, are you okay?"

Elaine's mother looked at her own mother, and then back at Elaine. "*Oui.* All is fine, darling."

Elaine's mother manufactured a slightly more pronounced smile. She was only partly successful at preventing a tear or two from falling. Elaine, from the corner of her own eye, caught a glimpse of the contents on the kitchen nook table. All seemed normal, except for the ashtray that was pushed aside holding two crushed cigarette butts. The lingering stench in the air also revealed itself to her. This was really wrong. From what Elaine knew, her grandmother did not smoke. Elaine's mother had often bragged in the past about how she believed her mother was the only French-born woman who never smoked, and Elaine's mother had not smoked since she learned she was pregnant. The back of Elaine's eyes filled with steam over what she saw. Infuriated, she turned her head to steal a look at her grandmother, who was now seated, and returned Elaine's penetrating glance with a nervous smile. Madame Charton did not want to let on what she thought Elaine did not know this soon in this moment. She casually turned away.

"Okay." Elaine smiled at her mother and kissed her again on her forehead. "I'm going upstairs to change out of these heavy clothes. It's warm in here." Elaine spoke to her grandmother in French. "*Granmère*, for how long will you be here?"

"I will be here for one week," she responded.

"This is marvelous! Mom will love that!"

Elaine kissed her grandmother in passing as she headed upstairs.

When Elaine returned to the kitchen, her mother had already left the table, and the ashtray was also gone. Her grandmother was still seated, back turned to the staircase, and even though Elaine could not see her face, the way she rubbed her mature, elegant hands together communicated quite a bit.

"*Ou est Maman?*"

"*Endormi.*"

"*Est-elle malade?*"

"No, no, darling, she had a very long week, and so I came down just to be of help and to surprise you. Your mother said you insisted upon coming home without her having to cajole you into doing so. Sit down."

Elaine walked to the stove and ignited the flame to heat the kettle and then she took her mother's place at the table.

"*Votre Français est très, très bon,* Elaine." Madame Charton beamed at her granddaughter. "But get this, eh, your old *grandmère* is trying to strengthen her English, so while I am here, English, okay?"

"Okay."

"You are no actress, and you are not, eh, naïve, are you, my dear Elaine?"

"I suppose I'm not."

"No, you are not. You are bold. Even if you might not, eh, fully know this, you are bold. Do you know who you remind me most of?"

"Who?"

"Your great-great-aunt Agnès. You, eh, did not know her because she died, eh, before you were born, but she lived a long time. She lived to be one hundred and one years old."

Elaine's eyes widened.

"Yes, and she was, eh, a woman *INCROYABLE*! She had a masterful sense of style, and elegance fit for a royal. And she was stunning like you. But, eh, I think you have better curves. You can thank your American side for that. I, eh, greatly looked up to Aunt Agnès because she was bold. She put the 'B' in bold! In those days, women were married to men they did not, eh, always choose. Well, they, eh, never chose, but if you were lucky, you liked the man chosen for you. Agnès was not interested, eh, in having a man be chosen for her, so she waited. All of her sisters had already gotten married and begun their families, and Agnès, the oldest, felt *absolument* no pressure. She used to try to tell me all of the time to follow my bliss, but I'd come to believe like her sisters, in that my bliss could only derive from having a home life. Her urges to me fell somewhat upon, eh, deaf ears, as they say in America. Anyway, at age thirty-six, five years after her youngest sister had her last child, Aunt Agnès met and fell in love with the man she married a year after that. He heavily courted her during that time, to everyone else's surprise. In normal cases, at her age, a woman was yesterday's headline, a forgotten thing, no longer considered. But he was so sweet, I have been told. They never conceived, but they, eh, adopted a lovely little blond baby girl two years later. This is why most everyone in our family has dark hair except François and Marithé. This, because they are descendants of Aunt Agnès.

"In her day, Aunt Agnès had a fabulous, marvelous life. She and her husband, Marc, were deeply in love and did everything together. They traveled all over the world, often bringing their daughter with them. Before she met Marc, Aunt Agnès was ridiculed, told that she would never marry or, eh, have any children. Well, she did both, on her terms. She ended up with five lovely grandchildren, and eight great-grandchildren. Aunt Agnès created more physical legacy than all of her sisters combined. This, because she was bold. Just like you are.

"You are your mother's child, but you are like Aunt Agnès. Your mother is like me."

Elaine looked surprised.

"Yes, very much like me. I seem like Aunt Agnès now, but in my day, I was, eh, very traditional. I urged your mother to follow her bliss, but most children do what their parents do. This is not to say that your mother is unhappy. I was, eh, not unhappy. Like your mother was for me, you inspire the sun to rise in her heart every time you smile. She is filled with joy because of you. Yet I know just as she knows, all that you can do, and all that you are, and we say to you, you know? Follow your bliss."

Elaine stood up from the table to halt the sound of the tea kettle while it was still only a murmur.

Elaine spent the remainder of the weekend in bed with her mother surrounded by newspapers, magazines, and an occasional trail of cigarette smoke that flowed in a single stroke out of the window as the chilly air acted as a vacuum for it. Occasionally, her grandmother would join them by sitting on the chaise lounge and watch bits of the television that was really watching them.

During their time alone, neither Elaine nor her mother let on to each other about Elaine's father, both waiting for the right moment, both wishing there didn't need to be a moment. Through Madame Charton's meaningful and metaphoric storytelling, Elaine understood more than she wanted to anyway, but she was grateful to her grandmother, and felt relieved that she was there for her mother.

On the last night, Elaine crawled to her mother as she sat on the edge of the bed and hugged her from behind. Her mother let her. While embracing her mother during that silent night, Elaine shed tears. She wondered if her mother was doing the same.

Elaine's mother chose to drive her to the train station that Sunday in the late afternoon. She tried to remain upbeat, and was actually in a better mood.

"It was really wonderful having you home this weekend, Elaine."

"*Oui, Maman.* I will return next weekend, if you'd like."

"No, no, darling, I am fine, really. Whatever is going on

will pass. It always does. Your grandmother's company will suffice. But I will call you."

"Okay, *Maman.* I am glad she is here as well."

"We can wait until Thanksgiving holiday . . . It is only weeks away . . . I trust you will continue to keep yourself fully *protected* as best as you can until then, yes?"

Elaine's heart shot directly to her stomach, and she turned her blushed face to the window.

"I suppose I can."

❧

Sagrario knew that the second Monday after the Fall Dance was excitedly anticipated by her fellow seniors and lower-class Old Girls, yet dreaded by the majority of the New Girls. If the Name-Writing Tradition was considered a warm-up, then this day's tradition was full on. Sagrario even had a short conference about it with Dr. Knoll as rumors of fright amongst the New Girls began to swell. "They will be fine," assured Dr. Knoll. "We've got a great group of girls."

Each Old Girl was on call to dispense encouragement and TLC to her New Girl if she fell apart before or during the activity. Anxiety loomed over the lacrosse field where the New Girls were instructed to stand at attention and wait. Two Old Girl juniors, wearing Ray-Ban aviators, MES hooded sweatshirts, and cut-off Levi shorts with black leggings underneath, walked the line of New Girls with looks of intimidation that made girls like the one from Wisconsin try not to stand out. But there was nowhere to hide! Carrying dodgeballs, the Old Girls warned that all New Girl freshmen had better give each other enough time to call their parents during freshman phone hours because they were going to "feel it." One girl began to cry, and so her Old Girl had to walk her to Main to calm her down.

Because she put the most effort into not being seen, one of the junior Old Girls noticed the girl from Wisconsin and chose her to be the first to participate. The girl from Wisconsin was escorted to the center of the field, and then the entire senior class stepped out onto the field, seemingly to hurl dodgeballs, or at least that's what most of the New Girls believed. The junior Old Girl who escorted her out onto the field whispered in her ear, "This might be a little brutal, but I think you will survive."

The girl from Wisconsin looked like she was going to pee in her pants.

Then, the junior Old Girl did something that the New Girl from Wisconsin did not expect: she handed *her* the dodgeball! Then she screamed through a megaphone, "Chrisna Garrison, the cheese head from Wisconsin! You have three tries to hit your Old Girl! You cannot cross this line!"

The junior Old Girl's partner ran across the barrier line.

She continued. "Blows to the face are not permitted! Do you understand?"

Chrisna, shocked, did her best to readjust her disposition. Though her copper-brown skin did not show any signs of this, the blood in her face immediately rushed to her head. She was barely audible. "Yes!"

The junior Old Girl was unimpressed. "I. Cannot. Hear. You! Scream out YES!"

"Yes! Yes! YEEEESSSSSSS!"

Right then, a loud speaker began to play rock music, and the timer on the field was switched on. The junior Old Girl slid her sunglasses to the top of her head and smiled at Chrisna. "I told you you would survive this. Now go get 'em, sweetheart."

The group of New Girls finally relaxed and began to cheer, and the seniors did their best to cradle and protect Chrisna's Old Girl without breaking the rules. Chrisna's first try was a bust. By her third try she narrowly missed her Old Girl, a kind-faced senior from New Jersey, and hit Stephanie instead. Sagrario, remembering Chrisna from the chapel, caught eyes with the New Girl and offered a reassuring smile. Sagrario then turned to Stephanie, and the two laughed, holding their positions on the back line that was reserved for the tallest seniors.

"You know, I have never, ever, not been hit by a dodgeball," Sagrario revealed to Stephanie. "Even when I was little, or *supposed* to be little, I was an easy target."

"You must have been tall your whole life," Stephanie assumed.

"My entire life. Off the charts tall."

"I'm new to the tall-girl world. In two years I grew nearly four and a half inches. Now I am five ten, though, and my doctor says I have another inch or two to go."

"Get out! I thought I was pretty much alone! One more to go and I am six feet."

Stephanie laughed. "Let's see who makes it there first!"

"I don't mind it. The only thing that bothers me is that I can never blend in with the crowd," Sagrario admitted.

"Who are you telling? Sometimes I feel like I stick out like a sore thumb."

Stephanie was hit again by another New Girl. She rubbed her arm.

"Nowhere to hide, nowhere to run. They will soon know all of your secrets just because they will always see you," she added.

"Yeah, everybody *sees* me, but I wonder what it is they see," Sagrario replied.

"They will see what they want to see, and assume they know the truth. They think your size has you all figured out."

"Or that your feelings aren't fragile because you are tall."

"Feelings?" Stephanie interrupted. "Oh, we have *feelings*? News flash!"

Just then, Sagrario's New Girl shot the ball straight at her shoulder.

"I guess I'm out."

"Sure wasn't hard for her to make that shot," commented Stephanie.

"Of course it wasn't. We are easy targets, remember?" Sagrario smiled at Stephanie and walked to the edge of the field to the "out" section. She was the first Old Girl who had been officially tagged.

How Brooklyn fared the Dodgeball Tradition was anybody's guess. She considered it great luck that her New Girl tagged her only at her feet. *My baby is being protected*, she thought.

Brooklyn was so fatigued about the following day's private workshop with Winsome and BJ Fortunato that she was not sure that she'd be able to make it. Winsome consoled her all that Monday night, encouraging her that the session was only preliminary, and if they could help it, they should not change the date of their meeting with BJ Fortunato so no one would suspect anything out of the ordinary.

To their surprise, and to Brooklyn's sincere appreciation, the private session did not entail much physical movement. In fact, BJ Fortunato directed them to sit on the floor of the stage with folded, crisscrossed legs and perform voice exercises inspired by feelings she guided them to cultivate. BJ Fortunato told the girls that although this exercise did not involve running around, the intensity of the session would leave them most likely wanting to take a nap afterward. She encouraged them to be sure to have a snack after the session, and do just that.

"All right. First question. How would you breathe if you were being chased by a wild animal? What kind of sounds would you make? Would you speak any words during the chase? If so, what would you say?"

BJ Fortunato instructed them to keep their eyes closed during the exercise. After they completed this request, she went on.

"Now let's take our time. Let the feeling move slowly into you. Give me sounds of pure joy. Think about what gives you pure joy."

Winsome thought about the times when her little brother, Colin, looked her in the eyes when he told her a story. His first time was at age seven, and this was a milestone for her family because he had yet to be so engaging. Winsome was especially joyful because he'd chosen her to be the first person with whom he connected so strongly. Colin told her about the line of cars he'd formed in the hallway and asked her with enthusiasm if she'd like to see it. After she followed him there, he told her the specifics about each toy car. He told her about why he thought some had stripes painted along the sides, and why he thought others had fins connected to the backs. She could not believe it. The best part was that both her parents were able to witness the moment as they peeked in from the den entrance when they heard Colin's voice. Winsome and her parents knew from that experience that Colin had a shot.

Winsome could not hold back her tears, laughing throughout. Keeping her eyes closed, she congratulated Colin. "Good job, little brother. Good job." She continued to laugh and cry aloud as if in a trance.

"Yes, yes, good job, Winsome. Good job," whispered BJ Fortunato.

BJ Fortunato's voice broke Winsome out of her state, and still keeping her eyes closed, she shook her arms and wiped her face to prepare for the next emotion.

BJ Fortunato dug deeper.

"Now, how would you react if you were devastated about something? Would you scream? Would you be able to muster words? Imagine. And take your time. Let the feeling flow freely through you, just as you would pure joy and fear. All feelings are equally important. We must learn not to run from, but fully experience the spectrum of emotions. Proceed."

There was no need for Brooklyn to imagine. She'd already been devastated and was living with that state of mind most all day, every day. She'd cried herself to sleep so many nights, including the night before, so she did not know how she was going to create more tears so soon. But she was not without water. In an instant she began sobbing unto herself, rocking back and forth, quivering lips, and runny nose. BJ Fortunato was struck by this, because she had never seen Brooklyn so emotional before. BJ Fortunato always had faith that Winsome had incredible range, but she believed that Brooklyn would find herself struggling in her attempts at going *there.* That belief was immediately dispelled.

Winsome's and Brooklyn's eyes were closed and BJ Fortunato's were not. She noted their language, body movements, and subtle sounds they made with each emotion. BJ Fortunato had been a drama teacher for a long time, and having been taught by some of the best teachers in the world during her career as an award-winning stage actress, she knew authenticity when she saw it.

"She's been bloody balled up for years," BJ Fortunato whispered to herself, assuming that Brooklyn's outpour was a result of years of repression.

Brooklyn could not stop crying, even when BJ Fortunato tried to quietly interrupt as she did with Winsome. When BJ Fortunato placed her hand upon Brooklyn's shoulder, she shuddered.

"Do you need to take a break, Brooklyn?" asked BJ Fortunato, concerned.

"No, no, I'm all right . . ." Embarrassed, Brooklyn tried to wipe all of her tears away in one swoop, noticing that Winsome was also staring at her with tears in her own eyes. Brooklyn responded defensively, but kindly, "I, I was just thinking about when I heard that my grandmum died. She meant the world to me."

BJ Fortunato at once understood. "Oh, Brooklyn, how could I forget that time for you! Poor thing." She said the same thing to Dr. Knoll about Brooklyn when Brooklyn had to, at a moment's notice, fly to London for the funeral.

"Well, I think we all need a moment to reflect. Good job, excellent job, girls."

By this time, Winsome had grabbed Brooklyn's hand, for she knew what Brooklyn's tears were really about.

BJ Fortunato continued. "Now, what I have just instructed you to do is only a percentage of what will be expected of you when you perform your duet. You've already submitted your outlines, and so I base all private sessions on what I believe will be needed to execute the job well. You two have chosen a doozy of a project.

"Performing as a child and the spirit of a deceased parent is more than encompassing. Dealing with the loss of a parent is incomprehensible for those who have never experienced this sort of tragedy. But it is your job to convince the audience that you know what that feels like. And anyone who might be sitting in the audience who actually does know what that feeling is like must feel as though you are speaking for them. Understand?"

With Brooklyn still sniffling, both girls nodded in agreement.

"Now, take those feelings that you have shown me, *those* feelings, and have another go at your first two scenes."

Despite the fact that Winsome was very pleased with their first two scenes written as was, she knew that they had not written them with tears in their eyes. She did not object.

On the way back to their dorm room, Brooklyn and Winsome held hands. Their bond as friends grew more powerful that day, and as connected at the hip as they were, they were inaudibly, and individually, shocked that they could become even closer.

8

Mothers

The faculty was sure to time a decent-sized holiday shortly following the Dodgeball Tradition. The actual tradition itself was only ten percent anxiety and ninety percent excitement for the New Girls, but the two-week anticipation that led up to that day called for some time to regroup with their families. The gossip and rumors of past Dodgeball Traditions had many of the girls so riled up, and though in the end they realized that, just like the Name-Writing Tradition, all was in good fun and camaraderie, somehow the Old Girls, especially the seniors, were able to convince them that the very next tradition was going to trump the last one. And so traditions were handled this way for the remainder of the school year: the New Girls would be calmed down only to transition into nervous anticipation, all in the name of Madame Ellington's treasured school spirit.

Sagrario spent her entire vacation working to pay various bills, including some of those that involved Isabella. At work she paced on and off about Isabella's pregnancy. By the time there were only two more days left in the holiday, Sagrario's pacing was joined with serious prayer that God would allow her to be present when Isabella gave birth. Sagrario felt obligated to return to campus by Sunday evening so she could complete the final essays to add to her nine college applications. Like most drama in her life, Sagrario kept Isabella's pregnancy a secret, not even confiding in a fellow MES girl whom she'd known since their first day of orientation at the academic scholarship program in which they were chosen to take part during their seventh-grade year. That old friend had acclimated to the MES world in a social way, and would surely divulge Sagrario's secret to her new Upper East Side friends. The last thing Sagrario needed was for her family to be stereotyped as some welfare-illegitimate-baby-ghetto-street people. Sagrario was no one's charity case.

Isabella had gone into false labor just three days before, and Sagrario's mother said that was the same thing that happened to her when she was pregnant with Isabella, and she ended up giving birth to Isabella two days later. This was one of the few times Sagrario ever wished for an outcome to resemble that of her mother's.

When Sagrario's mother gave birth to Isabella, her temperament was nearly tranquilized. Life seemed okay, and there were no eruptions from Isabella's father for a while. Sagrario was doing extremely well in school, and her mother even became involved a little bit with the PTA. This lasted for nearly a year, and then she became pregnant with Louis. Around this time, Sagrario's father was released from prison, and not being able to go home to Sagrario and her mother created tension. Sagrario heard Isa's father slamming her own father over the phone, telling him things like, "This ain't yo home," and "I be running things over here!" and "*Te mataré* if I see yo face near here," and things like that. Sagrario never cried. She chose to bury herself deeper and deeper in books. The first empowering words she heard in person with her own ears that actually stuck were from her first-grade teacher, who told the class that they could be anything they wanted when they grew up if they did well in school and put their minds to it. A seven-year-old Sagrario took those words fully to heart. For someone so young, Sagrario devised a plan, and that plan was to make everything better for her family. She had been putting her mind to it ever since.

The turmoil between her mother and father and stepfather was still not over after Louis was born, and when Sagrario's father was denied entry to see her mother when Louis arrived, he circled the hospital building over and over until he built enough anger to take out his frustrations on the first person who stood in his way. Unfortunately, the person in question was a police officer.

Nearly a decade had passed since that incident, and while Sagrario's father sat in prison, Isabella's father was shot and killed during a drug deal. Louis was hardly old enough to assume any serious responsibility at home, but Sagrario watched him grow up fast, too, taking out the garbage and such in the absence of any older male figure in their home.

It was an early Friday afternoon, and Sagrario was hauling groceries up the six-story walkup in which her family had been living since Louis was five years old. When Sagrario opened the door to the apartment, she heard an unfamiliar sound: silence. Her mother was working, and Louis was out with friends. There was no loud television playing, and no loud talking over the phone. Save for the traffic sounds in the streets outside, she could probably hear her earring drop to the floor. Sagrario appreciated the peacefulness and reciprocated that state of being by removing her shoes at the door and moving about the house in a hushed manner. After quietly putting away the groceries, she walked to her mother's bedroom where Isa slept and observed her from the doorway. Sagrario looked at the sleeping Isabella, remembering that it was not so long ago that she impatiently watched her nap when Isa was just a baby, eager for Isabella to wake up so they could play. To a young Sagrario, Isa was her favorite doll baby. "*No puedes*, she is too little, *niña*," her mother would softly warn. Sagrario would reach into her baby sister's crib, just to hold her hand and be there until she did wake up. Now that Isabella was due to give birth any day, Sagrario found herself feeling the same bit of eagerness to be able to be there when Isa's baby was born. *I can't leave her alone, I just can't*, Sagrario thought to herself as she stood in the doorway. She walked over to the bed, knelt down beside it on the floor, and gently placed her hand atop Isabella's. Isa moaned a bit, then she woke up.

"*Hermana*, when did you get here?"

"I just got home, *mi muñeca*, waiting for you to wake up. I brought you a few things to eat, so whenever you are ready, let me know."

"Thank you, *hermana*. I don't know if I am hungry or drained or what."

"Exactly how do you feel?"

"Other than drained, I feel all right. Contractions are no joke."

"That is what I hear . . ." Sagrario took a deep breath. "You know, *muñeca*, I have been meaning to tell you how sorry I am that I have not been here for you."

"*Hermana*, it's all right. I know you have school. Sometimes I wish I went to that school with you. I wouldn'ta got pregnant."

Sagrario looked down when Isa said this.

"What's going to happen to me, *hermana*? Ignacio loves me, but he ain't exactly the most mature, you know? He ain't gonna take care of me and the baby . . . I feel like, I feel like I'm gonna end up like *Mami*. I wish I had the sense to leave like you did."

"*Muñeca*, you cannot think like that. Everyone is different. I had to leave for me, and what I am doing, I am doing for you and Louis, too. Maybe one day all of us can go to college. Just because you have a baby doesn't mean that you can't go to college."

"How am I supposed to do that with a baby?"

"I will help you. If you want to go, I will help you get there. I promise."

"*Hermana*, you always been like a mother to me, and I thank you for that."

"Thank you, *muñequita*." Sagrario leaned over and kissed her sister's forehead. "You know, Isa, this baby you are having, I told you it belongs to all of us, and the both of you will be all right."

"I only believe that because the words came out of your mouth."

The sisters smiled at each other and squeezed each other's hands. Staring into each other's eyes, Isabella shed the first tear. Sagrario lowered her head upon Isa's chest and wept continuously. Isa's tears fell into Sagrario's hair, and Isa cracked a joke.

"I've been crying all in your hair, but you know tears are better than shampoo!"

Sagrario looked up, face wet from her own tears, and added, "Apparently they are better to clean your face, too!"

Sagrario wrapped her arms around her baby sister and whispered in her ear, "*Te amo*," to which Isa replied, "*A ti, tambien.*"

Sagrario's mother's room was small and crowded, though having been the larger bedroom for the girls to share while Isabella was pregnant. Louis slept in the living room on the pullout. Sagrario's mother had draped rosary beads on the headboard, and placed a framed picture of the Virgin Mary above the bed. Stillness was their backdrop.

Suddenly, Isabella felt a jolt in her stomach, and what felt like a puddle of water began to grow beneath her. Her water had broken.

Sagrario had prayed to be able to be present during the birth of Isabella's child, but she did not know that God would give her a front-row seat right from the start. She rang everyone she could remember, starting with Isa's doctor, and then their mother, then Isabella's boyfriend, Ignacio. Sagrario wished her father was home to be there for the family. Aside from that fantasy hope, Sagrario could not reach any family over the phone. But there was no time to wait.

Sagrario packed a bag for Isabella and rode with her via taxi to Albert Einstein Hospital.

By the time they arrived and Isa was examined by the nurse, they found out that she was already eight centimeters dilated. The doctor told Sagrario that her sister was in heavy labor, and that the baby would arrive any minute. This news only heightened Isa's already emotional state. Holding her hand as they loaded Isa onto another stretcher, Isabella begged Sagrario to remain at her side. Isa's doctor gave permission, and a nurse quickly instructed Sagrario how she should physically prepare herself.

Sagrario coached her sister through labor like she did when she taught her how to ride a bike for the first time. "Come on, Isa, you can do it! Come on, *muñeca, Dios esta contigo*!" In just under an hour, but what seemed like only a few minutes, Nayanna Sagrario Inez Nuñez Vallesquez was born. Sagrario was the first to hold the baby, and then she laid her onto her mother's chest.

Entering the waiting room, Sagrario was met by nearly twenty relatives and friends.

Sagrario's mother charged up to her first. She paused as if to embrace Sagrario, then she immediately switched gears. "Isa, is she all right? How is the baby? *Cómo es mija?*"

Sagrario answered her mother, feeling hurt that she was being spoken to as if she was not also her *hija*. "She's fine, *Mami*. They are taking her to another room in a few. The doctor will be out to tell us when we can go back in."

Sagrario's mother received the information from Sagrario with a firm nod. For a beat they locked eyes upon one another. Again, Sagrario's mother abruptly moved past Sagrario and continued on to congregate with the group. Sagrario stood there alone, now feeling inadequate.

To pass the time, Sagrario imagined her father there as well. Knowing that she'd just coached Isabella through labor, he would have prepared a cup of coffee for her and immediately asked how she was feeling. He would have known that Sagrario, very mature for her age, but not yet a woman herself, would have dispensed her entire lot of energy to her sister and could therefore use some comfort, too. Sagrario was not sad or angry, or elated. After what she experienced, she was simply overwhelmed, and her father would have sensed all of these things, and would know what to say to soothe her. Yet, in reality, Sagrario only had her mother, and for as long as she could remember, the attention her mother had always given her had little to do with being gentle.

Elaine's mother had shed and adopted her melancholy on and off since Elaine's grandmother returned to France.

Though Elaine did not see the physicality of these transitions, she could easily sense her mother's wavering emotional state with each phone call. With only a couple of days left of the Thanksgiving holiday to spend at home, Elaine did her best to compensate for the affection and attention her father had not been giving to her mother. "*La Vie en Rose*" was playing on loop in the living room, a song with which Elaine had become all too familiar. Édith Piaf was Elaine's mother's go-to singer in times of chagrin, but Elaine had not heard this much of the famous French sparrow's voice since they moved back to the United States for good. By default, "*La Vie en Rose*" had become a favorite of hers as well, though she wished her mother would mix it up a little, like play Grace Jones's cover here and there. Elaine considered this version to be more modern and sexy. But her mother was not feeling sexy. By the way she slurred her words as she sang along to Ms. Piaf, Elaine realized that her mother was not only sad, but was also drunk. Elaine scanned the room and found the culprit: a bottle of her mother's favorite Cabernet Sauvignon. Sitting on the sofa in the living room, Elaine's mother brought her glass close to her lips to take another sip, but Elaine took hold of the stem and gently removed the glass from her hand. Her mother returned the gesture with a sloppy smile. Elaine wanted to cry.

Elaine's mother cupped her own hands in her lap and stared at nothing in particular, then said, "If it were not for you, I would not be able to see my life with such positivity."

Elaine responded, "Mom, you will be all right. Nothing can be so bad that you forget just how beautiful and special you are."

"You know what they say, 'Beauty is in the eye of the beholder.'"

"Well please only consider what I behold in you, because that will never change."

Elaine's mother examined her hands. "When I was your age, I kept a good head about myself, too. I could see nothing but the good. Then life intrudes on your idealism and reminds you of the spoils ahead."

Elaine joined her mother in examining her hands. "Yes, but the spoils make you appreciate what remains fresh." Elaine had no idea how she came up with something so wise.

Her mother looked into Elaine's eyes. "You keep hold of that perspective, my dear girl. Never allow anything to break it loose from you. If you do, you will spend the rest of your life chasing that feeling because it will no longer be something that you can easily pull from your own heart. And that makes happiness very complicated and difficult to achieve after that, when you believe you have to find it outside of yourself. Don't let that feeling break loose from you."

With that, Elaine's mother stood up, then stumbled, then regained control. She leaned over to her glass that Elaine had placed on a side table, lifted the glass, and drank the remainder of what was left. She handed the glass back to Elaine then staggered off to her bedroom.

Elaine, still seated and holding the glass, raised it in the air as if to toast, and drank the drops her mother left behind. "*La Vie en Rose*" began playing yet again, but Elaine imagined the old tape she once watched of Grace Jones sauntering on stage wearing that rose-colored, metallic, spaghetti-strapped gown with her long, muscular, outstretched arms flanked with the elbow-length African metal cuffs, buzzcut hair, magnetic smile, and prototype teeth. Each word she sang brought attention to her sculpted cheekbones that protruded under flawless, deep-chocolate-brown skin. Grace Jones sang the song impeccably, perhaps lip-synching over a prerecorded track that she belted out to perfection. She wiggled and danced, and almost laughed her way through that performance she gave in 1977. This is the way Elaine wished her mother could handle the current time in her life. She wanted her mother to find that priceless feeling of positive for herself and reconnect it to her heart and saunter and laugh her way through it.

⁂

Stephanie was thrilled that she was not required to "eat dinner as a family" on her last free night of Thanksgiving holiday. She intended on returning back to school the following day when boarders were set to arrive, to share ideas with a few peers about personal essays on college applications. Stephanie wished her mother would just finish up already. Her little sister had already been dropped off at a sleepover, and with her parents soon gone, she could conduct self-evaluation for as long as she wanted. She did not understand the fuss with putting so much effort into making up a face that had been seen more unmade than made, assuming her mother was doing all of this for her father. Stephanie figured if her father did not love her mother by now, it was probably a little too late to impress him. But whatever.

Stephanie's mother hum-sang "It Must Have Been Love" by Roxette while she powdered her face like she was dusting a knick-knack. She loved that song because she said it made her feel like Julia Roberts in *Pretty Woman*. She began the first verse as if she were doing her best imitation of Marie Fredriksson, raspy voice and all.

Stealing glimpses from a crack in her parents' bedroom door of her mother in action gave Stephanie the perfect view to clearly see how far along her mother had been progressing in her face-making process. It took her to hit the climax of the song before she was finally finishing her cheeks.

Stephanie thought her mother was pretty enough, but she never saw her as being sexy like Julia Roberts. And Stephanie never felt inspired to adorn her own face watching her mother apply makeup. She was thinking while watching her mother that the act of applying makeup was a waste of time. Stephanie was the kind of girl who wiped her brow rather than dabbed her face with a napkin. Makeup on her face would hardly last. The year before, when her mother sent her to a beauty counter to have her face done before a cousin's spring wedding, Stephanie's makeup was already severely smeared by the time she returned home from the mall. Then Stephanie's mother badly applied touch-ups to overshadow the mess Stephanie had made, and this only reinforced

Stephanie's anti-makeup attitude. Stephanie wanted to take that flower her mother tucked on the side of her hair and burn it. She smiled to show manners at her cousin's beautiful outdoor wedding, and she was happy for the surprise downpour of rain because then she had an authentic excuse for a sudden makeup-free face.

"He's not gonna know what hit him!" Stephanie's mother smiled to herself as she pouted and puckered her semi-glossed lips.

Stephanie grimaced and shifted her thoughts back to the college essays she was going to keep working on the following day. The last thing she wanted to envision was her mother stepping to her father and laying on him a big wet one.

Sagrario stood outside her family's apartment building on Townsend Avenue and looked up at the window that was a part of the tiny apartment that her mother sweat day in and day out to maintain. The sun was shining especially bright that day, despite the fact that winter's chill had come early. She used her hand to shield the sun from her eyes and shook her head. Sagrario had accomplished most of what she set out to do for Isabella by cleaning the house and arranging her mother's bedroom to be as comfortable as possible for when Isabella arrived home the next day. Sagrario felt sad that she would not be there for her niece's very first days at home, but inside, she believed that the sacrifice she was making was going to prove a big difference in the end. This is what she had to tell herself when guilt would set in about not witnessing key moments in her family's life.

There were only so many ways one could spruce up a tiny and old apartment already filled with one adult, a part-time high school senior, a teen boy, another teenaged girl, and a newborn baby. Each time Sagrario traveled home, more and more she found herself in deep thought about her family not living in that apartment building in the South Bronx. As Sagrario ascended the stairs of the apartment building, she daydreamed about the present day being fifteen years from now, and she would be a young success story in the legal world, and the walk-up would be an elevator ride in a high-rise apartment building in Riverdale, where Sagrario would be visiting her almost thirty-year-old sister and her doting husband, and she would be gifting them with a dainty and beautifully wrapped package of overpriced baked goods from Balducci's instead of a large plastic bag filled with processed food and generic toilet paper from C-Town.

As she climbed the stairs, she thought about a quote she read by Oprah Winfrey that said, "You do not get the life you want, you get the life you believe." Sagrario thought about her mother and father's lives, and if this theory was true, they must not have believed in much for themselves. *Look at their lives, look at where they ended up*, she thought. She then considered her wealthy classmates, and how they were more than likely going to end up with a promising future and beautiful place to live. She figured that they must have been raised to believe one thing, and poor people like her parents were raised to believe another. She assumed that people like Caitlyn's family must have believed for generations that they deserved a good life, and therefore always lived one. Sagrario, as far back as she could remember being told, realized that her line of people must have only believed they were good enough for project housing. Sagrario was very grateful to have beaten those odds of belief.

But then Sagrario thought more about her mother, and how she gave up that life of project housing and chose to pay more rent in a smaller building. Family members and some friends called Sagrario's mother "uppity" for moving out, even though it was only five blocks away. Most everyone took offense to the separation at first, questioning whether Sagrario's mother thought she was too good for the projects. Sagrario remembered her mother packing them up and whispering to her, Isabella, and a five-year-old Louis at the time, "*No me importa. Mejor. Entender? Sea lo que sea. Mejor.*" Sagrario realized that her mother at a time did in fact believe that she was better than smelly staircases, and though project buildings did have elevators, she would rather climb six flights of stairs every day than risk her life or those of her children by living in a threatening environment anymore. The project housing building in which Sagrario was raised until she was nearly nine years old became a battleground where innocent bystanders had been gunned down more than enough times that year when her mother decided to move away. Sagrario's own cousin was gunned down in crossfire when he was less than ten years old.

Sagrario wondered what happened to her mother that made her halt her aspirations at the building in which they currently lived. What happened to make her stop believing? Could it have been the devastation of losing Sagrario's father to the prison system, or the trauma caused by Isabella and Louis's violent father? Perhaps as far as Sagrario's mother was concerned, as exhausted as she always was, by now they had as good a life as she could provide.

When Sagrario reached her family's apartment, the shiny number she daydreamed that was carefully mounted on the door morphed back into the dull and rusted iron letter/number combination that sat above a peephole whose lens was foggy.

Sagrario turned the key to the lock and opened the door. She was surprised to see her mother sitting on the floor with her back turned. At first, Sagrario paid her no mind as she made a beeline to the kitchen, hoping the sound of her doing something to benefit the family would keep her mother's wayward criticism at bay.

Mami still spoke.

"Sagrario. You have to read all of these books *para graduar . . . antes de universidad?*"

Sagrario could not believe what she was hearing. Was her mother sitting on the floor flipping through actual books of hers? Sagrario put down the groceries in hand and walked into the living room overcome with a bubbling pride that her mother was sounding somewhat supportive.

"Yes, *Mami. Todo.*" She smiled.

"Well, looking at these prices on the back, it is like *dos meses de* rent on this floor alone. *Y yo sé que tu tienes más!* This is how you spend your hard-earned money? *Estos libros?* For something that will not be used ten years later? *Que loco.*" She stood up, dropping the most expensive book at her feet. "*Los bebes no comen libros,*" she commented quietly in Sagrario's direction as she passed her heading into the kitchen.

Sagrario wanted to cry from the letdown, but instead she chose a different perspective. Sagrario reminded herself that she watched her mother open a few of her books, something she'd never seen. Regardless of if her mother understood them or not, she knew that Sagrario was investing in something greater for her life. And though Sagrario's mother did not express it, she knew somewhere deep down that it was she who planted the seed in Sagrario so long ago. "*Mejor.*" Sagrario felt that her mother's belief to leave the projects might have inspired her to dare an even bigger one.

Standing in the living room staring at those books, Sagrario shed a tear anyway.

Back on Long Island, Brooklyn cried practically every night after spending her days with Winsome's family for the Thanksgiving holiday break. Although she'd once again convinced her parents, namely her mother, that she did not need to go home, part of her wished that Winsome's doorbell would ring, and that her mother would be on the other side. Keeping this secret to herself was not easy, and there were days when she wondered if she could hold herself together on her own. Still, she invited no other support except that of Chris or Winsome. Throughout the levels of uneasiness and sleepless nights, she had made the decision to keep her baby, and she was not backing down.

Winsome wished she could visit Brooklyn or someone else during Thanksgiving break to avoid talking to her father, but Brooklyn's physical condition won priority, and the girls decided that it was Brooklyn who needed the most refuge. Winsome was a little sad that Brooklyn did not engage much with her family (and of course the two girls concocted the flawless explanation of "school exhaustion" about why she did not engage), but this time apart for the girls provided an opportunity for Winsome and her father to catch up. Brooklyn at least shared some things about what she was going through with Winsome, yet with regard to the incident at her father's restaurant, Winsome had gone radio silent. It was time for Winsome to put some of her feelings on the table. Winsome's mother Odetta was poised to act as mediator between father and daughter. She was able to help move the rock of their issue, but not yet the mountain.

Odetta, though, was successful at keeping Brooklyn's family at bay, confirming to them over the phone, "She needs to rest, rest, rest . . . She'll be right fine by the time she heads back to school." The girls were so convincing to Winsome's medically trained mother that though she more than once prepared a broth for her to sip during the days when Brooklyn complained that she felt nauseous, it did not dawn upon Mrs. Sinclair that what Brooklyn was going through had anything to do with a baby.

With everyone giving Brooklyn space, she had time to sit in bed and think about her life. In less than a year she would be a mother. A *mother.* Gone would be the days of being totally free. Of course she would have help, but from the day she gave birth, no matter what she did or where she went, she would always know that she was responsible for another life. That knowing panicked Brooklyn some, but she could resolve those feelings by believing there was some great plan for all of this. She had not become pregnant intentionally, so this was meant to be. But had she been more responsible, could she have prevented it? If she could do this all over again, knowing what she knew now, would she have been?

Winsome walked in the day before their holiday was over to Brooklyn sobbing again on the bedroom floor, pillow lodged in her mouth. Winsome ran to her best friend and held her in her arms.

"Brookie, what is it?"

"Winsome, one day soon, someone is going to call me, irresponsible me, Mother."

9

Humbled

Stephanie was glad to have the first and second big traditions behind her, and she, along with the rest of the MES girls, could focus on finishing strong for the second quarter. This time was especially important for seniors, because the results of the exams played a large part in their future collegiate careers. For MES and other all-girl boarding schools, symptoms that exam time was soon to arrive were immediately revealed by the dominating choices of wardrobe. For most, impressing a boy was hardly a consideration or objective this time of year, even for the debutante beauty queens. Easy drawstring pants, loose-fitting sweaters or sweatshirts, sneakers, or some other comfortable shoe was the look. L.L. Bean and J.Crew catalogues were the trusted fashion guides, and empty Birkenstock boxes filled the hallway recycling bins. Pony tails, headbands, and baseball caps kept the girls' hair tamed. For Stephanie, this chosen exam uniform felt right at home.

Stephanie took Eric's advice seriously and put more focus in trying to be who she really was. In her hand she held tightly to a trifolded, enveloped letter she'd written to Hedda. This wasn't just any letter, however. It was the essence of Stephanie's feelings for Hedda, handwritten on two sheets of her mother's nonpersonalized Crane's stationery paper. She walked across the senior dorm bridge from the day-student room past her peers with her usual strong presence, but if Stephanie's anxiety could be exemplified outside of her nerves, she would literally be shaking like a leaf.

Holding the letter in her hand as if it were velcroed to her palm, Stephanie was determined that she was not going to drop it on the floor. She struggled with so much guilt while writing it she believed that even if someone else held the envelope in their hand, the words would jump off the pages and be revealed. When she made it to Hedda's door, she knocked once, and in between the first and second knock, Hedda opened it with an ear-to-ear smile on her face. Stephanie, accustomed to Hedda's usual emotionless stare, was unprepared for this sort of greeting from her, and so she aborted her mission and crumpled the envelope in her hand as tightly as she could.

"Hi, Stephanie . . . What is going on?"

Hedda had even spoken to her first. Now at a complete loss for words, Stephanie folded her hands behind her back and lied. "Oh, hey Hedda, I was wondering if . . . I could borrow a few pencils. I left my pencil bag at home."

Hedda obliged Stephanie, nodding and retrieving a handful of sharpened pencils from her room. As soon as she extended her hand to pass them to Stephanie, Stephanie thanked Hedda in an abrupt fashion and hurried off, braid floating behind her like the tail of a mustang.

If things were to have happened as planned, Stephanie would have controlled that moment with Hedda, and in Stephanie's mind, Hedda would have been so taken by her heartfelt letter that she would have wanted to spend the remainder of the day with Stephanie, and Stephanie would have suggested they study together during evening study hall. Because none of this transpired, Stephanie's overwhelming sense of confusion about what had just occurred drove her to drive herself back home and study alone in her family library.

Without Stephanie and Hedda, evening freshman study hall was in full motion. Sagrario arrived early to find a place at a table farthest from the door. She enjoyed studying in the dining hall with the freshman class, as it brought back fond memories. It was regarded as the time of day when overachieving freshman students like herself could spend more time zeroing in on subjects they were sure to master, a time when social freshman students could figure out an inaudible way to spend the two hours filling each other in on campus gossip, and a time for the rest of the class to simply complete as much of their homework assignments as they could in a guaranteed quiet and disciplined fashion. But because it was finals week, however, the dining hall that served as regulated and required study time each weeknight for freshmen was also filled with other students, mainly seniors who used the two hours of near silence to pour and triumph over their academic challenges.

Sagrario observed when the freshman class, like clockwork, at the stroke of ten, mad dashed back to the dorms to either complete the remainder of their homework, further socialize, or most importantly, try to achieve as much phone time before "lights out" at ten thirty. She remembered how much she anticipated junior year because freshmen and sophomores were not allowed mobile phones, and so they practically tripped over themselves to be first in line for the hallway pay phones.

As the freshman class clamored to exit the double doors of the dining hall with key social members (including Winsome and Brooklyn's New Girls) leading the way, the room soon regained its mid-nineteenth-century New England elegant, yet institutionalized feel. Left with their feet still planted on the Victorian-inspired carpet were Sagrario, who was completing her own self-created French quiz at one table, and Elaine, who was gathering her belongings at another. When Elaine turned and realized that she and Sagrario were the only people remaining in the room, she approached Sagrario for a chat.

"Now that I don't have to whisper, how's it going?"

Sagrario looked up at Elaine, a bit surprised that she was being asked the one simple question of how she was doing.

Elaine was smiling, waiting for a response.

"Fine, fine." Sagrario returned an honest smile.

Elaine glanced at Sagrario's writings. "How is French studying coming along?"

"It's not bad. I'm happy that my mother's native language

gives me a bit of a head start," she stated almost dismissively, "but forty tenses? *Dios mio.* You are lucky to have a French mother. I'm not even at the AP level. It must be a breeze for you."

"It has its advantages, but you are better off than I am, actually. I only speak two languages."

Sagrario, quick to rebut Elaine's statement, froze. Elaine's admission about herself revealed something poignant to Sagrario. Her mother *had* given her something very valuable that placed her ahead. "At home, we speak what I speak!" Sagrario remembered her mother telling her when she returned home from elementary school. Though Elaine was correct about the dual language teachings putting her ahead, Sagrario still did not want to fully claim it.

"Yes, but my Spanish is not like your French."

"Doesn't matter. I cannot travel to Spain speaking my perfect French and get around as easily as you could your native Spanish, but you could travel to France and also communicate there. You totally have the upper hand in this match, my friend. But can I help you with your verbs? Sure. My mother taught me a long time ago how to master the tenses with a song. It's silly, but it works. I don't have the best singing voice, but you would get the point." She chuckled.

Sagrario was tongue-tied again. Had she fallen asleep at the table and was presently dreaming? Did Elaine Hammond just offer to help her with French? Sagrario could not remember the last time anyone questioned whether she needed help with anything.

"Sure, if you have the time," agreed Sagrario.

"No better time than the present! Meet me in my room at around ten thirty. I can at least get you through the first half. It's not hard at all. No worries."

And just like that, Elaine was off.

Sagrario remained seated at her table, astonished. She did not move until the janitor began switching off the lights.

❧

The following day was chilly, though disguised by the sun's illuminated shield over the MES campus. Students either rushed to and from school buildings underdressed, or those who were aware of the temperature withstood the wind, walking at a comfortable pace wearing layers of fleece and wool. During lunch, the dining hall that usually served as either a revolving door for quick takeout stashed in napkins, or as a sit-down hour for students who actually had time to dine and socialize, was packed with everyone indoors. It was simply too cold outside.

Winsome was holding court at a table with three other black girls munching on sandwiches or the special of the day, baked rainbow trout. Victoria had just exited the buffet line looking for a place to sit. Winsome motioned her over.

"Victoria, over here. You can sit with us."

Victoria nodded in agreement and approached the table. As soon as she sat down, Winsome began to inquire. "So Victoria, I haven't seen you around campus a lot. You are always rushing from one place to the next."

Winsome pushed a spoonful of cereal, her lunch of choice, into her mouth, and a drop of milk dribbled down her chin. She wiped it with a napkin. Winsome's fifteen-second revelation did not inspire Victoria to acknowledge anything. Instead, she kept her head focused on nothing in particular while taking small bites of her bagel.

Winsome pressed on. "Is everything all right? I saw you and your boyfriend at the dance holding hands down the hill. You guys look so cute together. You are like this little tomboy waif who has the dapper guy madly in love with her. It's like a story in a romantic novel . . . or a stage play." Winsome smiled sincerely.

As soon as Winsome mouthed the word "boyfriend" to Victoria, basically summing up a chunk of her relationship dynamic in less than one paragraph, Victoria seemed to focus on what Winsome was saying.

"I don't know what you mean."

Winsome continued. "Oh come on, Victoria, I know you're a shy one, but it's no secret that you've got this super adult love affair. I think it's cool. I've not had a boyfriend since the beginning of junior year!"

The three other girls laughed to themselves.

Victoria quietly turned a deep shade of pink. She whispered in an angered tone through her teeth to Winsome. "Would you PLEASE stop saying that?" Victoria stood up, tray in hand and her food barely touched. She stepped away from the table, shoved her tray onto the nearest conveyor belt, and scurried out of the dining hall.

Winsome was about to scoop a spoonful of cereal in her mouth when Victoria did this. But she felt Victoria's anger so intensely through her hushed words that she could not make her mouth meet with the spoon. Winsome, not having a clue how she'd managed to make Victoria so upset, wished she'd not talked so much. She wished she would have paid more attention to what she was eating, which was no longer appealing, and not because it was now soggy.

❧

Stephanie, who had resorted to packing a bag lunch over the past few days, made sure to tighten her book bag, because while rushing to arrive to school on time, the half-closed bag often lost its contents all over the car seat. Stephanie was not exactly lying when she told Hedda some days prior that she'd left her pencil bag at home.

Since her shocked encounter with Hedda, Stephanie had been studying in the gym, as she had quickly become the distant one in their relationship.

Hedda further moved into Stephanie's previous role of initiator by unexpectedly appearing in front of her at the squash courts.

At the moment she saw Hedda, Stephanie began shoving her belongings back into her backpack and blurted out while brushing past Hedda, "Oh hey, Hedda, I'll get you some new pencils tomorrow."

Before there was too much space between them, Hedda whisper-shouted, "This is not about the pencils, Stephanie."

Stephanie stopped in her tracks. With Stephanie's back still turned to her, Hedda lowered her tone. "I know what it's like . . . to really like someone, to love someone, and they don't love you back."

Stephanie turned around, giving Hedda her full attention.

Hedda continued. "I know what it feels like to love someone that your parents don't think you should love."

Hedda walked slowly closer to Stephanie. As Hedda edged closer, she divulged more.

"And in your heart, you still love them, because that is all your heart can do. Sometimes our parents are right about the person we fight so hard to love, and other times, they are not right, and we should not feel bad about it."

By this time, Hedda was face to face with Stephanie. "I saw you at the dance, and you looked beautiful."

Stephanie's eyes filled with tears.

Hedda went on. "You were standing there, waiting for her, and she never came . . . But know that she did not come because she does not think that you are beautiful, and smart, and nearly perfect in every way. She did not come because the one whom she fights to love, the one whom her parents might be right about, won't love her back. And until she can get over him, her heart won't let her love anyone else."

Hedda bowed her head, tears falling rapidly onto the glazed wood. Then she looked up into Stephanie's eyes. "Okay?"

Stephanie wanted to offer a sense of understanding to Hedda. "Okay."

Hedda reached out her arms to Stephanie, who dropped her book bag at her side and accepted Hedda's full-on embrace.

It was unusually empty in the squash courts. Silence dominated the room so much that Stephanie could almost hear Hedda's tears bounce off of the floor.

After being embraced by Hedda, Stephanie still did not know exactly how to respond. There she was, being held by the love of her life to date, and though this love of her life was holding her, Stephane knew that even if there was no boy who occupied Hedda's heart, it could never be filled with love like that for another girl. But Stephanie still let Hedda hold her. And Stephanie held on to Hedda not just for the love she felt inside for her, but also for the love that she now knew the Luke Perry lookalike did not give.

Hedda backed away slightly from Stephanie and stared straight into her eyes, and left with her one last gift: she leaned into Stephanie's face and kissed her gently on the lips, like a summer's breeze gently blowing out a candle. There could be no *thing* between them, she knew, but Hedda's kiss symbolized having been understood and appreciated by someone whom Stephanie considered so important in her life.

The next day, in Señora Luz's AP Spanish class, there was

a big exam, which was extremely important, especially for Winsome, because she intended to study Spanish Golden Age Theatre in college, and she considered all of the Spanish leading up to that opportunity serious training. She mostly loved the oral presentation part of the exam, where she was able to perform aloud using a Castilian accent.

Winsome arrived slightly early to seat herself in the front of the class to go over her oral piece in her head. Slowly but surely, other students arrived, and when Señora Luz greeted the class and took stock of the room, Winsome took inventory as well. Seated in the far back, perhaps as far away as she could seat herself from Winsome, was Victoria Lee with pencil in hand, staring at her desk. Winsome was so busy rehearsing her presentation that she had not seen Victoria walk into the classroom. The two girls never really spoke to each other outside of basic hellos and forced smiles if they caught eyes with one another. But the two classes the girls happened to share during their senior fall semester sensitized Winsome more to Victoria's existence, which compelled Winsome to zone in on her every once in a while. And because of what happened in the dining hall the day before, Victoria had been on her mind more than a little bit.

The exam proved exactly what Winsome had intended, and upon completion, she smiled at Señora Luz with A+ confidence.

Victoria was already heading down the hill when Winsome stepped outside of the Language House. The few birds that remained in town as the weather had become increasingly colder seemed to serenade Winsome's victory as she smiled into the sun. Holding her hand across her brow, she spotted Victoria nearing the traffic light at the bottom of the hill. She thought again about the dining hall incident and reminded herself that she had not meant to embarrass Victoria and desperately wanted to tell her this. Winsome missioned down the hill and tapped Victoria on the shoulder while calling her name.

All of the other waiting students rushed across the street when the light changed, but not Victoria. She turned around, not looking Winsome directly in her eyes, nonetheless, appearing sad. Winsome gestured anyway.

"Victoria, I'm really sorry about what happened in the dining hall. I didn't mean anythi—"

Victoria cut her off, perhaps preventing Winsome from naïvely saying too much again. "Hey, it's all right. It's not your fault that you don't understand."

With that, Victoria turned back to the street, looking both ways while ignoring the red light, and ran across the street to the senior dorms.

Victoria flew past Sagrario, who was walking from the dorms toward Main Building. Victoria flew so fast by Sagrario that the two barely waved. Walking slowly also toward the senior dorms was Brooklyn. At her speed there was no opportunity to miss engaging with Sagrario, and it was true that Sagrario never quite forgot Brooklyn's fainting episode in front of the chapel.

"Hey Brooklyn, what's up?"

Before Brooklyn could respond, Winsome, who spotted her best friend being potentially cornered by Sagrario, zipped across the now green light and slipped her arm in Brooklyn's.

"Hey Sagrario, how's it going?"

"Doing well, Winsome," Sagrario offered, a bit startled at Winsome's abrupt interruption. Still, Sagrario's focus was on Brooklyn. She angled her head in Brooklyn's direction.

"Oh hi Sagrario, how goes it?"

"Actually, I was wondering about you. It's been a minute since you passed out in front of the chapel. That was scary. Did you ever find out what was wrong?"

Brooklyn was unprepared to answer, and so Winsome stepped in once more.

"Oh, isn't that when you told me that you hadn't drank any water all morning from the night before?"

Brooklyn caught on. "Oh, yes, I felt so dehydrated that day. All good now. And you, Sagrario?"

Sagrario was only slightly more prepared. "Me? You know I always have a ton going on. But I'm good."

"That's good," answered Winsome.

"Are you two going to do a special presentation for theater this semester? Last year's was awesome."

"We're working on it," Winsome again responded.

Because Brooklyn did less speaking, Sagrario focused more on her. "Well, as long as everyone is doing okay." She seemed suspicious.

"All good over here. Talk to you later, Sagrario." Brooklyn nodded and waved.

The girls left Sagrario standing alone, and she processed the moment. *Was Winsome physically holding up Brooklyn while they stood there?* The two were now officially on her radar.

Sagrario thought about Winsome and Brooklyn all the way to the Main Building, to her mailbox inside, and back to the front steps. She sat on a bench in front of the Main Building and flipped through papers and mail. She opened an envelope from the business office and her eyes grew wide like an owl.

What? This cannot be! Sagrario thought to herself, panicked. The space in her mind that she just carved out for Winsome and Brooklyn instantly vanished and was replaced by what she was reading. Somehow, Sagrario had done some serious miscalculating. She knew that she was behind on her current tuition payment, but she was just alerted that there was a clerical error that brought even more owed forward from last semester as well. She felt doomed. Sagrario had already completed most of her college applications, and she'd been working incredibly hard to be on time with her Madame Ellington payments to be ready to send them along. This semester had been trying for Sagrario, especially because Isabella had just given birth. Yet despite the load she carried, Sagrario could see the light at the end of the tunnel because she believed she had a solid plan. But these extra charges owed threw Sagrario more than a curve ball.

Sagrario began to tap her feet and take deep breaths to keep from crying. Out of nowhere, she let out a laugh. *Dios está jugando conmigo, estoy segura de esto.* She tried to reassure herself, but she also knew how meticulous the business office was, and if they caught some sort of error, they were always expeditious about letting a student know. Sagrario remembered during her sophomore year, due to submitting so many random payments just to keep up with her end of her financial agreement, she was told at the close of the spring semester that she overpaid for the semester by two hundred dollars, and was asked if she wanted to pay it forward for junior year. The timing could not have been more perfect because she was soon to begin working at the law firm and needed a couple of new shirts. She chose to take a reimbursement check. This clerical error was not like that time.

Bringing herself back to her current reality, Sagrario immediately began thinking of how she could make up the difference. Nothing came to mind. While she sat on the steps tapping her foot, Sagrario became nauseated with the realization that if she paid for her college applications, she would have no money left for tuition. If she did not become current with tuition, the school would not release her transcript, and she would risk missing important application deadlines. Sagrario thought about the dreams she had for her family, the dreams she had for herself living in Midtown, taking her father to lunch at one of the swanky restaurants nearby. She thought about Isabella, and how she vowed to help her get through community college so her baby could have a brighter future. In Sagrario's mind, those things would be impossible if she did not complete the education for which she set out. Just as she was feeling defeated and was going to allow that tear to make its way out of her eye, the front door of the Main Building opened. Out walked Dr. Knoll.

"Sagrario! Hi! How is everything going?"

Like the leader Sagrario had always been, she perked up and stood, ingesting the tears so tightly they became lost inside of her.

"Dr. Knoll, all is well! Yes, I was just going over some paperwork for school." Sagrario wished that she could confide in Dr. Knoll what she had just read, what she was going through because of what she had just read, but she choked. And because Sagrario was so good at covering up her issues, Dr. Knoll did not notice anything wrong at all.

"Well, good for you, Sagrario. You are such a star." Ingrid Knoll placed her hands on Sagrario's shoulders as if she were talking to her own child. "I want you to always remember that no matter what, you will shine. We have yet to see how brightly." After declaring this, she held eyes with Sagrario until Dr. Knoll believed her words stuck. She wished Sagrario luck on the remainder of her exams, and then made her way to her home, as she was in anticipation of a meeting there.

"Thank you, Dr. Knoll!" Sagrario waved to her as she watched Ingrid Knoll walk elegantly and assuredly down the road to the Headmistress Residence.

Sagrario might have been standing on her feet, but inside she had been brought to her knees. All of the work she had done, and it culminated in this. She could not let that happen. Something had to happen. And fast.

10

Faith

Sagrario was at least happy that Christmas holiday was soon to arrive, and she pressed autopilot to complete the helming of the annual Christmas traditions, remaining exams, and other campus responsibilities only to return to the South Bronx and work her heart out at her holiday job and try to figure out any other possible solutions to raise money for her outstanding tuition balance. This upcoming break might have been considered a vacation for most, but Sagrario knew that for her, there would be no time to rest. Many of the seniors had completed and turned in their applications early to avoid being burdened during the holiday, just as Sagrario had intended to do, but she was forced to prolong her submission until the actual deadline. This was still wishful thinking on her part, considering that she would be able to make a deal with the business office by submitting a one-time promissory note agreeing to submit a lump sum by the beginning of January, and to become current on the full balance by February. She had no idea how she would fulfill this promise, but she believed that her chance meeting with Dr. Knoll was more than purposeful, and if Dr. Knoll believed in her, Sagrario could believe in herself.

While packing the last items in her duffle bag, disappointed that she'd missed the last free shuttle to the train station, Sagrario received a godsend: Elaine offered to share a taxi ride to the train station. Sagrario accepted and was relieved, knowing that her few dollars saved would allow her to buy dinner on her way home. Elaine, who had never thought to share a taxi to the train station with anyone, contemplated asking Sagrario some nights before when they chose to share study sessions together prior to their French exams, which were held two hours apart but on the same day. During study breaks, the two girls talked about their lives at home, with Elaine divulging more, having grown comfortable talking with Sagrario. Elaine really appreciated Sagrario's view on things.

When Elaine confided in Sagrario about her parents' separation as a result of her father's infidelity, Sagrario advised Elaine that she had to now wear two pairs of glasses in her family: one that looked at her parents as people who were going through a difficult time, though her father might be the one at fault, and the second that continued to see and love her mother and father as her parents, and not get in the middle of their issues. Sagrario had mastered this way of consideration because she had to deal with her mother with two sets of eyes and two minds, and almost two hearts, her entire life. This was what prevented Sagrario from hating her mother despite the way her mother treated her and her father. This was what restrained any resentment Sagrario could have had for her father, whom she loved dearly, for the many ways that he abandoned his family. Sagrario had to view her parents as people, too, with problems that she did not cause. Sagrario's late grandmother used to comment all of the time that Sagrario was born with a great sense of understanding. "*La niña entiende todo . . . Su corazón* stays clean because she understands everything." Sagrario's advice to Elaine made sense and felt right for Elaine to do, and it calmed her anger considerably. Elaine wanted that same enlightened spirit to be with her as she traveled home for the holidays. Sagrario, the youthful sage, who was secretly grateful to have saved ten dollars from the shared taxi ride, was unaware of the immeasurable value she served for Elaine.

In spite of the wisdom she had to offer Elaine, Sagrario had no time to focus on meaning in her own life. The moment her feet were firmly placed back on New York City concrete, she hit the ground running. Her first four days at home were literally comprised of a series of hi's and byes, quick kisses on Nayanna's forehead, and short conversations of encouragement to Isabella. Originally, Sagrario was only going to work two days straight and then take two days to relax with her siblings and niece, but her emergency financial burden forced her into overdrive. She heard that one of the holiday salespersons dropped a total of five days, and those hours became open for the remainder of the staff. Sagrario jumped at the opportunity. Two of the five days were scheduled consecutively following her first two days. Sagrario would have tried to take all five days, but the remaining three days were scheduled on days and times when she already had to work. Sagrario accepted the two extra ten-hour days with gratitude, believing that God was meeting her halfway to fulfill her school debt. After that fourth day, though, Sagrario was exhausted from folding and refolding T-shirts and denim, and sweaters, and keeping up with all of the various accessories the Gap produced and placed in various bins, bowls, and wooden boxes around the entire store. Sagrario thought if she had to ask one more person if they needed help, she was going to scream.

Sitting in her mother's room, surprisingly, with Nayanna all to herself, though the house was filled with generations of family, Sagrario hummed while watching her niece as she held her up to sit on her stomach. There were no other people in the room, but there were lots of coats and pocketbooks on the floor surrounding the bed, as that bedroom had been the designated place to store coats. By choice, the television was not on because she wanted to hear any sounds Nayanna made. Sagrario was so proud of her niece's cooing.

"You are so smart already, mi *sobrina preciosa.*"

She lifted up the baby and kissed her. Just outside of the bedroom door Sagrario could hear the goings-on about the house. She heard her name mentioned in conversation, mostly by the older relatives who acknowledged that she was a hard worker. There was not a lot of chatter about how hard she worked in school, but Sagrario did not mind. She was at least being acknowledged in the positive.

Sagrario stared in the eyes of her niece, whom Isabella said gave her first real smile when Sagrario came home, and wondered what she made of all that surrounded her. Occupying the house during this holiday gathering were the usual suspects: Sagrario's mother and siblings, two siblings of her father's, and all of their children. Between these aunts and uncles there were twelve children. Between those twelve children were six grandchildren—all under the age of five. There was a pallet in the center of the living room floor where babies rolled around, and the older kids played videogames while some adults looked on conversing loudly, sometimes having a go at the videogame. The smaller bedroom was filled with men screaming about baseball playing on the television, the kitchen crowded with women and smoke from food being prepared, and two teenaged girls were hunched in a corner on their cell phones. Ignacio, baby Nayanna's father, and his mother were new additions to the lot. There was no room to move, nor space for another human being. The mixture of music, babies, laughter, chatter, and yelling all rolled into one big SOUND.

"You will go to college, you will." Sagrario kissed her niece again and held her close to her chest. Through all of the noise outside, it was a wonder that she actually heard the door buzzer.

Sagrario stood up with the baby and ventured out of the bedroom to alert the house of the doorbell in case everyone's ears were engulfed in their own chosen audible distraction.

Isabella also heard the door and rushed to answer it.

"*Primo* Manuel!" Sagrario looked on as his arms stretched wide enough to envelop Isabella's still-shapely post-delivery figure. "I didn't know you were coming to visit us! *Cómo estás?*"

When Sagrario's mother heard Isabella scream Manuel's name, she, in one motion, drained piping hot potatoes, wiped her hands on her apron, and made her way through the people in the kitchen, through the people in the living room, and moved Isabella out of the way to stand directly in front of Manuel. She looked him up and down, and then at once, the blank expression on her face transitioned to one joyful, yet dismayed. She took a moment to address him.

"*Manuel, hace mucho tiempo que no te he visto.*"

"*Yo sé, Titi.*"

"*Cómo estás?*"

"*Bien, Titi.*"

The music was so loud it was as if they were reading each other's lips to communicate.

"*Ven aquí mi sobrino, mijo. Ven aquí.*"

Manuel took two steps toward his aunt and she yanked him the rest of the way into her bosom. Sagrario watched her mother as tears streamed down her cheeks onto Manuel's shoulder.

"*Te amo mijo, te amo,*" Sagrario saw her mother mouth.

With her arm wrapped around him, Sagrario's mother yelled to the crowd, "*Mijo está aquí!* My son is home!"

Sagrario had never experienced anything close to that level of affection when she returned home from school. Though going to school away was her idea, spending two months trying to acclimate within a new environment proved isolating at times, and when she called home, she made sure to never let on her anxieties, fearing that her mother would force her to enroll in a local school as she'd wanted from the beginning. Sagrario had stepped off the Peter Pan Bus with a wide smile, which was for the most part real, but when she laid eyes on her mother, holding hands with Isabella and Louis, she had no smile for Sagrario, nor did she offer to help with her bags. But for Manuel, the son of her mother's favorite brother, Chico, who was now deceased, she welcomed him back as if he were a king. And Manuel did not leave to go to school. His return was from having disappeared after ten years in and out of juvenile detention centers and two years in a real jail for armed robbery. Sagrario's mother's promise to her brother to raise Manuel as her own was a failure, and as soon as Chico was put in the ground, Manuel's inability to be controlled grew stronger by the day. Yet despite her feelings for her mother and her blatant and constant disregard for Sagrario, Sagrario also did not hold anything against Manuel. He was a troublemaker, and much of the family did not trust him, but she, like her mother, loved him very much. Manuel's feelings for Sagrario were also strong, and Sagrario's mother often competed with her for his attention. Sagrario always relented, and Manuel routinely fled Sagrario's mother's clutch to be close to her. This time was no different. As Sagrario's mother held her eagle-like grip on Manuel's shoulder, grinning as though her most prized possession had fallen from the heavens, Manuel's eyes were fixated on Sagrario only. Sagrario pretended to hold her attention on Nayanna, planting kisses on her tiny hand, as it was wrapped around

Sagrario's finger, but she could not help but meet Manuel's eyes a time or two.

Manuel released himself from Sagrario's mother and, while waving to various family members, made his way to Sagrario. He first looked at Nayanna and then back at Sagrario. Sagrario corrected his unspoken assumption.

"Isabella's. Her name is Nayanna. *Preciosa.*"

Manuel coughed. "Yes, she is precious, just like *mi amor* who stands before me."

"Manuel, where have you been? You've been gone since I started high school. The family thought you were dead."

"Trust me, there were times when I wished I was. But I am home now and doing real good. You still go to that rich-people school in Connecticut, huh?"

"Yes, I still attend Madame Ellington. This is my final year."

"Wow, you really gonna finish. I knew you would. You always been special."

"Not around here, but yeah, I am trying to be on my way."

Sagrario's mother was nearing the two of them. As she parted the small sea of people to reach them, someone pulled her back into a group of people talking. Still, Sagrario chose to cut their conversation short.

"Well, I'd better be headed back to the room. Nayanna looks sleepy, and I know she won't rest with all of this noise."

"You are on Christmas break, right? Wanna go to lunch? You workin' in the city?" Manuel suggested an option to see her again.

Sagrario leaned into him, offering a location, date, and time. Manuel nodded.

By this time, Sagrario's mother's eyebrows were furrowing as she grabbed Manuel's arm to lead him into the kitchen.

Wednesday afternoon, Sagrario sat shivering on a cement stump in the center of Rockefeller Center waiting for Manuel. She praised the cup of hot chai tea that one of her coworkers offered her during her previous break, and regretted that she was so preoccupied that she let it go cold. Only five minutes earlier she was praying for time to move faster so she could be freed from folding shirts and be able to see her cousin Manuel, but after sitting in the cold for this short time, she would not have minded going back in to pop her cup in the microwave. The weather did not annoy Sagrario as much as the time passing by, though. Her break was only thirty minutes, and Manuel had already wasted five minutes of it. After nearly five more minutes, Sagrario hopped off the cold hydrant stump, and Manuel walked up to her at exactly that moment. He extended to her a flower bouquet and smiled. Sagrario forgot the stern scold she'd prepared for him.

"Mani, I only get a half hour for lunch, you know."

"I know, I know, and I'm sorry. It's just that I had a meeting uptown right before this and it got held up."

"Okay, so what was this meeting about?"

"You wanna get some pizza or something since you don't have a lot of time left? My treat."

As they walked and talked, Manuel began asking Sagrario questions.

"So why you workin' here during your break? And you said you working almost EVERY DAY of your break?"

Sagrario held her flowers to her nose and turned her head. "Yes, it's no big deal. I just have a few things to handle at school, and I'll be good."

Manuel easily persuaded Sagrario to tell him about her financial troubles. Despite all that she knew about him, Manuel only represented love for her. When he was around, he always did right by her. She confided in him everything.

Manuel stopped short on their walk. "Why you ain't tell nobody? I knew there was a bigger reason why I came back home right now . . . Look, I can get you work easier than this and make you way more money. Guaranteed."

Sagrario looked at Manuel disapprovingly.

"It ain't like that, aight? This is real good stuff. Matter fact, there is this dude Thomas from Gun Hill Road that I was gonna put on after I left you, but something about him keeps telling me that he won't be responsible, and the job ain't even hard, but it's important. You would be perfect for it." Manuel continued. "And it would not interfere with your rich people's school."

Sagrario thought for a minute, then picked back up on their walk. She wanted to know more. "What would I have to do?"

Manuel continued to persuade. "Just take a package from here to there. You ain't even gotta open nothin'. Ain't gotta ask no questions. Just pick up, drop off, and get your money."

"That's all? Well, what's in the package that's so important?"

"You can't tell nobody this. But it's diamonds."

"Diamonds!" Sagrario quickly covered her mouth.

"Yes, diamonds. That's why you have to be very careful. See, my boss has jewelry shops all around the country, and he prefers to have his merchandise hand-delivered by people who don't look like they would be carrying diamonds, you know, so the diamonds won't get stolen. That is why he chose me and I am choosing you."

Sagrario began to feel important that Manuel would choose her for such a high-profile job over another person. She told him what her school balance was, and Manuel brushed off the amount, saying that she would triple that before she even graduated.

Sagrario was beyond impressed. She could not believe that a blessing like this would present itself at this time. Sagrario thought about what her father might say, but he would be wrong. Manuel had come to save the day. Sagrario could hardly contain herself. She threw her arms around Manuel and kissed him on the forehead.

"When do I start?"

Manuel smiled. "I will call you tonight and we'll talk."

Sagrario's face was masked with a giant grin. Transfixed in a slight daydream about how her life was going to change for the better, she was jolted from her state by the loud honking of a taxi horn on the street. She glanced at her watch, acknowledged the time, and cut their meeting short.

As she walked backward toward the Gap, she screamed, "No time for pizza! I'm five minutes late! Don't forget to call me! I love you!"

Manuel waved to her until she turned around and ran toward the store. He stared at her all the way with a smile on his face.

All while folding T-shirts and jeans, Sagrario thought about Manuel, and the imaginary warning looming over her head from her father, the only family she knew for sure wanted what was best for her. She weighed her options on and off over the course of the work day. Sagrario knew in her heart that her cousin had a reputation of being up to no good. But she also believed that his love for her was genuine, and believed he would never involve her in anything unsavory, or put her in harm's way if he could help it. He knew what she had at stake. That being said, she decided that what she agreed to do might have seemed questionable, but it wasn't *bad.* Sagrario convinced herself that as odd as it might have seemed, God was using him as a tool to help her remedy her school debt. She'd been giving more money to Isabella, and God knew that she desperately needed the money to pay for school, and up until now she had always been a faithful servant of her belief and faith in God. *And it is true that God can speak through the most unlikely to reward one for their good faith and works, isn't it?* she thought to herself. It was that faith that brought forth the good fortune to land Sagrario at the Madame Ellington School in the first place. It was that same belief that gifted her with the courage to rise up to the top of that supremely exclusive group better than the best cream, with accolades and credibility to spare. Sagrario could not empower a notion that this whole thing was set up to ruin her life. She just couldn't. She was on her last gasp of hope during this crucial leg of her life's race. She was going to use her faith and belief to make her side job with her cousin Manuel a good thing.

More than family love, too, Manuel and Sagrario shared an undefined devotion that remained between the two regardless of the distance between them. They were the only ones who evoked this feeling from one another, and Sagrario depended upon this closeness to further entrust in her cousin's plan. Her father did not know Manuel the way she did, and she believed that Manuel was committed to her. And for all of the things that Sagrario had been through in her life, she was determined to win.

After being given the simple commands by Manuel the next day, Sagrario made two pickups and drop-offs through the Bronx to Queens, and one from the Bronx to Brooklyn. She was paid handsomely in cash each time. As opposed to celebrating her financial success at a New Year's Eve party, Sagrario volunteered to babysit her niece while the others traveled to Washington Heights to celebrate with extended family. Sagrario lay on the bed using one hand to hold her niece on her belly, and the other hand to fan the one-hundred-dollar bills she had just been paid. She was so happy that she had made enough money to pay off her surprise school debt, and well in advance of the February date on which she agreed. Sagrario gently kissed her niece atop her head and sang to her while watching a muted *New Year's Rockin' Eve* on television.

Tía lo arreglará todo . . .
Con Dios todo estará bien . . .
Un día será tu turno para la universidad . . .
Con Dios todo estará bien . . .

On Sagrario's last night of Christmas holiday, Manuel, who only met with her during her lunch breaks and at strange times in secret locations near her home, rang her unexpectedly.

"*Querida*, what time is your bus tomorrow?"

"Nine in the morning, why?"

"Well, I was having dinner with my boss, and I was telling him that you were headed back to Connecticut tomorrow for school, and he told me that he has several jewelry shops in Hartford, and that he could benefit from your services from here to there. Plus, get this, he said that he would pay you triple what he pays you to do in-state drop-offs for just this one time. How does that sound?"

Sagrario thought for a minute. She promised herself that she would never bring any "home stuff" with her to school. This is why she told her family that she could not talk on the phone during the week, to keep her school energy focused on school. And why she was always one of the first to arrive on campus after any holiday: to have the ability to decompress before the rest of the student population arrived. Everyone in Sagrario's immediate family depended on her excelling and becoming successful, even if her mother resented the process. Sagrario's home life represented chaos and extreme limitation. She could not risk any of that energy spilling into her

God-given, life-saving education at Madame Ellington, even if it was going to make her extra money.

"Mani, I don't know. You know, I am Student Head of School, and I always have a ton of things to do as soon as I get to campus. I won't have time to travel through Hartford."

"No, *prima querida*, see, it is not like that this time. All you have to do is bring it with you to the bus station in Hartford, and someone will meet you there to pick it up."

"That's all?"

"Yep, that's it."

"For triple what I was paid before?"

"Triple."

"Okay, I will do it."

As always, Sagrario took an early bus to school, yet this time, she carried a small brown backpack filled with what she was told were diamonds. When she arrived at the Hartford train and bus terminal, she collected her belongings and walked inside the terminal to meet her contact by the vending machines as she was instructed to do. There was a man waiting there who looked too suspicious for Sagrario's taste. All of her other connects in New York were kids who looked fairly normal, just like she did, but this guy had a grimy feel, and there was no mistaking that he was her connect because he spoke to her in a whispered command.

"Sagrario. I know that is you. Get over here."

Scared, Sagrario approached him. He was tall, gangly, and had dark lips and thick, long dreadlocks pulled back in a ponytail. His heavy eyebrows and gold tooth made him look more villainous than the regular Joes she'd met thus far working for Manuel. This man looked like a thug, not like someone who would work in a jewelry store. Plus, he seemed on edge. Sagrario noticed how he continuously checked out his surroundings as he stood there. When Sagrario was face to face with the man, he commanded her to follow him to his car parked outside. When they arrived at his car around the block in a minimally populated area, he told her to get in the car and put her bags inside, too. Sagrario told him that she didn't need to do all of that, that they could just do like the others and make an even exchange.

The man was not interested in Sagrario's idea. "What do I look like? A goddamn fool? Get in the car."

Sagrario was frightened and did as she was told. The transaction in the car was, from beginning to end, very short-lived, yet each second in the car with this strange character lasted much longer in Sagrario's anxious, terrified mind. Her eyes moved slowly and deliberately while observing the interior of the car and identifying specifics about him, like the three piercings he had in his right ear, and the tattoo he had behind it. When he sat down and turned in her direction, Sagrario noticed that his eyes were stained red. In the car, the man did not seem as sure of himself as he did in the bus station. He fumbled with his keys and nervously attempted to operate the radio twice, which he gave up after failing the second time. He never smiled, but this behavior made him more vulnerable. This calmed Sagrario slightly. Soon after he sat down, he commanded her to give him the bag, and then he pulled out a wad of money and handed her eighteen hundred dollars in cash.

"Now you can leave."

Sagrario grabbed her bags and ran as fast as she could away from that car back into the crowd of travelers. When she arrived at her gate, she found that she missed her connecting bus to school. Desperate to get out of there, and armed with more money, Sagrario took a cab instead.

The cab ride back took longer than Sagrario expected, in part because of traffic, and the other part because of Sagrario's wandering mind. All that she had told herself the short time before that convinced her to engage in Manuel's plan began to fill with holes. The questionable parts of this idea grew stronger. *The first few times were easy, so what just happened was a fluke, right?* Sagrario tried to belittle her experience with the thug. Maybe this guy just had a bad day, but Sagrario could not help but remember what he looked like, and had to acknowledge that he might always have bad days. Maybe he was a last-minute substitute for the real person whom she was supposed to meet. This could not be too good to be true, could it? Graduation was near, and "I have to graduate," Sagrario kept telling herself almost loud enough for the cab driver to hear her. Sagrario clenched the eighteen hundred dollars in her hand, closed her eyes, and with all of her might, tried to refill those holes with faith.

11

Inhale

By the time Brooklyn knew it, she was more than just feeling pregnant, she began to look pregnant, too. Standing in front of her bedroom mirror unclothed, she turned to the side and noticed that her lower belly had protruded a little. Brooklyn was a moderately built girl, and so her widening abdomen could easily be camouflaged with heavy sweatshirts and sweaters that both she and her fellow classmates had grown accustomed to her wearing since the beginning of the year. And there was little commentary about her sloppy attire because even the most fashion savvy of the senior class relaxed their efforts in that area more often than not. Brooklyn's face remained the same, and her arms, legs, and rear end were all relatively unchanged. Luckily, it was only her midsection that could visually reveal the secret. As Brooklyn ran her long, unpainted fingernails across and over her growing belly, she closed her eyes and wished to feel a kick or push from the baby to assert its presence. She noticed small, wrinkly lines that had appeared on the lower half of both sides of her stomach. She had seen these same lines in a magazine, and discovered they were called stretch marks. Had she not read about the possibilities of them disappearing, she might have been more alarmed about it. Brooklyn considered these lines her baby's silent communication that he or she was growing well. Up until this moment, Brooklyn had not been to visit a doctor for fear of her secret being disclosed, and so hadn't fully acknowledged the baby growing inside of her. Completely coming to terms with the reality was challenging; not having heard its heartbeat by this point made her nervous at times. But signs like stretch marks appearing and her growing appetite led Brooklyn to believe that what she was experiencing was not all in her head. She kept a copy of *What to Expect When You're Expecting* hidden in her bed, and as her pregnancy progressed, the book became her doctor's appointments and trusted ally when it came to her health.

Brooklyn could not obtain prescribed prenatal vitamins, so she researched the vitamins that comprised them and took each separately, along with extra vitamin D and calcium, which was suggested by a highly rated pregnancy website that warned of in-vitro babies virtually robbing their mothers of calcium. Her daily walks around campus from class to class constituted a healthy dose of physical education. Up until this moment, Brooklyn also had not fully recognized and embraced her pregnancy because she had to get through classes, exams, and college applications without shifting focus to her emotional state. There was much work to be done, and Brooklyn did her best to handle it all. Before she became pregnant, a more ambitious Brooklyn would have applied to nearly double the schools to which she actually did. The truth was, she was simply too tired to attend to all of the paperwork, as she barely survived exam week.

Brooklyn had vowed not to obsess about her weight during her pregnancy, and so one afternoon she stepped on a scale—the first time since weighing herself at Winsome's house during Long Fall Weekend—and realized she had only gained nine and a half pounds. She stepped off and back onto the scale more than once, hoping the numbers would change. After her fourth try, as if to tease her, the scale did shoot back a different number—one ounce less than the previous number. "Bollocks!" she cried to herself. Brooklyn slumped onto her bed and sighed. She felt bloated all of the time, and still, at nearly six months pregnant, she had gained less than ten pounds. Within seconds this truth set in, followed by strong trepidation, and that feeling compelled her to gnaw on her thumbnail. Whittling it down to almost a nub, Brooklyn tore through *What to Expect When You're Expecting*, desperately in search of a sentence that would assure her that her weight was fine. The book did its job of patting her on the shoulder and confirming to her that her lack of serious weight gain was nothing to worry about. She read that many women gain the majority of their weight after the second half of their third trimester. Brooklyn also figured that as long as she had gained enough weight to constitute the actual birth weight of a healthy child, she was doing fine. *Maybe I will just look, as they say, "all baby,"* she thought.

Brooklyn stood up from her bed and in front of her mirror again, taking stock of her relative fullness. She wondered what her life would be like when the baby was born. Would she marry Chris? What would her parents say? Despite how most traditional families operated, Brooklyn was actually more concerned about her mother's opinion. Her father, though more celebrated as an athlete than her mother was as an actress, had his feet firmly planted on the ground, unlike her mother, and would therefore likely not be concerned about how their family image might be affected. Also, Brooklyn's mother was her own mother's child, after all, and believed wholeheartedly the words of Brooklyn's maternal grandmother: image is everything. Brooklyn thought about the best spin she could give her mother so that she would have a head start on what to tell the outside world once they found out. In Brooklyn's mind, her being pregnant was not all bad, however. She could have become pregnant by an American. Image was one thing. Bloodlines were another.

Brooklyn sorted through a fair share of research, and she read about the number of actresses who had delayed pregnancy so as to not lose a working opportunity, whose bodies were then too old to house their previously stored eggs when they were "ready" to conceive. She thought about her own mother, who led a similar path, later having to experience three rounds of IVF as final attempts to become pregnant, which still did not work. As chance and a natural flow of things would have it, Brooklyn and her twin sister, Manhattan, were actually conceived the old-fashioned way on a drunken and chauffeured drive through New York months after her parents had given up on the idea of trying for a baby at all. Brooklyn's parents were lucky, but not out of the woods. If her mother had not remained on her back for most of her pregnancy, the twins would have never made it. For those reasons and then some, Brooklyn felt more and more confident about her choice to keep her baby, and believed that at her age she was in an excellent position to give birth without complications, and she would then have her bright career to anticipate. What she really needed, though, was for time to speed up so she could meet the baby she was trying so hard to control, yet also realize. She figured that she was due in early May, and if all happened according to plan, she would have time to properly execute her performance with Winsome, plus, she would look fit to walk with her graduating class in June. Brooklyn had it all carefully considered in her seventeen-year-old mind and believed that she had convinced both Chris and Winsome.

She turned to the side to see a profile of her belly again, and suddenly, her bedroom door swung open. With nowhere to run, Brooklyn jumped into Winsome's bed because it was closest to the mirror.

In ran Winsome with all of her dramatic thunder. She looked to her bed and then realized that Brooklyn was in it, which rendered her puzzled.

"I thought I locked the door," explained Brooklyn, "but even if I hadn't, what a way to come in!"

"Sorry . . . But if you knew what was going on, you would be screaming, too!" Winsome could hardly contain herself.

Brooklyn sat up in bed. "What's going on?"

Winsome composed herself and began, "Well, I had no idea about this, so that meant you didn't either, right?"

Brooklyn nodded. "Winnie, you are being long-winded! Get to it!"

"All right, all right! BJ Fortunato entered our first act in this contest they were holding at Tisch . . . and we won!"

Brooklyn jumped up and out of bed forgetting that she was unclothed. Winsome nearly shrieked. When Brooklyn realized what she'd just done, she shrieked for Winsome.

"Sorry, Winnie." Brooklyn calmed down as she covered as much as she could with her bare hands while reaching for her robe.

Winsome could not help but stare at her best friend's body. From the back she looked exactly the same, yet from the front, she now had a visible pouch that looked like more than a result from overeating. Winsome had not seen Brooklyn this undisguised before, because Brooklyn had done a fine job of making the baby issue second to the tasks that she believed needed to come first. Winsome took a pause from celebrating their theater win, faced with this evidence of the real, live silent drama happening in their double-occupancy boarding-school dorm room.

"So, what's happening with—"

Brooklyn interrupted Winsome, whispering, yet trying to sound secure. "With the baby? I feel fine. Better than the first three months. The book says this is the period when I will be the most tired, so I am glad that it will be over in a month. Then I will be heading for the countdown."

"When will you . . . tell your parents?"

"I don't know. As close to May as possible. Sometime around Spring Break, or during, or right after. I read that many times the baby can be due at a certain time, but ends up coming early. Maybe I can ask them to come visit me here so that I can tell them in person, and we can fly private back home. I'd like for the baby to be born in London. My mother would like that."

"How can you be so sure? What if the baby comes late? How can you calculate something like this? Do you think you will be able to just fly home for the weekend, have a real live baby, and then fly right back here to finish out the semester? Have you thought about changing your mind and seeing a doctor?" Winsome could not help but finally express some level of serious concern.

"Winnie!"

"I'm sorry, Brooklyn, but I've not had near a comment since you told me about this at the gas station during Long Fall Weekend. If you will hear my truth about all of this, I'm scared shitless for you . . . I'm sorry I said that."

"Winnie, NO DOCTORS. Have you forgotten about the idea that telling a doctor just might make matters worse? If I went to a physician in town, it would only be a matter of time before the school found out. And if the baby chooses to arrive early, I have to cross that bridge when I get to it. Chris and I have it under control." That was a lie. The truth was, Brooklyn had been avoiding Chris's calls for over a week.

Winsome sighed, feeling left out. "Okay. But I keep telling you, if you need anything—"

Brooklyn interrupted her again. "I know, I know."

Tying the sash on her robe, Brooklyn attempted to lighten up the mood. "Now tell me about the contest!"

Winsome sighed in compliance, trying to pretend that she had moved on as Brooklyn had wanted her to. "Well, we get to have two of the Tisch School's finest theater graduate students act out our first scene, in New York, and the chair of the theater department is going to give us advice!"

Brooklyn sat down slowly.

Winsome continued. "But wait, there's more. After we finish our second act, which we will have to complete earlier than is due at school, that same theater chair will review it as well, and if we rework it in college, it could be submitted early for a Little Eugene O'Neill Award. Only college students qualify for it, but what if we were an exception!"

"So you mean, we'd be getting recognition in New York even before we left high school?"

Winsome nodded.

Brooklyn stood up and embraced Winsome, and then began to cry. "You do realize that I am only crying because of our win, not because I'm pregnant."

Holding Brooklyn close, Winsome retorted, "Yeah, tell that to someone who hasn't held your hair over the toilet!"

Both girls laughed.

"Boy, that seems like an eternity past," sighed Brooklyn.

"We'll have fun again, Brookie. Soon come. Soon come."

Winsome's mobile phone interrupted their embrace. It was Winsome's mother.

Something her mother was saying must have been as heavy

for Winsome as when Brooklyn discovered her weight on the scale, because like Brooklyn had just done, Winsome lowered her body slowly onto her bed. After about ten minutes of saying only "Yes" and "Uh-huh," Winsome hung up and remained seated on her bed in silence.

Brooklyn joined Winsome and exercised a moment of patience before she inquired. "What's up, mate?"

Winsome let out a deep sigh. "It was my mother. She was talking a mile a minute about how she is worried about my relationship with my dad and she feels it has been strained by what happened in October. She felt that I was so closed when she tried to get us together over Thanksgiving, and my father is torn up about it."

"But didn't you all talk during Christmas? All that time at the restaurant?"

"Nah, it was no better. We only scratched the surface. I stuck with you most of the time, remember?"

Brooklyn nodded.

"My mom also said there is something he wants to talk to me about if there is time when we return from Spring Break, but I am done talking. I just want to leave it alone already and move on!"

Brooklyn could not help but feel the slight tension through her best friend, and although she knew there was nothing she could do about helping to mend Winsome's compromised relationship with her father, she still offered an apology as if all of the drama was her fault.

"Not your cross to bear, Brooklyn. But thanks," Winsome whispered sincerely.

Winsome also explained that her mother, on the other hand, did express relief that it was she who was in the restaurant when the man entered and not her older sister, Claire, and how grateful she was to Winsome that she had not yet shared what happened with Claire, because she would not handle it well. Winsome's mother reminded her that she was cool like her father, and so she believed that God knew who to choose to be there.

Like Brooklyn, Winsome's new priority was to adhere to the responsibility of keeping a difficult, complicated issue out of the consciousness of someone she loved. Winsome leaned her head upon Brooklyn's shoulder, and Brooklyn placed her hand in Winsome's. Focusing their attention on nothing in particular, they held hands and allowed the quiet to have a turn.

Later that afternoon, Sagrario stood at the counter at the school book boutique and hummed to herself the song she sang to her baby niece on New Year's Eve while waiting for the bookstore clerk to hand her a receipt for her books. Caitlyn walked up behind her carrying a few books and a sweatshirt to purchase. When Sagrario noticed Caitlyn's presence, she stopped humming. She turned around and smiled at Caitlyn, who, after nervously returning the gesture, actually spoke to Sagrario.

"Hi, Sagrario. How are you?"

Sagrario, having experienced interest in her well-being

twice in two months now by people other than Dr. Knoll or another faculty member, was again at a loss for words. To have exchanged with Elaine was a surprise, but to then be greeted by Caitlyn Lovette? Sagrario scanned the room and realized that they were the only ones in it. *I suppose she can't be embarrassed to be seen talking to me*, she thought.

Sagrario smiled and answered, "Doing well, Caitlyn. And you?"

Caitlyn looked to the floor and back at Sagrario and sighed. "Fine. Just fine."

To interrupt the dominating awkward moment, Sagrario smiled once more and turned back around. She wanted to pay for her books and leave. She did not want to keep Caitlyn feeling more backed in a corner by engaging in continued conversation with her.

The clerk returned holding a lengthy receipt. She lifted her glasses, placed them on the top of her head, and leaned over the counter to speak discreetly with Sagrario.

"Sagrario, darlin', I don't know what seems to be the problem, but it says here that I cannot give you these books until you pay this past-due bill. I'm so sorry."

The clerk handed the bill to Sagrario, and Sagrario covered her mouth, whispering to herself. *What? This cannot be.* Just like with her school-tuition bill, the number looked beyond her immediate reach, and Sagrario did not realize that she'd let the tab grow so big. It was not Isabella's fault, but because of the new baby in the family, Sagrario's normal routine of handling school business and home balance had become imbalanced.

Then Sagrario, forgetting who was standing behind her, tried to reason with the clerk.

"Okay, I see this bill, and I will pay it. But I really need at least one of these books to begin the new semester now."

"I understand, Sagrario. Why don't you run to the business office and have them write you a note, and then I can honor the request, okay?"

The clerk was embarrassed and felt bad for Sagrario, but her hands were tied.

Sagrario tried to hold back her tears. She'd recently given the business office a big chunk of her money to pay toward tuition in order to ensure that her transcript would be released to colleges. What was left, she divided between her and her family, and what was allotted for herself would only put a small dent in her bookstore bill. She sighed.

Caitlyn again made her presence known. "Sagrario, I can pay for your books, whatever the cost." Caitlyn reached in her tiny wallet and pulled out a platinum American Express card.

Sagrario turned around and looked Caitlyn in her face, then down at her perfectly manicured fingers that held out her impeccable credit card. Sagrario was stunned, and not in a good way.

She turned back to the clerk and hastily apologized before exiting the store in a rush. Caitlyn ran behind her.

"Sagrario! Wait up! Did I say something wrong? I'm sorry! I just was trying to help!"

Sagrario was beginning to feel an uneasy sensation that rushed and filled up in her belly then rose to the top of her head.

Tremors were forming inside, piling one by one, eager to escape underneath a guise of rage. No one knew how difficult life was for Sagrario, even those who shared four difficult walls with her in the South Bronx. The dual lives she led were pure pressure. On the one hand, trying to appease her campus community, and on the other, maintaining a breath-holding patience to make sure that her family's needs—her mother's, her sister's, and her brother's—were met first. Sagrario knew that she had made it this far, yet just as she could see the finishing flag in the distance, life decided to laugh aloud and point its "you-are-still-not-good-enough" finger in her face in the form of someone who would try to sum up her entire journey and struggle with a credit card. For Sagrario, Caitlyn's audacity embodied everyone who thought they could encapsulate her life in a dollar amount, a label, a metaphor. There was no metaphor that could express the weight she'd been carrying on her shoulders for seventeen years, all the while maintaining an upright position. Sagrario stopped walking swiftly and allowed an inch between hers and Caitlyn's face.

"Thank you, Caitlyn, but I am no charity case."

Caitlyn interjected. "I . . . I don't think you are a charity case, Sagrario. I just don't want you to be behind. Bad things happen to everyone. Trust me." Then Caitlyn flashed an honest smile that still could have been taken in a condescending way depending on at whom the smile was directed.

Sagrario gave permission to her tremors that had by that time truly transformed and no longer needed to be cloaked. Out came full-on rage.

"What is it with you, huh? What BAD has ever happened to YOU? You and your stupid rich boyfriend aren't getting along this week? Or, or Mommy has decided not to fund one of your weekly shopping trips to New York? Or let me guess. You compare me not being able to pay for school books to your favorite chocolate truffles being on back order?"

"Sagrario, I didn't mean to belittle you at all! I was only trying to help!" Caitlyn began to cry.

On cue, Sagrario thought. *People like her are allowed to cry at the drop of a dime. She never has to think about being strong.* Sagrario could not remember the last time she felt that she could cry freely because of her own hurt feelings. This privileged response from Caitlyn only angered her more.

"Do you want to know MY biggest problem? No, you don't want to know. You would not be able to handle it!"

As Sagrario's forehead gushed with sweat beads, her breathing began to feel like a pant. She tried to calm herself down. "It's fine, Caitlyn . . . You don't understand. It's fine. I don't need any help . . . I'm sorry."

Sagrario turned and walked away, leaving Caitlyn sniffling with a wetted, flushed face.

Caitlyn mumbled humbly and quietly underneath her sobs, "And I am sorry that I live in such a fucking bubble."

Sagrario parted with her head deliberately held high. This made it easier for her unprivileged tears to not completely give herself away to others before she made it to her dorm room where she could deal the best way she knew how: alone.

12

Outed

By late March, Elaine and the senior class as a whole were itching for a freedom scratch. It was the time of year where there was one more major hurdle to jump, and then their Madame Ellington experience would be complete. Just like that, in came April, and acceptance and declination letters by the droves from universities and colleges were deposited and removed from student mailboxes. There were screams of excitement, tears of letdown, and overall emotional volcanoes simmering within the senior dorms that would seep out more and more the days leading up to that explosive time of graduation.

Elaine could not speak for anyone else, but her emotions were on a high for more than the obvious reasons. She was also preoccupied about her mother, and where her father was concerned, her only regard for him revolved around his effect on her mother's well-being. Elaine was discouraged that her mother had not fully shared all of her intentions regarding how she was going to handle her marriage, or lack thereof, and Elaine still had aborted several attempts to initiate the conversation. Elaine did all that she could to take her mind off of her family, and had she been overloaded trying to decide what school to attend in the fall, like many of her peers, her parent's concerns would have had to take a back seat. But Elaine had been accepted into her top three choices, and she already knew which school she was going to attend. With nothing much left to engross her, her mind was at liberty to be absorbed with her mother.

Ironically, after a couple of days thinking obsessively about her, Elaine was triggered to focus on another female in love distress whom she knew about: Hedda. No longer able to pretend that what she heard in the bathroom over Long Fall Weekend was not real, Elaine guided the courage she could not cultivate to confront her mother to divulge what she witnessed with Hedda to Sagrario.

Sagrario, who was still milling in her head about what had happened with Caitlyn, welcomed the opportunity to shift her focus to someone else's issue, so she could push her own problems way down.

Both girls sat on a bench in front of the local diner and ice cream shop, Kindly's, at Elaine's request to ensure that no one on campus could hear their conversation.

"So, are you still thinking about where you want to go next year?" asked Elaine, opening up the conversation.

"Yes, I have my dream, and I still have not heard back yet. Any day now." Sagrario forced a weak smile.

Though Sagrario and Elaine had been bonding over the recent months, it was still clear to Elaine that her budding relationship required Elaine to be patient and wait for Sagrario to share only what she chose. Elaine did not pry, and did not talk about her own college results to make Sagrario feel any pressure. "Well, that's good. I think we are all still trying to figure things out. I am just happy this part is almost over."

"Me too."

Now confirmed that Sagrario was not interested in discussing college applications, Elaine changed the subject. "Speaking of transitioning, have you ever thought about how Hedda has gotten on here? I mean, she is one of only two New Girl seniors, and at least the other girl has a support system because she's a day student, right?"

Sagrario immediately placed her imaginary Student Head of School hat on her head. "Yeah, I think she has had a challenging year. I hear that she has a boyfriend whom she misses a lot—I have been keeping an eye on her. She seems to have connected well with Sofija . . . Is there something I don't know?"

Elaine told Sagrario she knew about Hedda's connection with Sofija, the Ukrainian senior, but Sagrario interrupted.

"Stephanie seems to like her a lot and really tries to cater to her, I've noticed."

From hearing this, Elaine started thinking about how much Sagrario fit her position as Student Head of School. She was sincerely concerned with all things Madame Ellington, yet, like many leaders of groups, she was not keenly aware of the specific goings-on. Elaine excused the fact that the details of campus gossip tended to bypass the threshold of Sagrario's door.

"Yes, Stephanie has been an awesome Old Girl, Sagrario,

but all of Stephanie's kindness has not been able to keep Hedda from blessing the bowl."

Sagrario angled herself more in Elaine's direction. "She's what?"

"Yes, and I have known since Long Fall Weekend. We both stayed on campus and I got to know her a little bit. I sort of walked in on her, well not exactly, but I heard her. On two separate occasions."

Sagrario had heard of girls at school battling issues with bulimia and anorexia. Her class had one student who ended up having to finish her junior and senior years at home because she became so skinny. But that was one issue Sagrario hoped could have been left behind. Madame Ellington, as she knew it, had been revitalized, and the idea of individual pride and support was at an all-time high. Loving and respecting one's self had become such an unofficial motto, she did not realize that there were any students who could have fallen between the cracks. The girls were practically trained to be built-in support systems for one another.

"Why did you not come to me sooner?"

"I don't know, and I have wrestled with this a lot. I think that with all I have going on with my mother, I have put all of my protective spirit into her. I'm sorry." Elaine looked away, realizing that waiting months to break her silence about Hedda's eating disorder was not a good thing. Her eyes watered on the spot. She also felt a sense of shame because though she wanted to protect her mother, as with Hedda, she felt that she had failed at that, too.

"Hey, I didn't mean it like that, it is not your fault." Sagrario did her best to take it easy on Elaine. She liked her a lot, and also, she had no intentions of repeating the scene she experienced with Caitlyn.

"What are you going to do? I am okay if she finds out that I am the one who told." Elaine figured since she waited so long to say something, she had to be all in.

Sagrario understood how Elaine being outed could damage her new connection with Hedda, and thus turned her down. She told Elaine that perhaps if she knew what was going on with Hedda, she might not be alone, and so there would be no problem expressing (if asked by Hedda to reveal the messenger) that one of her fellow seniors who was worried about her shared the information. Elaine was amazed at how well Sagrario knew how to handle situations and people. She felt good about speaking up.

Sagrario hugged Elaine and thanked her for sharing. Elaine held the hug a bit after Sagrario let go, for she could not resist a prolonged embrace to help soothe her own preoccupied mind about her mother. Before they parted ways, Sagrario reassured Elaine.

"It's going to be all right. It really is. Just wait and see."

Adding to the extreme amounts of estrogen in the air was Brooklyn's baby, who was, by this time, eight months housed inside of her. However, her outer appearance still had yet to catch up with how far along she was. In fact, she spent time staring at her naked self in her mirror as often as she could just to prove to herself that her baby was there, growing. With help from all of the pregnancy books she had been reading, and the dozens of examples and explanations about women who experience a similar process, but still produce healthy children, Brooklyn tried to keep her panic about carrying so small at a minimum. *If I can just make it to term*, she thought, *everyone's disappointment will turn into happiness once they see the baby*. Yes, she'd been away from home since August. Yes, she said she wanted to go home for Christmas and then changed her mind at the last minute, using her and Winsome's senior project as the excuse. Yes, the aforementioned "last-minute" change of heart was planned in advance to bluff her family. And yes, she really did miss her family, most importantly, her twin sister, Manhattan. But Brooklyn knew that if she placed herself so much as within a two-hundred-mile radius from her, Manhattan would feel the difference in Brooklyn enough to speak on it and blow her cover.

Brooklyn's biggest wish was to know if she was carrying a boy or a girl. Without having an ultrasound, however, she would never know until the baby was born. Still too afraid to go home, Brooklyn also abandoned her previous plan of going home during Spring Break with hopes of giving birth in London and decided that she would yet again travel to Winsome's. Brooklyn intended upon asking Winsome to try and finagle something at the hospital where her mother worked, hoping to catch a glimpse of her baby. More important than knowing the sex, though, Brooklyn wanted to calm her nerves that her baby, boy or girl, was okay. She was also in deep thought about her mother's impending trip to New York within weeks and her specific request that Brooklyn meet her in the city so they could spend some time together.

"It's ridiculous that you have purposely stayed away so long this school year, despite your dedication to your senior project. Manhattan absolutely misses you! And I'm sure you have not found a suitable graduation dress yet," her mother urged.

Brooklyn was prepared to avoid her mother like a plague when she arrived in New York, and she would send a photo of an acceptable designer dress to her mother. As for Manhattan, Brooklyn would brave another phone call with her twin sister, devising an interruption to cut their conversation short as she'd done the week before. It is true that her loved ones were becoming skeptical, and Brooklyn had thus far not crossed but successfully avoided every bridge that revealed itself to her. As it pertained to Chris, Brooklyn had to talk him out of nearly jumping off the ledge of spilling their secret when he became visibly upset about her non-growing belly. For her baby, Brooklyn had lied repeatedly to her family, and with Chris, she threatened to deny him visits to their baby if he told anyone what was going on. This she did not really mean, but Chris believed her and continued to keep quiet. Brooklyn told Winsome that she was well aware her actions were Machiavellian, but she believed any mother would do whatever it took to protect their child.

It hurt Brooklyn to speak such harsh words to Chris, and she was deeply pained about the games she was playing with her family, but she felt she had no choice. She had her plan in mind and believed it would work. Ever since she decided to go through with her pregnancy, she had been establishing for herself a way that she would handle everyone and everything concerning the baby. She believed that she had to be calculating to succeed. She had learned how to be calculating from her mother. Brooklyn was her mother's child.

Winsome, who was labeled by her mother as her father's child, chose to take Brooklyn's grave matter into her own hands. Witnessing Brooklyn struggle more and more every day trying to keep up with the lies she told herself and everyone else, coupled with trying to live in the present and complete senior year, Winsome knew her best friend was unraveling at the seams. Luckily, because Brooklyn was a theater girl, her random emotional episodes could be chalked up to her natural sense of drama, but Brooklyn was growing sloppy at covering her tracks. For one, she was almost seen naked by a fellow senior when Brooklyn accidentally dropped her towel while brushing her teeth in the bathroom, and then Winsome found herself telling people all sorts of stories on Brooklyn's behalf about why she could not attend a tradition, or why she had not been seen in the dining hall. She even took on a great deal of responsibility with Brooklyn's New Girl, standing in as an ear or to give advice when she experienced a challenging moment. And Winsome was a very good actress, so creating diversions for Brooklyn was not difficult, but Winsome felt that Brooklyn was becoming completely entangled in the web she had created for herself. Something had to be done. With one shaky hand on the dorm pay phone, and the other covering her mouth over the receiver, she confided:

"Is this you? Though I know she is here with me, I cannot help but feel guilty telling someone with the exact same voice."

Manhattan took a deep breath on the other end of the phone. "I know what is wrong with my sister, Winsome, and I am glad you called."

"You do? Did Brookie tell you? Now I feel extra guilty. But Manhattan, I just couldn't bear—"

"Winsome, of course Brookie did not tell me anything. She will barely even speak to me. How far along?"

Winsome was silent. *Is this how twins work?* she asked herself in her head. Winsome did not know what to say. Was Manhattan asking how far along in her pregnancy was Brooklyn? Winsome gasped. "She is in her third trimester."

"That's about right."

"Can I ask, is this some twin voodoo stuff, or are you just clairvoyant?"

"Not that I know of. But when Brookie was out having nightcaps with Chris this summer, I knew she did not protect herself each time, and she was ovulating during that week. We both were. She's such a free spirit and never pays attention to that sort of thing, but this is where we differ. She did not have her period the next month, and while I suspected exactly what was going on, she believed it was from stress about her senior project with you."

"And you're not scared?"

"Scared? Why should I be? She is obviously going to keep it, and so until the baby is born, there isn't much to be alarmed about, is there? Sure she has not seen a physician, and she has obviously done well hoodwinking everyone at the school . . . Sure that wasn't hard," Manhattan commented with a hint of sarcasm.

"It was, is, hard, Manhattan." Winsome uncovered her mouth and took a pause as two seniors and a freshman were laughing on the way out of the dorm. "Your sister is totally not herself, and I am afraid for her emotionally."

"Well, there is not much I can do with her not wanting to tell me the truth, is there? Not much I can do with her shacking up, *going to school* in Ameeeerica!"

Though Winsome sensed Manhattan's resentment, she still tried to provide balance.

"Listen, Manhattan, I happen to know firsthand that if your sister could talk to anyone in the entire world, it would be you. You have no idea how much she cries at night, how ashamed she feels for not telling her family. She did not want to put that load on you and make you promise not to tell your parents. She was only trying to protect you."

Manhattan remained silent.

"And one last thing, Manhattan. Brooklyn told me that her biggest regret is not even getting pregnant, it was that you were not with her when she found out."

On the other end of the phone, on the other side of the pond, out came from Manhattan, the once-described deliberate snail, a heavier, trembling breath, revealing to Winsome that she was now crying. Her tone shifted from night to day. After taking a pause, then collecting herself, Manhattan asked, "Is she all right?"

Winsome was grateful that Manhattan finally let down her guard. "You know your sister, but sometimes, I am not so sure."

Manhattan continued on with her real concerns. "How is she getting on, not seeing a doctor? She is such a free spirit! She thinks everything can be fixed with a home remedy! I read how lots of women give birth every year having not been seen by a doctor, but if there are complications that a doctor does not see beforehand, things can be very bad."

"She seems fine, although she is not gaining a ton of weight. But she eats like a horse, not like a bird as usual. This, Brookie says, is how she is assured that the baby is fine. She reads all sorts of baby books that tell her what to expect as she goes along."

"She is planning to travel home for Spring Break, yes?"

"I don't think so. She said she was going home with me again."

"Then I've got to do something. This cannot wait until your graduation."

"No, no. Sit tight. Don't move. I will call you back."

Winsome hung up the dorm pay phone. She paced and paced about what she had just done, trying to convince herself that by calling Manhattan, she had not just committed the greatest sin amongst best friends.

Though she advised Manhattan to sit tight and be patient for her next phone call regarding Brooklyn, Winsome could not delay another day to finally peel away the layers with her father about their own family crisis. She did not understand why her father would want to wait to deal with what was happening, especially since they only scratched the surface during both Thanksgiving and Christmas holidays. Now that Brooklyn had canceled their long-planned trip to London, Winsome thought that spending it on Long Island trapped in some ongoing family drama with her was an awful alternative. Brooklyn had been ultra-respectful about the ordeal since their run-in with the thug at Winsome's family's restaurant during Long Fall Weekend, and had not further inquired about what she saw. Yet Winsome knew that somewhere in the back of Brooklyn's head she thought about it, because that day still weighed heavily on her own mind. To avoid Brooklyn being further entangled in the mess, as well as to ease her own growing stress about it, Winsome found a remote place on campus and dialed her father's mobile phone.

"Daddy, it's Winsome."

George Sinclair sounded startled by the call, though he answered seemingly on reflex. "Winnie, what's the trouble?"

"There is no trouble with *me*, Dad."

There was a tension-filled silence in between the words

spoken next. Winsome hoped that her father would jump right into it because he understood that unless there was trouble with her, she would normally not call home on a Saturday afternoon. The operative word being *trouble*, Winsome anticipated that her father would take the hint and get right to it. He did not. Mr. Sinclair commenced to making irrelevant small talk about subjects he knew Winsome cared little about.

Frustrated with her father's unwillingness to express that he knew what her call to him was truly about, Winsome broke the silence. "What's going on with the restaurant, Dad?"

Winsome heard a commotion from the other end of the phone, like her father had knocked something over. "Right. Well, I've had to make some adjustments. It's no big deal, really. Didn't your mother tell you that we would discuss it during Spring Break?"

"Yes, she did, but that is almost three weeks away. Of course I can handle whatever is going on, so why give me so much lead time?"

"Because I wanted to have a proper sit-down with my daughter about what happened, is all."

Winsome was not convinced. "And you cannot have a proper conversation with me over the phone? What has happened with that man since he showed up?"

There was a silence again, only this time it did not last as long. Mr. Sinclair spoke up abruptly as if he was trying to cut off Winsome before she said something first. "Nothing has happened with him. But something has happened with me, with the restaurant."

"Okay, 'something'? Dad, why are you being so vague? What is so big that I cannot be told over the phone?"

Mr. Sinclair took his first of many deep breaths during the conversation. This one sounded exhausted. "Do you know how long it took for me to build my restaurant, Winsome?"

"No, Daddy."

"It took me three whole years to just convince myself that it was acceptable for me to even think about accomplishing something like that, three and a half years to raise the deposit money, and another two years to complete renovations. All the while holding down a square job to put food on the table for my family. During those days, our only priority for you all was ensuring that you received proper nourishment. Whether we ate the same thing every day for a week was not the worry. Your mother's perspective was, 'Anything more to eat than what constituted your right nourishment was a big bonus,' and I agreed. But we were proud because lots of families around could not consistently provide that. More than that, I had a dream. A dream to do more for you all. I wanted your mother to be able to go to nursing school like she wanted, even though I knew that I would never have a shot at attending any university myself. This is why I read any and everything I can get my hands on to make sure that I stay educated. Remain connected. Remain informed. And that dream of mine, that restaurant that I know to you doesn't look like much, was my opportunity to show what I could really do in this world. I need you to understand this first before I go on and tell you the possibilities for the next level of that dream. And I wanted to do this in person, but here we are."

Winsome did not know exactly where her father was going with this story. Some of it she remembered, like being in the first grade and eating peas and rice, a beef patty, and callaloo for what seemed like all of the time, but she was not fully following her father, so she probed more.

"I hear you, Dad, but I still don't understand . . ."

Mr. Sinclair breathed a frustrated-sounding sigh, and interrupted Winsome again. "You don't know this, but right before you entered Madame Ellington, I almost lost the restaurant. Yes, that is correct. Almost lost it. Until one day, a supposed friend of a friend of someone they knew in Jamaica said he knew a guy from back home who'd become wealthy in America and was looking to invest in businesses here. He said he thought my restaurant would be a perfect fit for his portfolio. I met with the guy, and actually, I went to school with a cousin of his, and so there was that connection. It was all nice and clean, he liked that we were family owned and had a steady movement of customers. He invested immediately, and that is how we paid your first year's tuition. Because all flowed well, I did not ask any questions."

"So what became the trouble?"

"Last summer I realized that he was tied into some illegal things, and I feared that he had been using my business as a front. When I confronted him and he didn't deny it, I told him I wanted out of the partnership, and that is when things went south. Someone was killed, he sent the cops in the direction of the restaurant, and then began trying to intimidate me by demanding more money. This is why that man visited when you were in town. I had to do something, so I called the authorities. They contacted him and he threw me under the bus, so now I am seen as just as criminal as he is."

Winsome tried to interject, but an angered George carried on.

"And I just might lose my restaurant for good because of it! I had no idea that the investment was shady! But who will believe me? I am just some man with no college degree! Just as sure as my name is George Omar Sinclair, they will take my place of business from me! Take it all. Practically ten years I worked myself to the bone just to be able to hang a welcome sign. I quit my job and cooked every patty, curried every piece of goat, because I could not afford enough staff. I built that place with my two bare hands! Nobody ever gave anything to me, and the one time I allow myself to be vulnerable, and this only to secure a good education for my children, the rug gets swept right from under me?"

Winsome's father was, by this point, very emotional, and he then switched gears.

"And this, this is why, Winsome! Why I urge you to have stability in your life! Because when you don't have security, you will be forced to compromise. I didn't want to go into partnership with anyone for a business I built with my own two hands. But I had to, to properly provide for my family. Do you understand?"

"Yes, Daddy, I do," Winsome mustered through sobs she no longer cared to shield.

Mr. Sinclair let out one last, angry sigh, making Winsome feel to be the sole target of his frustration.

"And so you want to follow that rich British girl and try your hand at acting, is it? That is what you want to do with your life? Struggle? That will be your fate because I will no longer be able to carry you. Who knows where I will be by then. I sacrificed my life for you and your siblings, and in the end, this is my reward. Well, thank you. But you know something? I have no regrets because I know in my heart that I did the right thing. Look at your old man who had somewhat of a plan, and where did it get him? Where will your 'plan' take you?"

Winsome was nearly hyperventilating by this moment and could not take anymore. She hung up on her father.

With a closed flip phone in hand, Winsome continued to cry. The area on campus where she sat was free of bystanders, but she did not want anyone within earshot to hear her crying and inquire, so she placed her phone between her legs and covered her mouth with both hands. Rocking herself back and forth, she could not control her crying, as she thought about someone wearing some kind of uniform taking the keys from her father, stripping down the awning that flashed *G. Omar Jamaica* above the restaurant, and the thought of watching her father load all of the things in his beloved office into unmarked boxes and onto a trailer, then to be placed somewhere in their crowded basement, never to be opened by him again. He would lose his zeal for learning; he would find no comfort in reading all of those newspapers in his home in an attempt to recreate a new morning ritual that he oh so used to cherish in his office at the restaurant.

The possibility of seeing her keyless father walk past the building where the restaurant would have once been housed, unable to unlock the front door and walk right in and claim the space as his own, shook Winsome to the core. Soon, guilt began to set in about her life goals. *He is right*, Winsome thought. *If I don't succeed as an actress, I will have nothing to fall back on.* In previous years, just as her father held close his passion and belief for his restaurant, Winsome moved on near blind faith for her career dreams. She knew in her heart she had serious talent and had worked hard as often as she was given an opportunity to, and many times, had created opportunities for herself to cultivate that "thing" she knew she possessed. But her talent was not like having a passion to sell food. *People have to eat to survive*, she asserted in her head. Winsome, with all of her passion and believed talent, could end up performing to empty houses for the rest of her life.

As she sat on a stone bench in the middle of a clearing on campus, Winsome spotted Victoria Lee walking in the distance, and Winsome was unmoved. It would take a million years for Victoria to stop and engage Winsome, she was sure, and so Winsome knew that she would be able to process her grief alone. To Winsome's surprise, within seconds, a million years had arrived. Victoria had edged herself all the way in front of Winsome and her face full of tears. As of yesterday, any engagement from Victoria would have easily piqued Winsome's interest, but today she was in no mood to converse with anyone. Not fully fanning Victoria away, she mumbled, "It's all right, Victoria. It's cool."

Victoria did not accept Winsome's response. "Why are you crying, Winsome?"

Winsome, not used to wearing the vulnerable hat, answered, "Because life isn't going so well right now . . . But I'll be all right. Don't worry."

Victoria did not respond to Winsome's comment with words. Instead she inched even closer to Winsome and sat down beside her.

Victoria's presence had arrived at the exact right moment. It was comforting, yet at the same time not intrusive. Winsome appreciated that Victoria gave way for her to be absorbed in her own thoughts and feelings. Winsome had always served as a caregiver to her friends and family, but this also meant that for much of her own problems she would almost be expected to go it alone. Victoria knew of no such stigma that had been placed on Winsome, and so in Victoria's tiny, judgeless arms, Winsome was allowed to fall and cry without subconsciously feeling weak.

"I only wish he understood me, my dad," Winsome sobbed. "Just because who I am is not what he sees for me does not mean it's wrong or that I will fail. I am different from the girls in my family. And that's okay!"

"Different is okay," Victoria confirmed. She held Winsome tighter.

"And I am not going to be afraid to be myself around him or anyone else anymore."

"You can be yourself." Upon saying this, Winsome noticed Victoria's eyes water.

Winsome peeked over Victoria's shoulder and noticed that the sun was beginning to shine through the clouds that had been looming all day. When she did this, Victoria turned her head around to acknowledge them, too. Then Victoria gently released Winsome, stood up straight, looked her in her eyes, and repeated almost verbatim what Winsome had just told her. "I know that life isn't going so well right now . . . But it will be all right. Don't worry."

Winsome knew that Victoria had very little knowledge about her life, and had no idea what had just transpired between her father and her, but Winsome believed Victoria Lee.

❧

"Sweetheart, I believe that you and Eric will be the nicest-looking couple at his school dance," smiled Stephanie's mother as she sat on their family room sofa unstitching a hem on a dress.

"Stephanie will certainly be the most beautiful. You are going to be wearing a classic handed down by your mother! Do we have enough film for the camera?" added Stephanie's father. Special occasions deserved negatives, not pixels, he always insisted.

Stephanie was annoyed. "Guys, it's not such a big deal, okay?"

"It IS a big deal, sweetheart! Madame Ellington doesn't have a big formal dance like this, so this will be the closest you will get to going to the prom. That is why wearing my dress will be meaningful!"

"Your dress is totally vintage and awesome, that is why I want to wear it, Mom. This dance is a joke."

"It is not! I am sure Eric doesn't feel like that!"

"Yes he does, he thinks it's ridiculous."

"So why are you going, then?"

Stephanie's little sister, Kate, who was within earshot, chimed in. "SO she can kiss boys! Ah ha!"

"Ewww! Stay out of it, Pipsqueak!" fumed Stephanie.

Now it was Stephanie's father who was annoyed. "Ewww? I certainly hope that's not the tone you still take regarding boys, Stephanie. You are very close to turning eighteen!"

"Yes, and imagine, one day you will be going on serious dates and he'll want to kiss you at your doorstep . . ." added her mother.

Feeling intruded upon, Stephanie screamed at her parents, and a nearby Kate, "Why is everyone so focused on my love life, huh?"

Later that day at Eric's house, Stephanie vented to him about her situation at home. She was grateful to finally have someone to whom she could air out her family grievances. By this time, Eric had become Stephanie's most trusted friend. Between him and Hedda, they served as her emotional sounding boards. Yet it was not always so feasible to talk to Hedda about her issues because Hedda remained Stephanie's first love interest. Though they had established a common understanding, Stephanie still at times could not avoid becoming lost in Hedda's eyes when she spoke. Also, Hedda being mostly a matter-of-fact advice giver, did not possess the wit, candor, and downright crude humor that Eric did. Stephanie needed that from time to time just to keep from crying about all of her heart's anguish.

The two friends lay on Eric's bed on their backs, Stephanie nuzzled underneath Eric's arm with him running his fingers through her hair. Together, they looked the epitome of beauty and contradiction: within Eric's chiseled, ultra-masculine body was embedded a gentle and sensitive character that often helped to soften Stephanie's temper. Stephanie's luminous eyes stared at the ceiling with a gaze as hard as steel.

Eric felt Stephanie's rigidness and decided to be straightforward with her. "I don't know why you just don't tell them."

"Because I can't. Are you kidding? My father would be devastated . . . You're one to talk. I don't exactly see a rainbow flag blowing in the wind from your bedroom window!"

"Oh no? Well, believe me, they know. I have left them every opportunity to know. I even slid a few male mags in my mom's laundry basket!"

"Oh my. What did she do?"

"She returned them. They were under my pillow."

"So they're not mad? Your dad isn't disappointed that his *only* son doesn't have a crush on the latest gorgeous movie star?"

"Sure he's not! And who said that I don't have a crush on a gorgeous movie star! Have you heard of the GORGEOUS up-and-coming Bradley Cooper?"

Stephanie punched Eric, urging him to get serious.

"All right, all right. Actually, we just had a little talk about IT, and boy am I relieved. It was my dad who brought it up. He says he doesn't care, as long as I'm happy, and my mom feels the same. My dad is an equal rights attorney. It would go against everything he stood for if he denied his own son because of his sexuality. He says with me God was testing him to see how committed he was to the cause. He told me that when you truly love someone, nothing is really challenging."

"Wow. But you're not out to the neighborhood."

"No, not formally, my mom says I can come out whenever I feel like it. I totally had the best platform at my bar mitzvah. But it's not like all of our neighborhood friends don't know. I was only bullied for years by Josh Stein because he said I was a 'girl in disguise.' He stopped saying that after I punched him and broke his nose!"

"I remember that! But I didn't know the reason why you'd done it!"

"He had it coming. I'm sure the other parents have talked about me and my girly ways, but not to my parents. My mom would have them for breakfast. The reason why your parents don't know is because, well, let's face it. Your parents might as well live on a commune. I mean, they are so Adam and Eve *before* the serpent. Their eyes have not been opened to the fact that they have pubic hair! I'll bet you and your sister were brought to them by a stork. They crack me up!"

Stephanie punched him again.

"Hey girl, you'd better stop punching me. Those volleyball

arms of yours might be fierce to look at, but they are also no joke! Don't think I won't fight you back! Didn't your mama teach you not to hit a lady?" Eric continued. "Switching gears, why won't you respond to Emily?"

"Because she scares me."

"How can she frighten you just because she likes you? Look. The girl is a dream to look at. Even I think so, and you know I usually do not acknowledge that sort of thing. She's smart, athletic like you, AND she has a little experience. When I met her at a get-together last month, I knew the two of you would hit it off. She moved here from Southern California when she was ten, and whatever glow she has certainly shines through. The girl looks like walking sunshine."

"Maybe that's it. Because she likes me."

"You should be happy! And no, she is not interested in you because I put her up to it. Somebody showed her your photo and she practically lost her mind. She could not wait to meet you . . . That's why she is on her way over here!"

"Holy shit! She really is coming?"

"Have you forgotten? I told you she was! And it IS SUNDAY! Hello! The dance is next weekend, and it's not like you don't practically live at your school! What time do we have? And I've got to find out if there is any chemistry between the two of you so my boyfriend can take her to the dance. That boy needs a beard like Madonna needs controversy. Plus, I can't have you all up in my mix at the dance because you don't have anybody to hang out with at my school! Chop chop!"

Stephanie bounced out of bed and stood in front of Eric at

the foot of his bed. She outstretched her arms, performed a rendition of Madonna's "Vogue dance" that ended with one hand on her hip and the other cupping her breast.

"What do you think?"

Clapping and sitting up in bed, Eric congratulated her. "Ultra-vintage! Sashay, Chanté! Love it! Now get home. When she arrives, I will send her to your house." Eric hopped up from his bed. "Remember, this is only a 'get to know you.' If you click, you will have next Saturday. Capisce?"

"Capisce."

Back in her bedroom, Stephanie marched back and forth holding a different bottle of perfume in each hand. She decided to use neither. She brushed her hair while standing in front of her window, waiting for Emily to arrive. When Stephanie saw Emily pull up in the driveway and exit her car, Stephanie ceased brushing midstroke. Emily was stunning, even better than her photo. How could someone that beautiful have a crush on her? Eric told Stephanie that Emily had attended one of Stephanie's volleyball matches and was smitten from the start. Emily was tall and blond like Hedda, but her hair was bone straight and layered. Stephanie peeked from behind her drapes as Emily looked up at Stephanie's house, in the direction of her bedroom. Newly broken-through sunlight shined on her shoulder blades, and Emily's eyes were so blue they nearly jumped out of her head. Stephanie suddenly felt thirsty.

The doorbell rang. Stephanie, listening at her closed door,

could overhear her father greeting Emily when she entered the house. He was very polite to her, as he was to all of Stephanie's friends. He acknowledged that he had never met her before, but was pleased to, and told her that Stephanie had just returned from her boyfriend Eric's house, as they were planning for a big dance the following weekend. Emily told Stephanie's dad that she knew all about it because she and Eric attended the same school. Stephanie's dad asked if a pretty girl like her had decided on the many suitors he was sure she had for the dance. Emily said she was working on it.

Stephanie was then summoned by her dad to greet Emily, and she froze again. "Coming!" she yelled from a crack in her bedroom door. When Stephanie descended the stairway that led right to the front door, which brought her closer and closer to Emily's perfect face, all she felt was more parched. With a cracked voice, she asked her father, who was still standing at the front door with Emily, if he could bring her a glass of water.

The two girls stood facing one another, with Stephanie measuring perhaps a few inches taller than Emily. They both stood there and stared into each other's eyes. Emily spoke first.

"You are so beautiful," she whispered discreetly.

Blushing, Stephanie whispered back, "So are you."

The two girls did not move one muscle, but with their eyes, they searched and examined every visible part of each other. Stephanie noticed a mole on Emily's left shoulder, and throughout their encounter Stephanie's cheeks and overall face shifted from various shades of pink. The spell that Hedda had unknowingly cast on Stephanie was broken.

"I brought a glass for you, too, Emily," Stephanie's father interrupted their chat. Emily thanked Stephanie's father.

Emily and Stephanie sat on Emily's bed for nearly five minutes, and still said nothing. Stephanie, whose hands rested on her own tight jeans, sighed here and there in between. Emily leaned over to smell Stephanie's neck, which startled Stephanie a bit, but she eased into it. Emily's breath on her neck felt like the most natural thing in the world.

"Boy, do you smell good."

"Thank you."

Emily slowly brushed her fingers up and down Stephanie's thigh, and Stephanie leaned in closer to Emily so she could have a better advantage to breathe down her neck. Heavy breathing led to licking, and licking led to eager caresses on thighs. With no warning, Stephanie turned over and straddled Emily on her bed, and they began a full-on make-out session. Emily cupped Stephanie's backside with one hand, and her other hand found its way up the back of Stephanie's tank top. Stephanie had never in a million years tasted a kiss so sweet.

Within seconds, the girls were no longer atop Stephanie's bed, but lying together in a bed of jasmine and surrounding greens. Throughout this everlasting kiss they clutched hands, bit ears, and ran fingers through strands of hair . . .

So mesmerized they must have thought the voice right above them was a harmless buzz of a butterfly, because Stephanie lifted her hand to shoo it away.

"I said, WHAT IN GOD'S NAME ARE YOU DOING?"

Both girls jolted upright to the stirring, yet emotional sound of Stephanie's dad's voice as he stood before them carrying a tray holding cookies and milk.

For Sagrario, the next two weeks whizzed by, and Spring Break was upon her and her peers. She understood that so many of the students needed it, especially some seniors, who'd been undergoing serious, life-altering transitions from the knowing that within less than two months, Madame Ellington would be a home of their past. Sagrario and the rest of the senior class had all received their school admittance and declination letters, and mostly everyone knew what college or university they wanted to attend. Sagrario had reason to exhale because as schools were concerned, her dream of being accepted to Harvard had come true. Knowing, however, that no one at home would fully understand what a great accomplishment this was, Sagrario pulled in her biggest cheers of support from Dr. Knoll and her new friend, Elaine. This was the last, biggest decision Sagrario and her class would be making to begin their young adult lives.

And for various seniors, there were other decisions concerning the details of their lives that were voluntarily, or involuntarily, made. Winsome had refused to talk to her father until she saw him in person that coming weekend. She was no longer angry with him, but she was experiencing feelings she could not define. This was the longest she'd ever gone without speaking to her father. Repeated calls from her mother did not help. Winsome, her mother, and her father needed to see each other, and when they did, they needed to fully open up about their feelings about what happened. During that time of estrangement from her father, however, Winsome and a very pregnant Brooklyn completed a masterpiece of sorts with the second act of their senior theater project. Winsome's emotions toward her father coupled with Brooklyn's hormone overload were a perfect combination to accomplish the goal. They wrote all night sometimes, which worked well for Brooklyn, because there were many nights when she could not sleep. BJ Fortunato was so impressed by their work that she offered to take them both to dinner to celebrate. The girls declined for fear that too much intimacy with BJ Fortunato would reveal Brooklyn's condition.

Stephanie did not attend the dance at Eric's school after all. There was no hiding what was witnessed in her bedroom by her father, and Stephanie's family had been in therapy about it ever since, although it was not she who suffered from confused or inexplicable feelings. She listened to her mother go on and on about faith, and listened ad nauseam about her father's small-minded guilt that he was at fault for trying to shield her from boys during her formative years in the first place, which clearly drove his daughter into the arms of a woman. Hearing this, Stephanie could not be more embarrassed, and wished she could be excused so her parents could together get through their own personal issues. Bearing witness to her parents' ranting to the therapist proved to Stephanie how clear and confident she felt about her life.

The Thursday before Spring Break, Sagrario, trusted First Student Head of School, did the responsible thing and requested a meeting with Dr. Knoll to share what she learned from Elaine about Hedda. Sagrario sat down on the cushy floral-print sofa in Dr. Knoll's office while Dr. Knoll ended a phone call with one of her sons. Sagrario only caught the tail end of the conversation, but what she heard was quite familiar—it was how Dr. Knoll spoke to her as well. Dr. Knoll was reassuring and upbeat, and although it seemed like her son might have been going through a small issue at school, surely by the time Dr. Knoll finished with what she had to say to him, he'd believe he could rule the world again. That was the way Dr. Knoll always made her feel. That was the way she made everyone feel. Dr. Knoll was sure to make eye contact with Sagrario the minute she arrived, smiling while holding out her hand to offer her a seat on the sofa. Right after her call, Dr. Knoll stood up, smoothed her skirt, and joined Sagrario to talk.

"Hello! Just the Harvard girl I wanted to see!" Dr. Knoll hugged Sagrario like a proud mother. "How do you feel?"

"Surprisingly, I feel calm about it. I thought I'd be flying off the hinges, but I'm calm. Maybe I'm just tired from all of the work that it took to get there."

"That is absolutely to be understood, Sagrario. You've done your share of hard work, and it has definitely paid off. After you receive a week's worth of proper rest and it really begins to sink in, trust me, you will fly off a hinge or two."

They both smiled.

"So tell me, do you want to start, or should I? No, no, you begin, you requested this meeting."

Sagrario cleared her throat and tried to remember how she was going to come out with it. The moment she said Hedda's name, she realized that Dr. Knoll was already on the trail.

"Sagrario, what do you know about Hedda Kaiser?" Dr. Knoll asked, leaning in as she sat next to Sagrario on her office sofa.

"I know that Hedda, well, she's new, and I don't think she has warmed up to the campus very well. I've stopped by her dorm room a few times inviting her to have lunch with me throughout the school year, but she always declined. I have seen her laughing here and there with Sofija Shevchenko, and Stephanie Johnson."

"Stephanie Johnson? She is her Old Girl, yes?"

"Yes, she is, but there is something about Hedda that neither of them might know." Sagrario thought that statement was a very diplomatic entrance to whatever question would come next from Dr. Knoll.

"That she has a serious eating disorder?"

Sagrario nearly choked. "Um, yes."

"Yes, I have only recently learned. I gather you came to me as soon as you found out?"

Sagrario nodded.

Dr. Knoll thought for a moment about what she was going to say next. Clearly she was having a very intimate conversation with Sagrario, Student Head of School, but still a student, nonetheless. Sagrario was a different kind of student and person, though, and extraordinary times called for extraordinary measures. Dr. Knoll loved all of her girls and felt particularly sensitive about the ones who were on their way out—the senior class. She needed an in-house, "in-dorm" ally who could bring a penetrating sense of positive energy to help those few girls feel fortified during such fragile times. Dr. Knoll decided that she would confide in whom she believed would serve as the most empathetic ear: the honest and noble Sagrario.

"Hedda's parents have flown in, and her mother will remain nearby on campus until graduation. I think Hedda's concerns derive from a different place. Feelings of inadequacy are part of it, but I think she just needs some good old-fashioned TLC. She comes from a big family. Her father has had two marriages. Somewhere in there she got a bit lost. Good for them that they have stepped up before it was too late."

Sagrario was at a loss for words. How could these details slip past her like that? She knew that everyone had some sort of hurdle to climb at all times, but these issues were full-on crises. She began to question how effective she had been as leader of her class.

"Dr. Knoll, I thought I was doing the right thing by coming to you as soon as I learned about Hedda, but now I realize that you already knew, and even had more to share with me. How could I be so in the dark? I live in the same dorm with these girls!"

"Because, Sagrario, you are all very brave and very smart, just like Madame Ellington wished for you to be. You think that you can handle your problems all on your own, and for the most part, you all do a good job at keeping things to yourself. Yet bulimia, anorexia, and other body-image issues are all very serious, and going it alone is never the way. There does come a time when any problem will hit a ceiling and you will have to reach out for help. And not if, but when that happens, there will always be someone there to help you through. It may not be a mom or dad, but help will be there. Sometimes it takes hitting that ceiling for some girls to know that, thus exposing everything, but bringing them closure at the same time."

Sagrario thought for a moment, and then asked, "Will she be able to attend graduation?"

"I am sure she will. But there is one student I am not so

sure of . . . I tell you, when it rains it pours. Caitlyn Lovette's father succumbed last night, and so she left on a flight first thing this morning to Texas. A heart attack put him in a coma right before the school's fall dance, and he did not make it through. If you have a moment, please send her a card. I am sure she would like to hear from you, I think she looked up to you a lot."

Sagrario sat silently with guilt compounding so heavily that a splitting headache immediately set in. She did not mean to be so curt with Caitlyn at the bookstore, and after their harsh encounter, they both purposely steered clear of one another in every way.

Dr. Knoll exhaled heavily, seeming relieved that she'd gotten out all that she wanted to say.

"Now, Sagrario, as Student Head of School, I tell you these things, but do not in any way take these issues on as your own. When you encounter your fellow classmates, just continue to be supportive as you have always been." Dr. Knoll already felt secure that she had Sagrario's strictest confidence.

Dr. Knoll stood up and smoothed out her skirt. Sagrario stood up after Dr. Knoll's lead and they embraced. Dr. Knoll, as usual, offered kind words to Sagrario before she left. "You are a good girl, Sagrario, and you will be a great woman. What God has in store for you, heaven only knows. You have done so much work in your young life. Now all you have to do is walk through that door." Ingrid Knoll pulled back from Sagrario to look her in her eyes. She continued. "Do you really feel good about your life?"

"Yes, yes, I do, Dr. Knoll." Sagrario tried not to veer her eyes away.

"Good, because you deserve to feel just like that."

Dr. Knoll embraced Sagrario once more and bid her adieu for her final short holiday as a Madame Ellington student.

Sagrario was in awe at how packed the bus and train station were the next day. It seemed like everyone was headed to New York or Boston that weekend. This, perhaps because the weather was forecast to be beautiful, and what better way to spend it than on the streets of New York City or promenading around Boston?

Elaine sat in traffic while on the phone with her mother, wishing she had her saint Sagrario at her side. Elaine felt like she'd taken her father's place as her mother's bickering partner. Since her father returned home a couple months previously proclaiming his love for her mother, their relationship descended quickly. Elaine believed that her father only came back to her mother because the much younger beauty broke up with him and he felt dejected. So much of Elaine's free time was spent in disagreement with her mother over her father, she could not remember the last time she experienced her mother's soft side. It did not help that traffic was at a standstill, because it only gave them more time to argue.

Sagrario declined to travel with Elaine to the train and bus station because she needed to arrive earlier, having received an unexpected request from Manuel to pick up and deliver a package upon her arrival to New York. Sagrario figured that this call was payback for Manuel fulfilling Sagrario's short-notice need to make some quick cash to pay for her previous bookstore tab. Sagrario promised herself that after her experience with the strange man, she would refuse to handle any more jobs in Hartford, but Manuel did help her pay her bookstore tab, and so she accepted the job. She supposed they were now even.

Sitting on the bench at the bus station, Sagrario thought long and hard about her talk with Dr. Knoll. She was being honest when she responded to Dr. Knoll's question about how she felt about her life. Sagrario always tried to focus on the good, and so she did really believe that her life had become more promising since she had earned the prize of Harvard. Thinking about her own life and blessings led Sagrario to think about the lives of her peers, most notably, those about whom she spoke with Dr. Knoll the day before. Learning about Caitlyn was the biggest blow. Although Sagrario's father was in prison, he was very much alive, and Caitlyn's was not anymore. Sagrario wrote in her datebook to remind herself to pick up a card for Caitlyn to mail to Texas the next day. She thought again about Hedda and her complications with her father and family, and how that led to her obsessing about her weight. Those issues were so complicated, and not as simple as the ones she had. *Poor people cannot afford to be complicated*, she thought. Nonetheless, Hedda's problems were still very real, and Sagrario sincerely hoped that she would see her, hopefully Caitlyn, too, on graduation day.

Shifting her thoughts to things more uplifting, she began

to think about what she would do with the money she stood to make in a matter of hours. After paying off her tab at the bookstore, she actually did not need any more since she was at a zero balance all the way around at school. Plus, she sent Isabella money just two weeks before. Sagrario thought about splurging a little and buying an actual dream graduation dress to wear, as opposed to wearing the cheap one that she wore to a relative's communion but had not worn to school yet. She could even buy new shoes, she thought. She could get her hair blown out really straight at a Dominican hair salon uptown and close out the year with a bang. *Wow*, she thought, *imagine how upper class I will look.*

Just as Sagrario was delving deeper into her lofty daydream, she was startled by a woman who greeted her as though they were friends, and Sagrario quickly caught on. The "friend" handed her a canvas duffle bag and immediately disappeared within the crowd. But the strange encounter somehow spoiled her visions. For reasons she could not explain, as soon as Sagrario received that canvas bag, her lofty daydream was spoiled completely. She sighed, looked down at the bag, and frowned at it. No longer did this bag represent something that would cover a necessity, so it had become meaningless. Her school bills were at a zero balance, and she'd gotten a good start on helping her family. She really did not *need* anything. Her usual law firm summer position was secure, and thus her finances leading to college in the fall would be covered. Her common dress and shoes would suffice for graduation. Sagrario could not justify making the easy cash for nothing at all.

Suddenly, the hand that held the strap of the canvas bag began to itch so much that she dropped the bag. Sagrario inspected the strap to see if there was something on it that would have irritated her hand, yet the bag was clearly brand new and looked as if it had never touched the floor. Sagrario's eyes grew wide and a slight panic set in that compelled her to stand up and scan the crowd to try and locate the "friend" so she could return the bag. She wanted to give it all back. She reminded herself again that she did not need a new fancy dress, and that where she was headed, in time she would be able to buy more fancy dresses than she could count. But Sagrario could not locate the woman. So she sighed unto herself again and decided that she would do the job to satisfy Manuel, but refuse payment and then be done with it all.

As Sagrario lowered herself back onto the bench, someone grabbed her arm as if they had no intention of letting go. Then, two other men stepped behind her, one picking up her travel bag, and the other taking the canvas bag from her grasp. Sagrario was in shock at what was happening. As the station became packed with people, she had no idea who witnessed her being arrested by three plainclothes police officers. Sagrario couldn't even cry. She was void of emotion, and the exhale that she so gravely wanted to have at that moment felt like it had been stolen.

Elaine had just pulled up to the train station as Sagrario's head was being lowered into the police car. Elaine noticed a brunette getting into a police car, but could not discern who it was. It was no matter; her mother was screaming so loud in French, it was a wonder that Elaine was able to make her way through to the terminal on time.

"*Merde, merde, merde,* Elaine! Why must you reduce me to this?"

"Because, Mom, you can't let him take what's left of your life away from you! And I'm not reducing you to anything! It's you who are settling for less with him!"

"Damn it, Elaine! If you must know, I have filed for divorce! Are you happy? I have filed for divorce and am moving back to France to DO SOMETHING with the life I have left. *Merde!*"

Elaine's mother hung up the phone. Now it was more urgent than ever for Elaine to sift through the crowd and get home.

Winsome and Brooklyn were still on campus. Winsome was stalling to avoid dealing with her family. Since much of the campus had left already, Brooklyn made her way to the dining hall to grab a few snacks to eat in the car on the way to the train. When she returned to her room, winded, there stood her live reflection without a baby bump.

"Hello, Brookie."

"Bollocks! Why in bloody hell are you here, Manhattan? I was on my way to Winsome's!"

"I knew that, and that's why I hightailed it."

"When did Winsome ring you?"

"A week ago, but I already knew it!"

"You *would* know."

"No, I was never confirmed, but you avoiding me like a virus made my belief true. Winsome did nothing but speak it aloud."

At this moment, Winsome strolled in mumbling something about wishing the Long Island Railroad would shut down for the weekend, and upon seeing the twins, she dropped her bottle of juice.

"What in blood-clot hell!"

"So you didn't know Manhattan was coming?" Brooklyn interrogated Winsome.

"No, I had no clue! I told her I'd call her. That was a week ago . . . I'm sorry, Brookie, that I called her. I didn't know what to do, and, well, look at you! You're in shambles!"

Brooklyn took a look at herself from head to toe. She was wearing heavy sweatpants, an oversized sweatshirt, and an enormous scarf. All in seventy-degree weather.

"Don't get your knickers in a twist! What's wrong with how I look? Nobody knows! That's the point!"

"But somebody *needs* to know so you can get some help! You told me the baby had not been moving!"

"But Winsome, you've witnessed how I've been eating! I am not feeding just myself!"

Manhattan interrupted. "But Brookie, your baby does not have to be moving in order for you to still feel hungry, I read. You can have those symptoms for months, even after you give birth. A nonmoving baby is not a good thing. You have to go to the doctor. That is why I am here."

"Oh, yeah, right, Hattie. So you are just going to waltz in here and escort your baby twin to the doctor, is it? Then report to our parents how you've once again saved the day, is it? You can stop using me as a way to prove how pious you are!"

"She doesn't mean it," assured Winsome to Manhattan.

"I know she doesn't. It's cool."

To Winsome, Manhattan seemed heartbroken for her sister, who stood before the both of them looking a mess. After months of not seeing her twin, Brooklyn was a shell of herself: hollowed eyes and pale skin. Brooklyn's boarding-school friends might not have noticed so well, but to a twin, this sight must surely have been devastating.

Manhattan urged, "There is a car waiting for us outside. Can you please come with me now?"

By this time, Brooklyn was sniveling and crying profusely. Manhattan asked Winsome to join along, and she obliged, somewhat grateful that her own family confrontation would be delayed. Winsome signed for the both of them while walking out of the dorms.

When a senior dorm parent noticed Manhattan as the last to enter the chauffeured town car, she waved, "Have a wonderful vacation, Brooklyn!"

"Bloody Americans, blow me," huffed Manhattan.

In the car Brooklyn learned all that Manhattan had done on her behalf. Through her tears, she muttered, "You prearranged for me to be seen by a gynecologist? I am convinced that Grande Dame has inserted her soul within you."

"It wasn't rocket science, Brookie. But I did have a go with the actress thing pretending to be Mum."

Manhattan reached for Brooklyn's hand. They interwove their fingers and smiled at each other.

"I'm nervous, Hattie," cried Brooklyn to her identical twin sister.

"I know. But you will be fine. I promise." Manhattan squeezed Brooklyn's hand. "And I will not tell Mum or Dad about this. That is your job. I did have to tell Maude something so she wouldn't spill the beans."

"What did you tell her?"

"I told her I wanted to go shopping with you for your graduation dress."

"What did she say?"

"Her exact words: *You're entering the gates of the United States by choice?* Can you believe it? The stodgy Brit's gonna take on the real Manhattan!"

The sisters laughed.

Manhattan's dry humor was just what Brooklyn needed to help calm her nerves.

When the girls arrived at the doctor's office, before long, a nurse entered the waiting area and announced Brooklyn's name. Brooklyn, Manhattan, and Winsome all stood up when she did this, but Winsome hugged Brooklyn as tightly yet as gently as she could, and opted to remain in the waiting area until her examination was complete.

"Remember, New York already knows your name," Winsome whispered into Brooklyn's ear.

Sobbing, Brooklyn covered her mouth and nodded her head.

Manhattan wrapped her arm around Brooklyn, and they followed the nurse to an exam room.

Brooklyn removed her clothing and lay down on her back on the table for Manhattan to see her for the first time while pregnant. Within seconds of laying her body on the steel observation table, Brooklyn watched her sister become overwrought with emotion. Brooklyn outstretched her arm to Manhattan and offered to soften the tension.

"Hatt, what if I am having a girl? Or a boy? Or BOTH! What if I'm having twinsies! I know that my belly is rather small, but there still could be two in there. One for you, and one for me!"

Manhattan tried to smile through her tears.

The nurse entered the room, greeted the girls again, and told Brooklyn about the procedure.

"Did you leave a urine sample in the cup?"

Brooklyn nodded.

The nurse asked Brooklyn a series of questions regarding her health, and this made Manhattan even more nervous.

"Can we please get on with it? You've taken her weight, blood, and blood pressure . . . We'd like to see about the baby, please."

Brooklyn turned to the nurse, who was kind and seemingly not offended by Manhattan's remarks. She tried to move things along.

She smeared a cold jelly substance across Brooklyn's stomach, then moved a flat metal device across her belly, using the jelly as a glide.

Astonished, Brooklyn turned her head to the monitor and saw a translucent baby figure cradled in what the screen projected as her womb.

She whispered, "That's my baby."

Tears streaming down her cheeks, she asked, "Is there another in there?"

The nurse smiled, and continued to glide the device across and around Brooklyn's stomach.

After asking Brooklyn to repeat when she learned she was pregnant, the nurse shut off the device, and excused herself.

Brooklyn asked calmly, "What's wrong with the baby?"

Seconds later, the nurse returned with the doctor, who apologized for hastily introducing himself as he turned on the monitor again.

"Are your parents arriving soon?"

Manhattan panicked. She demanded, "Why? What's wrong with the baby?"

After writing down a note from his observations on the screen, the doctor again shut off the monitor, sat down, removed his glasses, then scooted his stool close to Brooklyn. What he told her made Manhattan scream. Brooklyn could not find the strength to make another sound.

Where there was a possibility of two, there was only one, and that one was no more.

13

Vulnerability Equals Strength

When Brooklyn awoke from the anesthesia after the surgery, her mother, who was already in New York, had arrived in Connecticut. Brooklyn turned her head and her foggy vision slowly focused on the printed tunic her mother was wearing, and then on her mother's hands, which were clasped so tightly her knuckles were white. Melanie Abbott was seated beside her daughter on a lumpy-cushioned hospital chair. Though there was no evidence of tears, Brooklyn sensed her mother's sadness and regret through her inability to outwardly emote. This response to what had happened to her reminded Brooklyn of her mother's stone face when Brooklyn's maternal grandmother passed away. All of her grandmother's offspring cried during the ceremony, but not her mother, although everyone knew that she was Grande Dame's most connected child. Winsome comforted Manhattan in the waiting area, who, in contrast, had been sobbing right until the nurse entered the waiting room to alert the two that the surgery had been completed, and that Brooklyn was doing fine.

With a strained, weak voice, Brooklyn could only say "Hello." She rubbed her hand over her fruitless belly, which was still a bit puffy from the pregnancy, but Brooklyn was fully aware that her baby was no longer inside of her.

Brooklyn's mother sighed hard and reached for her youngest twin's hand to hold, which Brooklyn freely gave to her. Melanie tried to offer her words of comfort.

"You know, when I was pregnant for the first time, your father and I acted so prematurely. We bought out nearly a boutique's worth of baby merchandise, all to be told that I'd lost the baby two weeks later. By the second and third times, I'd become accustomed to miscarriages. You and your sister were our miracle babies . . . I am telling you this because sometimes it is not meant to be."

"Did you see my boy?" Brooklyn asked, attempting to hold back her tears.

"Yes, I did, and I said a prayer for my first grandson."

Brooklyn sobbed. "Mum, I'm so sorry! Everything was going so well, and school was doing fine, and I did not want to interrupt because I wanted to get to Broadway, and Chris was just so nervous, and I took all of the prenatal ingredients every day, I swear I did! I did not have one drink or a cigarette when I found out! I am so sorry, you must hate me now, Hattie must hate me! Dad must hate me!"

"No one hates you, we are happy that you are all right, love. And Winsome did the right thing by calling Manhattan. I am just glad that I was able to get here in time."

Brooklyn's mother continued.

"You are both our miracle babies. I am somehow partly to blame for all of this . . . Somewhere along the way I'd just lost sight of how important that was. What a gift that was. How could I have allowed for you to spend so much time away from me without seeing you? I should have seen you. Then I would have known, and we could have dealt with it better than this. Your father said we should have surprised you on campus right after Christmas break. He said we should have brought Hattie along, even Maude, but I said no. I said that the Sinclairs have been a great influence, and that if you needed us, you would call . . . But I don't know why I didn't need to see YOU. That is not how a mother should be. I've put my children second long enough."

Brooklyn said nothing.

"I will arrange to have Chris be with you, as you will both grieve this loss. As for school, I don't know, love. We will have to figure this whole thing out, all right?"

Brooklyn nodded.

The whole of Brooklyn was not in her own body. Actually, her consciousness, the real Brooklyn, was sitting somewhere in the corner of the room watching the scene between her mother and her bedded, hollowed self. Who would have known that life would turn out like that for her? For a girl who spent so long wanting to pursue theater, the majority of her senior year was comprised of superb acting, near-perfect direction of a plan, and a plot that would have earned her a Tony Award. Her young mind thought a career was all she really wanted, for she believed she had so much to prove.

Brooklyn's real self, her consciousness who sat in the corner observing the scene, watched an unfamiliar calm take hold of the bedded Brooklyn as she listened to her mother's sincere apology. This was a pivotal moment in the life of Brooklyn Abbott. Her mother for the first time finally SAW Brooklyn without her having to be on a stage, or wear a costume.

❧

She'd never sat in a sheriff's office before—only in waiting rooms of prisons anticipating a few precious moments with her incarcerated father. Now, for what she'd done, she was sure that she would soon be the one wearing a bland uniform hoping to receive visitors. Sagrario's reputation would be forever besmirched; all of her hard work would be unbelievable to cellmates and ultimately forgotten by all who could have remembered. Taking in the authoritative room around her, she never considered that there could be so many awards and plaques one could be presented for capturing criminals.

The leather on the seat on which she sat felt more like plush plastic. And the room smelled like old stacks of paper. Sagrario glanced at her watch and realized that had she made it to New York, by now she would be on the subway headed uptown to see her family. The city would have been alive with pedestrians, and as soon as she reached the South Bronx, she would have spoken to at least a dozen people she knew on her two-block walk from the subway. She would have been feeling a lighter pep in her step just because it was bona fide springtime, and thus even being home would have kept her smiling.

She would have soon laid eyes upon her niece, who was also her namesake, and Sagrario would be reminded what all of her hard work was for.

But she wasn't in New York, and she would not see her niece that day, and Sagrario did not feel a lighter pep in her step. She felt angry, alone, and scared. No one had offered her that one phone call, even though she wouldn't know who to call. Her family was a funny bunch. Finding out that she was arrested would have them, on one hand, resentfully, jealously happy that the "good one" didn't make it out either. But inside there would be other strong feelings that they would never muster the courage to share amongst each other, about how sad they were that any chance for a better life for any of them was destroyed.

When Sagrario was positioned in the police car, one of the officers asked her where she was coming from and where she was going. She told them she was coming from school and what school she attended, and when she arrived at the police station, all she was told was "follow me" by another police officer who led her to the empty office, in which she sat. That was over an hour ago.

After Sagrario told the officers where she attended school, all questions had stopped, which made Sagrario even more worried because she immediately thought of Dr. Knoll. Sagrario was just sitting in her office the day before, consoling her about her peers' dysfunctions, leading Dr. Knoll to believe that she had none, or if she did, they were all under complete control. Dr. Knoll asked her two times if everything was all right in her world, and both times, Sagrario answered favorably, declining to admit even a bullet point of the laundry list of things that were not okay in her world. Her life at Madame Ellington was very good, so she was not fully lying to Dr. Knoll. And with her bills being paid up for school, she felt especially stable there. Yet it was the means that got those bills paid that led to her sitting in the sheriff's office in Connecticut. It was the temptation that offered the money, but would somehow entangle school and home that was the culprit of all of this. Sagrario found herself in more than a precarious situation then, and thought she could keep them balanced. The two extreme lives had finally found an avenue on which to collide.

The doorknob slowly turned on the door of the sheriff's office, and in walked the sheriff with Dr. Knoll. This vision startled Sagrario so much that she jumped to her feet.

The first person's eyes she caught were Dr. Knoll's, who didn't look judgmental or angry, but she did appear sad.

"Sit down, Miss Nuñez," the sheriff suggested to Sagrario firmly, but kindly.

Sagrario sat down, lowering her body as quietly onto the plush plastic as she could. The sheriff sat at his desk in front of her, and Dr. Knoll sat on an even more uncomfortable-looking chair adjacent to Sagrario.

"We traced the contents of the bag you were carrying, and they connect exactly to the group of people we have been trying to bring to justice for quite some time. Do you know what group I'm talking about, Miss Nuñez?"

"No, I don't."

"I figured you would not. How did you get involved with these characters?"

Sagrario looked to Dr. Knoll for approval to divulge more. Dr. Knoll nodded "okay."

"Well, my cousin told me that all I had to do was bring a bag of jewelry to another person who owned jewelry stores. That is all I knew."

"Well, unfortunately, there was much more. You were being used as an illegal transporter of stolen property, Miss Nuñez. That is a major crime. People are sentenced to years in prison for this sort of behavior, and you are not too young to be tried in a court of law. Do you understand, Miss Nuñez?"

"I think—I think so. Yes, I understand."

"I hope you do. Do you want to know why Ingrid Knoll is sitting in here?"

"Because you could not get my parents on the phone?"

"No. Ingrid is here because besides my wife, she happens to be one of the few people I absolutely trust in this world. I have known Ingrid for most of my life, and if she tells me something, I know it is the truth. She tells me that you happen to be one of the few people she trusts wholeheartedly in *her* life."

Sagrario turned to Dr. Knoll, who looked into her lap.

The sheriff continued.

"And she says that if you were involved at all, you were in a completely innocent way, and that your involvement would be more for basic survival than to willingly commit a crime."

By now, Sagrario was tearing up heavily. She was ashamed of herself. "Yes, this is true, sir . . . I am sorry. I did not realize what I was doing. I was just trying to—"

"Graduate," Dr. Knoll interrupted.

The sheriff offered more. "I admire you, Miss Nuñez. It seems that from a very young age, you have beat odds that adults would not be able to move past. Your grades have always been impeccable, and you have served as a model student at the Madame Ellington School since you were admitted. You really have set a template for an ideal student. I think my own children, save for this mishap, could learn something from you."

Sagrario did not comment.

"Miss Nuñez, because of who you are, and because of whom you know, a living angel named Ingrid Knoll, you will receive favor, but you cannot be completely let off the hook. I am going to strongly suggest to another close friend at the courts that you serve six months' probation for your involvement in this mess."

Sagrario misheard what the sheriff said and cried, "Six months in *prison*?"

Dr. Knoll tapped Sagrario on her knee. "No, Sagrario, *probation*."

"Yes, probation," explained the sheriff. "That means you cannot have any run-ins with the police at all during that time—or any time after, or you will be punished to the full extent of the law. Do you understand?"

"I am not going to jail?" Sagrario asked in disbelief.

"No, you will not go to jail, and I will also ask that your records are kept sealed so this does not reach the college you plan to attend. What you did was a very real thing, Ms. Nuñez, but who you are is extraordinary, and this is reason for the extraordinary treatment. I trust you will never do anything like this again," urged the sheriff.

"No, sir, never ever again."

"It was both a pleasure and not a pleasure to meet you, Ms. Nuñez, and let us not mention that we had to come together in this way."

"Thank you, sir. Thank you."

Sagrario cried and cried and bid *gracias a Dios* over and over. The sheriff and Dr. Knoll allowed her this time, offering tissues to help dry her eyes. The sheriff was right, Sagrario had literally been saved by an angel.

In the car back to campus, Dr. Knoll did most of the talking.

"You have been mothering yourself and others for so long, dear Sagrario. Once again, I am the one who should apologize. I thought you were all right. Of course, even if you weren't, I left you no real opportunity to tell me because you were so busy being the one student who always held it together . . . I realize why I have always felt so close to you, so kindred. It is because there was a time when I was you."

Dr. Knoll divulged to Sagrario that underneath her prized haircut and flip-collared white blouses used to be a girl who was the youngest of six children born of two alcoholics who destroyed their lives and had their children taken from them.

She met the sheriff, whom she simply referred to as "Jason," while they were still in elementary school, and Ingrid lived in a crowded foster home. She explained how she learned to stay quiet and trouble-free and excel in school and to "stay awaaaaaay from booze!" she joked. She ended up working multiple jobs to afford her way through school and had never looked back. When she received an almost random opportunity to head the Madame Ellington School for Girls in Ruralton, it could not have happened at more a meaningful time, as the school was located near her hometown. It was during those early years at MES that she had been able to reconnect with her siblings and parents before they both passed away. Dr. Knoll said her return brought great closure to her life.

Sagrario listened to Dr. Knoll, astounded that she had similar experiences in life. Sagrario's gratitude toward Dr. Ingrid Knoll in that moment became even more meaningful. From Dr. Knoll's leaning on Sagrario regarding her fellow peers' dealings, to this day of Sagrario literally leaning on Dr. Knoll for her life, Sagrario had in less than two weeks experienced a full circle like no other. She learned through her acts of strength and vulnerability how to truly be a woman.

When they drove onto the gravel-covered driveway of the Headmistress Residence, Dr. Knoll turned off the ignition, took a deep breath, and exited the car. Sagrario followed.

Dr. Knoll stopped Sagrario short from walking up the porch stairs and opened her arms to her. Dr. Knoll gave her what Sagrario would always remember as the greatest hug of her life.

Dr. Knoll whispered in her ear, "It's time for you to rest, dear child. It's time for Sagrario to receive some rest."

When Elaine arrived home by taxi, her mother was resting in their family sunroom. She was sleeping so soundly that she did not hear Elaine enter their home, which was rare. To Elaine, her mother's coma-like slumber was a very clear indication that she was overwhelmed with exhaustion. Elaine did not dare bother her.

Sitting outside of the sunroom on a rocking chair on their deck was Elaine's father, drinking a cup of coffee and smoking a cigarette—something she had not seen him do in years.

As if he was expecting her, Elaine's father looked up and through the glass of the sunroom where Elaine's mother slept to the entryway of the sunroom where Elaine stood. Elaine's current disdain for him urged her to turn around and retreat to her bedroom. Her love and protection for her mother compelled her to walk outside and address him.

"How was your train ride?" Elaine's father asked, with a desperate grip on his coffee cup.

"Fair," she replied curtly.

"Sit down. Do you have a moment?" her father beckoned.

Elaine sat on a deck chair farthest from him.

"Your mother has taken a few sleeping pills that I imagine will keep her resting for a while, as she just fell asleep, but I also would imagine that traveling voices would arouse her, as I am elevating my voice right now to talk to you."

Elaine thought for a moment, then stood up and sat closer to her father.

"I am sure that will be better for her. Thank you."

"What would you know about what's better for her?" sniffed Elaine.

"I know quite a bit about your mother. Far more than you do."

"And what is that supposed to mean? I do not need to know more than what I know."

"Fair enough, but please know that when your mother left France to be with me, it was because we were very much in love. I did not force her to come here."

"I am sure she thought she was in love with you, as much as she believed you were in love with her."

"And I was, and I still do love your mother very much."

"So why would you do this to her?"

"It's complicated, Elaine."

"You risked losing your family for some whore, that's what's complicated."

"Watch your tone."

Elaine stood up. "Watch my tone? Watch MY tone? You have your nerve, Dad. Parading around here one day like you are sick of your life, and so you abandon it. Then the next, you come home, and for a moment, act like you want that same life back, but you don't. You are a coward, and you are such a coward that you couldn't just stay away. You had to drag Mom through the mud along with you. You are all right with her having to take medication in order to sleep?"

"Elaine, wait a minute. I spent my entire life devoted to my family. Yes, I expected to be with your mother forever, I did. I cannot tell you what went wrong with me that I jeopardized my life so much. I just don't . . ."

Elaine's father tried to curb his vulnerability by attempting to take a sip of his coffee, but his crying commenced before his lips reached the mug. Ultimately, he had to put it down. He seemed different from when he barged into their family home declaring that he wanted to come back. He was now more than broken. It was clear to Elaine that her mother's final decision to leave him had affected her father more than he even knew. He was the entitled half in the marriage, and never expected that she would do this, regardless of his offense.

Elaine's father seemed jittery and insecure. He even looked up at her a couple of times while he was crying, as if to be sure that Elaine was looking at him, which she was. Elaine sensed that he might have been looking to determine if she had sympathy for him. She was trying.

"Elaine, I love you with all of my heart and soul. I have lost my way, I have destroyed my family, and I will pay for that forever. No amount of money will ever take the place of you and your mother . . . I am begging you, Elaine, to . . . please forgive me."

By the end of his monologue, Elaine's father had ceased crying, but she believed he was sincere.

"As you speak, Dad, I am trying."

Elaine stood up and walked closer to her father, who was still seated, and cupped his head and leaned it on her stomach. He cried again.

Elaine's mother did not wake up until three hours later. When she did she seemed well rested. Despite Elaine's father's newfound humility, Elaine's mother was still determined to go through with a divorce from Elaine's father and move back to France. Elaine observed her father's obvious uneasiness about her mother's decision, but he had to accept the fork in the road he alone presented for their union. Seeing all of this transpire between the two people who meant the most in her life, just as she was approaching her own precipice of major transition, made Elaine think of Sagrario. She felt that considering the circumstances, she handled herself rather well and honestly, and as Sagrario had encouraged her to do before, Elaine was able to place anger and judgment at bay. Though the end of her parents' marriage union served as a casualty of their dysfunction, Elaine realized that aside from being her parents, they really were just two people in the world, and that these two people had individual decisions to make, and lives to lead. She figured she'd better move ahead with her own life and simply do her best to love them as her parents. She was not angry anymore.

Stephanie felt sick to her stomach. She resented her parents for making her consult with a church counselor about her "issue"—someone who only reminded her over and over again, "Jesus Christ is the only redemption."

Lying on her bed on her back, Stephanie envisioned Emily and her lying there together. She daydreamt about the way Emily's skin felt and smelled. Inhaling the imagined smell in the air, Stephanie smiled, feeling a sense of relief. Stephanie had never been herself with anyone the way she was with Emily. Stephanie's beloved Hedda had helped Stephanie to melt the ice of her frozen, veiled reality, but with Emily, that cold water became cool water, which transcended into warm water that trickled down her back as beads of sweat during that incredible moment of passion. Suddenly Stephanie felt comfortable with all of the curves she'd developed over the summer prior. Emily had given them all a sense of purpose.

Stephanie then looked around her bedroom at all of what she had on display that was supposed to represent herself as the ideal female teen: Magazine photos of hunky celebrities on whom she was supposed to have a crush? Check. Mementos, tchotchkes, and dolls strategically placed here and there to show how much she had transitioned from a typical girly-girl to young woman? Check. But these things did not represent Stephanie, and over the years, she just used them to derail suspicion, a sort of tangible deterrent, just in case anyone had any doubt.

Stephanie bounced off of her bed with one hop to the floor and a semi-sinister look in her eyes.

She casually stepped face to face with a porcelain-faced doll sitting prominently on her tall dresser, and with one finger, she unapologetically knocked her down and the doll's face crashed, breaking into pieces once it hit the spotless wooden floor. Stephanie smiled. She paced around her room, ripping posters off of her walls, swiping statuettes and feminine picture frames onto the floor. None of the quick instances of breaking glass or sounds of torn paper broke her state of mind, and she continued on until her room was stripped of everything that in Stephanie's mind communicated, *I hate myself.*

Then she piled all of the destroyed items and swept them to a corner of her room with her feet.

Stephanie walked to her closet, opened its door, and eyed her wardrobe, shaking her head. She reached for the passed-down dress given to her by her mother weeks before and pulled it off its hanger. Bundling the dress close to her chin, Stephanie declared, "I am not a typical girl."

Stephanie's bedroom rage, as well as her rapid footsteps descending the stairs, was surely heard by her mother and father, who were sitting in the kitchen. They both turned to each other, somehow knowing that what was coming would be as intense as the foot patterns that introduced Stephanie's arrival.

When Stephanie reached the final stair of the staircase, she clasped in her fingers the tiny cross pendant she wore around her neck on a thin gold chain, something given to her by her grandmother when she was only eight years old. Her grandmother died the following year of a heart attack, but when she lowered herself to hook the necklace around Stephanie's neck that year before, she told her, "Never forget that God loves you, no matter what." Armed with those words, Stephanie took a second to rethink the meaning of her grandmother's intention for speaking those words back then. As she approached the kitchen, she questioned silently to herself, *Did grandma REALLY know me?*

Her father and mother were as motionless as a photograph when she stood at the threshold of the door. The newspaper was still elevated between her father's hands. Stephanie's mother was sitting erect on a bar stool next to her father. Their eyes turned to her direction, but they did not move.

Stephanie walked into the kitchen and stood in front of them. Her father made a swallowing sound, and her mother let out a quiet sigh.

Stephanie released the necklace, dropped her hands at her sides, flung her hair over her shoulders, and stood her entire full five feet eleven inches.

"Mom, Dad, I am a lesbian."

Stephanie's father, almost as if he did not hear her, asked her to repeat herself. Stephanie continued.

"You heard me correctly. I am a lesbian. I am also smart, and kind, and honest, and loving, and proud. And I am your daughter."

Brooklyn knew that everyone was feeling heavy anticipation for her and Winsome's great big show. Brooklyn's parents spun quite a story after she lost the baby about her becoming unexpectedly ill, and so she had three weeks to physically recover from that experience. Brooklyn's father recommended that she not perform her senior project with Winsome, but Brooklyn chose to rise to the occasion. And despite not being on campus, Brooklyn knew her lines like they were etched in her brain. The day of their performance would be her first back on campus.

BJ Fortunato had submitted the second half of their written play to NYU with very favorable reviews from the Tisch School. Both Winsome and Brooklyn had been accepted to NYU as well, and so they felt secure about their possibilities in the city.

Winsome never did travel to Long Island back in April when Manhattan surprised them both and forced Brooklyn to attend the doctor's visit, and therefore missed a face-to-face opportunity to meet with her father. Winsome's mother did tell her that their family restaurant was going to live on, and that her father's "business partner" was deported back to Jamaica.

At first Winsome did not want to go home, but being around Brooklyn's family made her think about her own. Winsome sacrificed seeing them only because she knew how much Brooklyn needed her. Her parents understood and agreed that Winsome and her father would have their face-to-face at Winsome's second home: the Madame Ellington School campus. Winsome was her father's child, and their bond had never been threatened before, until Winsome began to express her father-inherited independent, daring-to-dream spirit. She had heard her father loud and clear when he shared with her about his dream of building a restaurant, about the ups and downs, how it was almost not going to happen. In the end, it did. Winsome was unafraid of how her road would turn while setting out for her own dream. She had read horror stories about rejection and lack of money, but right now she was willing to embrace the adversity to pursue what she believed in her heart she was born to do. Winsome was no longer going to hide or make apology anymore for the dream she had for herself, and she would allow her gut and experience to lead her where she was destined to go. She realized that how riled up her father got at her over the phone was only because he did not want to see her lose. His last words that day stung Winsome, but it was the overall courageous story he shared with her that made Winsome even more determined to forge ahead.

As Winsome approached the theater building alone nearly two hours prior to call time, she saw her father sitting on the steps of the building. The closer he came into focus, the more she was reminded of a much younger dad who sat on a bench wearing bell-bottomed slacks long after they had gone out of style, and reading a Jamaican newspaper as he waited for both her and Claire to finish elementary school for the day.

Winsome's father was a proud Jamaican, but today he looked tired and aged. First, he had been deceived by his *brethren*, and as a result, ended up being at odds with his daughter. The emotional toll of it all would take time to fully recover.

When Winsome was within her father's earshot, she called his name. Mr. Sinclair looked up, stood up, and outstretched his arms. Her father's open arms instantly magnetized Winsome—

she could not help but run to them, the same way she did in the first grade.

"I've only one thing to say to you," Mr. Sinclair whispered between heavy breaths and tears on the way. "I am sorry. You know I only want the best for all of my children."

Winsome whispered back to her father a phrase that over the months was something she had missed telling him: "I know. And I love you for this, Daddy."

The performance was breathtaking. What Winsome and Brooklyn delivered on stage derived from a place their fellow peers could not explain, and neither Winsome nor Brooklyn could have predicted that choosing the complicated subject of loss the summer before would be so relative and relevant to their lives at the present time. Brooklyn's character wailing about the loss of her mother was very real. She held her bosom and stomach while she wept lines like, *Had I known your time with me would be so limited, I would have allowed what we had to be more sacred!* Brooklyn's family, including her nanny, Maude, sat in the audience and cried with her, along with the remaining audience, who were not privy to Brooklyn's actual grave ordeal. The death of Brooklyn's baby had given her a different chance in life. On stage her words rang with sincere feelings of loss, and also quietly echoed with energy of promise.

The audience was dazed as Winsome delivered the final speech of the show:

When is it okay to cry?
What loss is worthy of a tear shed?

Is it only when someone transitions physically into the beyond, or when you simply feel abandoned by someone you deeply love?

What loss is worthy of taking your time to heal?

Are we not allowed to become lost in the love for something or someone, cultivating a true, present connection, not ever considering a future demise or sudden ending? Or do we tiptoe through love, working overtime to control our hearts, desperate to protect our inevitable grief? Can we ever really fully protect ourselves?

For those whom we love, I think we cannot.

Pain is what drives the purest love, because it is only pure love that can replace the hurt we feel inside.

Loss inspires gain.

Pain inspires love.

Without pain, we would not recognize love.

BJ Fortunato led the standing ovation.

After bowing and exiting the stage to a standing ovation, Winsome, whose character was not written to emote, left her metaphoric costume at the door and fell apart in Brooklyn's arms in the dressing room.

"Brookie, I love my daddy so much!" Winsome's emotions hit her like a tidal wave.

Brooklyn stroked Winsome's head as Winsome knelt in front of her. "I know, but I also knew that everything was going to be all right. You have the best dad in the world."

Winsome looked up into Brooklyn's red eyes.

Brooklyn continued. "And don't worry about anything that has happened, Winnie. Trust me, none of it will be in vain."

14

Exhale

Sagrario awoke that morning in her dorm room bed and looked around her empty space. There were boxes everywhere, most of which were labeled "I. K." because Dr. Knoll suggested that Sagrario leave the items she would want for college at her home and she would send them to Sagrario in the fall.

Sagrario lay in bed, whispering her speech as fast as she could to be sure she had it memorized well, then sat up to officially begin the day.

Amongst the bustling of students in the halls, Sagrario almost did not hear her name being called to answer the dorm phone.

"Hello? This is Sagrario."

"*Mi amor* . . . I'm sorry."

Sagrario almost lost her breath. It was Manuel.

There was so much she wanted to say, so much that she'd thought about over and over that she'd say to him if she ever spoke to him again. She wanted to tell him how terrible he was for involving her in something so dangerous and for nearly ruining her life, but then she also knew that she accepted the job, understanding somewhere deep inside what she was risking. It was not fully his fault, and she did not want to make it be.

"Manuel, where are you?"

"Where do you think I am?"

Sagrario knew Manuel was in jail. If she was caught, there was only a window of time before he would be, too, and certainly with his criminal record his punishment would in no way resemble hers. It was likely that Manuel was going away for a long time.

"I . . . I am sorry to hear that."

"Well, I am less sorry about my situation than I am happy that you got out okay. I never meant to do you no harm, *nena*."

"I know you didn't, Mani."

"It's just that, I always wanted to help you out one day, do somethin' for you and alla your hard work. You the only one in the family that made it this far, and even though what I had to offer wasn't alla way right, I never thought you would get caught. Not you. I thought you could make money for school and get through. I never meant to embarrass you."

"I appreciate that, Mani. I really do."

Sagrario's vexed emotions dissolved for her cousin. He might have done the wrong thing for most of his life, but with her he tried to right a few of those wrongs. If he helped Sagrario finish school, his actions for how he did it would make what he did to get her there okay. In a way it was the same thinking as Sagrario's previous repeated attempts at filling the holes of doubt lingering inside about her job with him with faith. They both tried to justify the logistics of paying Sagrario's tuition bill.

"In your heart you are a good man, Mani, and I love you for that."

"Will you forget about me?"

Sagrario shed a tear. "Of course that is not possible. Hook or crook, you will always be my family, *y te amo*."

"*Te amo* every day, *mi prima*. Just make sure you don't mess up at whatever big school you goin' to. Keep gettin' them good grades, too. I'm countin' on you to represent."

Sagrario and her cousin Manuel both knew that in order for her to do what he asked, she would have to steer clear of him for a long time. Sagrario was used to Manuel stepping in and out of her life as she grew up, but this time, their separation was her choice alone. The feeling was liberating, yet sorrowful all the same. After hanging up the phone, Sagrario held her hand on the receiver for a few moments, their last embrace.

Sagrario was not the only one bringing her senior year to a close in a meaningful way. All of the other girls were also making their preparations for the morning graduation ceremony. Being a day student, Stephanie did not have the choice of sleeping in a hotel with family, but she chose to sleep overnight in the dorms, reminiscing about years past, and she even confided in Hedda about Emily, excited about the fact that they were both headed to Wesleyan University. Hedda joked, "But I was your first kiss!" Stephanie was relieved that Hedda was recovering well and that she was finally opening up, albeit during their final hours as Madame Ellington students. Their recent bond promised possibility for a continued friendship, even though it would soon be an international exchange.

Winsome was dressing herself alone in her dorm room, as Brooklyn remained with her family at the Old Inn. As she buttoned the last button on her linen blazer, Victoria Lee knocked on her slightly opened door, walking in without waiting for Winsome to answer.

"Hi, Winsome. I wanted to give you something."

Winsome turned around, barely recognizing who stood before her. Once a waifish, boy-like figure who roamed sadly and quietly on campus, Victoria had evolved into someone new, someone who looked her in the eyes when she spoke. Victoria appeared comfortable in the white spaghetti-strapped dress she wore. Winsome's mouth gaped open.

Victoria handed Winsome a flower. "It is called a *mugunghwa,* a flower well known in Korea. I know we have calla lilies to hold during the procession, but I think it will look beautiful pinned on your dress. I want to thank you for encouraging the girl in me."

Winsome tucked the flower in her blazer's front pocket. "Victoria, I have always seen you as beautiful. That is why I was not surprised that you had a boyfriend. You'd have to be blind not to see your beauty in and out, though you were so modest about it!"

"It has been hard to feel proud of myself, really proud of being a girl. Not easy for me to express it out loud, so I did my best to hide. I became very good at it. But that time with you on the bench, seeing those clouds overcome by the sun . . . I don't know, the sun sort of overcame me, too."

"Wow. I never would have thought. That is so powerful. What does your boyfriend have to say?

"We actually broke up not too long after the dance. But it is okay, I will see what other prospects Stanford has to offer so I can one day have a real relationship out in the open. Have a fresh start." Victoria smiled.

"Stanford? Congratulations!" Winsome gushed.

"Yes. I also want to be closer to my parents. We have a lot of growing to do."

Hearing Victoria put Winsome in an even stronger state of mind. After the two hugged and Victoria left, Winsome reflected on the recent turn of events with her, and how inspiring was Victoria's newfound confidence. After their talk on the bench, Winsome had cultivated the strength to confront her father in a real way. This made her feel proud to know that both she and Victoria were empowered in that shared moment. Victoria's obvious inner joy served as confirmation for Winsome that being herself at all times was the only way she would win.

~

The sun lit the large pond that served as the backdrop of the graduation ceremony like a halo. Sagrario stood at a distance and viewed the sea of hundreds of people who were in attendance, some sitting or standing with anticipation. In any given row, she could hear various cultural and geographical accents, dialects, and languages, and see every skin tone known to man. There were younger siblings, grandparents, aunts and uncles, great-grandmothers sitting patiently with clasped hands, and toddlers who tried to stand on laps to steal a glimpse of their beloved Madame Ellington School graduate when they marched down the calla lily–lined aisles. Even Sagrario's mother looked like she could not deny feeling the self-evident happiness in the air.

Sagrario spotted the Lovette family arriving on campus with Caitlyn, as she was one of the few who opted to sleep her final night in a hotel with her mother, brother, and her long-time nanny, Miss Annabelle.

She watched Caitlyn walk her family to their row to be seated, then turn to head around to the music hall to soon be led back to the garden with the senior class. Sagrario stopped short of her people-watching and made a beeline for Caitlyn. When Sagrario reached her, she almost grabbed her arm, but relented. Caitlyn turned around anyway.

"Caitlyn. Hi."

Caitlyn spoke softly. "Hi, Sagrario . . . Thank you for your kind card. Yours was the one that meant the most to me from those I received from Ellington's."

Sagrario was stunned. Ingrid Knoll was right about how Caitlyn really felt about her. "Wow. Thank you, I mean, I am shocked, I mean . . . I am so sorry about your dad, and I am just, sorry."

"It's okay, or at least it will be. Believe me, my life has changed leaps and bounds in less than three months. I chose to attend Columbia University of all places. Nothing surprises this Southern belle anymore." She offered a consolation smile.

"Congratulations. Great school, and you will be surprised at a whole lot living in New York City. I'm proud of you. Would you be willing to hang out sometime if we are there at the same time? I will not be far away."

"That's right, you're going to Harvard. I knew you would get in. It's been your number-one choice since freshman year, right?"

Sagrario could not remember ever confiding in anyone besides the school college counselor and Dr. Knoll an aspiration like that, except once during freshman year when a group of girls were asked what their dream school was by a visiting speaker. Caitlyn was a part of that group, and she must have remembered since then. Sagrario was touched.

Sagrario reached out her arms and gently pulled Caitlyn into a hug.

"It's going to be all right," Sagrario whispered into Caitlyn's ear.

"I believe it will be," Caitlyn whispered back.

After the families were seated, and the procession music commenced, Sagrario and the rest of the senior class appeared in various elegant visions of white, all holding small bouquets of white calla lilies in their hands.

As each girl walked past the audience to sit in the graduates section, fathers and mothers grabbed hold of each other's hands, grandparents patted mothers and fathers on backs, siblings smiled, and some screamed out names. Sagrario led the group, and she caught eyes with her mother, who she noticed was holding rosary beads in her hand.

Ingrid Knoll began the ceremony. Accustomed to having all of her major speeches written one week ahead to allot for any changes needed leading up to the given day, there was no year like the current year that could have benefitted from her preparedness. The significant events involving a handful of students in the senior class compelled Dr. Knoll to shift a few lines in her welcome, but Sagrario's episode changed her tone almost completely. Where she'd previously written an introduction about her Student Head of School that detailed Sagrario's traditional sense of dependability and academic excellence at Madame Ellington, Ingrid Knoll chose to speak more from the heart about who she believed Sagrario was as a young woman and leader:

"When I think about the definition of a leader, I do not think cold and unapologetically direct, or shrewd, or unemotional. I think the opposite. I think understanding, compassionate, giving, selfless, honorable, risky, vulnerable, and strong. That, too, would be a fitting definition of Sagrario Nuñez, who, for me, is the personification of the word 'leader.'

"Throughout this year, I have watched her perform incredibly as an academic student, and I have also watched her handle challenges that many adults who are considered pillars of their communities could not. She executed these feats with grace and honesty, and the Madame Ellington School is proud to have your name, Sagrario Nuñez, listed prominently in its archives."

When Sagrario stood up, so did her mother, fixated on her daughter, and she would not move until Isabella pulled her to sit down. Sagrario walked slowly to Ingrid Knoll and hugged her. Dr. Knoll gripped Sagrario's back and whispered in her ear, "For the last time, it's now your turn." Ingrid Knoll tried to hold back tears, but it was hard. She released Sagrario and walked back to her seat with her head slightly bowed.

Sagrario readjusted the microphone upward and politely cleared her throat. She took a moment to observe her surroundings, peering at the family section and to her graduating class. Looking for no one in particular, her eyes happened upon Caitlyn, who nodded to Sagrario and smiled.

Sagrario began her address:

"Good morning, and greetings to Dr. Knoll, the faculty, my fellow class, New Girls, Old Girls, family, and friends. I am most grateful to have served as your Student Head of School at the Madame Ellington School this year.

"More than a century ago, Madame Ellington wanted to create a place where girls from all over the world could grow into women without outside distraction, be cultivated as leaders without moving their eyes off the ball, and fine-tune their intelligence without acknowledging any limits. I can attest that more than a century later, her goals are still being met.

"I came to the Madame Ellington School not at all knowing

what to expect. I had never heard of boarding school before then, and I honestly did not know if I could make it to where I stand right now, but with the help of God and those who love me, I did. Each and every one of these young women is soon to embark on a new journey in their lives to get where she wants and deserves to be. I used to think that money would be the only problem one could have attending a school like this, but I learned that difficulties and challenges come in the forms of many, many dynamics, and we have all had our hills to climb. I, for one, am very proud to be a part of this class, and I know that we all will go on and go far.

"Dr. Knoll, you have no idea how valuable you have been to all of us in our senior class. I think we have earned the academic right to be here four years ago, but in order to stay here, to thrive here, it took leadership to help us keep believing. You have been a leader, a mother to all of us. Thank you.

"To our faculty, you are all the greatest. Thank you. To our family and friends, loved ones present and not, I say on behalf of the senior class, thank you. For all of the things you showed us how to do right, thank you. For all of the things you have shown us not to do, thank you. Thank you for being who you are, because you have helped to push us forward.

"Before I step aside, I would like to address my fellow seniors in a way that I had not intended earlier, so please excuse that I am compelled to speak from my heart: I want you all to acknowledge yourselves and give light to the fact that you did it. Each and every one of us, through our various challenges, however big or small, has forged ahead to do exactly what we entered this school to do—become a woman. I noticed, though, that the older we become, the less we want to reach out for support from our peers, but that is exactly when connections should strengthen the most. Each grand obstacle deserves its appropriate village. When I least expected it, there were those who stood up for me and helped to nourish my outlook and remind me that brighter days are always ahead. It is because of our camaraderie that we have arrived to this point. Wherever we may go in life, during our years at whatever college or university we have chosen to attend, shall we never, ever forget the Ellington way.

"Thank you all again."

Sagrario could hardly believe it. Her surroundings felt surreal. Before she gave her speech, she had stepped outside of herself and watched herself address the crowd. She watched her mother become so moved by her that she could no longer sit down. She looked into the eyes of her peers, some of them still unsure, but she believed they were all going to be all right.

The entire senior class stood up and cheered, followed by the faculty, followed by the audience.

Ingrid Knoll stood up and again wrapped her arms around Sagrario. "I am so proud of you, so proud," she whispered in her ear. Of all the years serving at the Madame Ellington School, overseeing the full lives of all of those girls, Sagrario Nuñez's triumph meant more to Ingrid Knoll than all others combined.

Flying calla lilies accentuated the breeze as the graduates, with diplomas in hand, surrendered to the next chapter of their lives.

Sagrario happened upon Elaine and her mother, and the moment Elaine saw Sagrario, she pulled her mother to meet her. Elaine's mother congratulated Sagrario on her speech. Sagrario was awed by seeing Elaine and her mother together. Elaine looked almost parental over her tiny mother, and Sagrario could understand at least in this way why Elaine was so protective over her mother.

In the bathroom to prepare for after-ceremony photos, Sagrario ran into her own mother. She'd been holding rosary beads so tightly until her hands had become red. Amongst all of the proud parents, Sagrario's mother felt guilty and ashamed. Her firstborn had beaten the odds with little to no direct help from her.

Sagrario stood still, having avoided her mother since she gave a distant greeting to her when her family arrived on campus that morning.

Sagrario's mother looked humiliated. The demanding and bitter woman Sagrario knew at home now appeared shrunken, overwhelmed by her surroundings, and intimidated by her own daughter. After a few attempts, she softly uttered her first words. "*Mija, lo siento . . .*"

Sagrario cut her off and turned around from her reflection in the mirror to look her mother in the face. "It's okay, *Mami. Está bien. Estoy aquí,* and this is what is most important."

Sagrario led her mother out of the bathroom and into the crowd, where she again spotted Elaine and her mother. Though Sagrario had spent much of the last few months serving as emotional counsel for Elaine, she was at once reminded of Elaine's naïve appraisal of her mother, bringing to light a sincere and substantial gift from her mother for which Sagrario previously showed little regard. Now she understood how it had and would continue to greatly benefit her life. Sagrario grabbed her mother's hand and smiled enough into her mother's eyes until the look of worry and intimidation calmed on her face. Sagrario's mother breathed, "*Gracias,*" in the best way she could without breaking down. After reengaging with the Hammonds, Sagrario declared confidently in perfect French, "Madame Hammond, this is my mother, Rosario."

Elaine's mother then commented on how well Sagrario spoke French.

Sagrario replied, "The reason why I am able to speak French so well with you is because my mother gave me a valuable head start."

Acknowledgments

Like the girls from around the world who make up this story, I have also been blessed with a group of international women who have read the book while I was fine-tuning all of the details. I am filled with unlimited appreciation to all of you for taking the time to read my words: Julie, Elaine, Vicki, Banu, Madame, Syreeta, Lisa, Lisa, Diana, Kemi, Wendy, Hyuna, the lovely, intelligent, and confident woman-to-be from her mom's and my alma mater, Miss Porter's School, Nicole, and my darling niece, Trinity, who is also well on her way.

And a special note of gratitude to Paula Wallace, Founder and President of The Savannah College of Art and Design (SCAD) for reading this manuscript the moment it hit her inbox, and sharing her empowering takeaway with all of you.

Belief makes the world go round, certainly my own. Thank you from the center of my heart for yours in me: my championing husband, my big sister Alisha, Grandma Liz, Auntie Dos, MIL, Mark, Abby, Reeta Dee, Christian P., Ayten, Jenn A., Aldon, Alice M., and Grandpa Smokey.

Sincere gratitude to the solid team inclusive of powerful women at Lanier Press, Taylor Brown for another inspired cover, and to photographer Drexina Nelson for such an honest capture.

To Girls and Women Everywhere: It Is Always a Perfect Time to Be Us.

Other Books by Chrishaunda Lee Perez

300 Miles: From Rock Bottom to Solid Rock

Share the Dream: Building Noah's Ark One Prayer at a Time

www.ingramcontent.com/pod-product-compliance
Lightning Source LLC
Chambersburg PA
CBHW030516310726
48979CB00010B/1693/J
* 9 7 8 1 6 3 1 8 3 3 6 6 3 *